LOVERS FALL BACK TO EARTH

Copyright © 2018 Cecelia Frey

Except for the use of short passages for review purposes, no part of this book may be reproduced, in part or in whole, or transmitted in any form or by any means, electronically or mechanically, including photocopying, recording, or any information or storage retrieval system, without prior permission in writing from the publisher or a licence from the Canadian Copyright Collective Agency (Access Copyright).

We gratefully acknowledge the support of the Canada Council for the Arts and the Ontario Arts Council for our publishing program. We also acknowledge the financial support of the Government of Canada through the Canada Book Fund.

Cover design: Val Fullard

Lovers Fall Back to Earth is a work of fiction. All the characters and situations portrayed in this book are fictitious and any resemblance to persons living or dead is purely coincidental.

Library and Archives Canada Cataloguing in Publication

Frey, Cecelia, author
    Lovers fall back to the earth / Cecelia Frey.

(Inanna poetry & fiction series)
Issued in print and electronic formats.
ISBN 978-1-77133-481-5 (softcover).— ISBN 978-1-77133-484-6 (pdf).—
ISBN 978-1-77133-483-9 (Kindle).— ISBN 978-1-77133-482-2 (epub)

    I. Title. II. Series: Inanna poetry and fiction series

PS8561.R48L68 2018   C813'.54   C2018-901519-5
                                            C2018-901520-9

Printed and bound in Canada

Inanna Publications and Education Inc.
210 Founders College, York University
4700 Keele Street, Toronto, Ontario, Canada M3J 1P3
Telephone: (416) 736-5356 Fax: (416) 736-5765
Email: inanna.publications@inanna.ca Website: www.inanna.ca

LOVERS FALL BACK TO EARTH

a novel

CECELIA FREY

inanna poetry & fiction series

INANNA PUBLICATIONS AND EDUCATION INC.
TORONTO, CANADA

... and there, eloping skyward
with the wistfully-fragrant
tree branches dipping
farewell
although they too
must know

the lovers will fall
back
to earth given
the time and the
temptations looming
ruby-eyed
in the imagination

—Pat Allan, "Collage"

TABLE OF CONTENTS

I. THREE SCENES FROM A STORMY NOVEMBER NIGHT	1
1. On the Island	3
2. A Prairie City	17
3. Across Town	29
II. WHAT HAPPENED AFTER	41
1. A Winter Morning	43
2. A Morning in Early Spring	115
3. A Series of Events in Late Spring	160
4. Two Years Later	219

I.
Three Scenes from a Stormy November Night

1. On the Island

THE SLICK WET PAVEMENT held the tires tight on a course that led smack into the cement barrier. Helena turned the wheel as hard as she could, away from the embankment, away from the ocean. Beside her, Amanda clutched at her throat. Human sound was suspended. The car's motor, the squeal of brakes, the storm — that was all there was.

At the time of the accident, the sisters were fighting. They were returning from Amanda's bingo night out with the girls, activities that Helena regarded as an excruciating waste of time and that Amanda enjoyed immensely. Wasting time always put Helena into a foul mood. Besides, the lack of oxygen in the smoky hall had caused a raging headache that was further intensified by the beer.

It was nearly midnight when they left Cha Cha's Bar & Grille. Needles of sleety rain driven by a fierce wind pinned them for a moment to the door that banged shut behind them. Helena held up an umbrella and under its protection they struggled their way to the car and climbed inside.

"Jesus, I don't know how you can *stand* that *smoke*." Helena's low flat tone was punctuated by dramatic emphasis of certain words. "Think of what it does to your lungs." She shook the umbrella out the driver's door, folded it down, and tossed it into the back seat. "And your clothes and your hair. And your complexion! I feel positively *grey*."

"We should have done something else." Amanda's tone was

apologetic. "Or you could've stayed at home. Reuben would've liked the company."

I wanted to be with you, Helena could have said. I didn't want to share you with those other women. "Don't worry about it," she said instead. "It wasn't a total failure. I got some material for my thesis." Through the windshield, there was only the blackness of rain against the brick wall of the building they had just left. She turned the key in the ignition and switched on the headlights. "I should have known better than to drink beer," she said. "I hate beer."

"You used to like beer."

"Since when?"

"Back in the Cave days. We used to drink pitchers of it. You used to smoke, too."

"That was when I didn't know any better, like a lot of other things I did in those days." Helena looked up at the rear-view mirror. There, too, her eyes came up against a black wall, alleviated only by the red blur of tail lights that barely penetrated the thick gusting rain.

"Twenty years ago. The Philosopher's Circle. Remember how they named a table after us. The six of us. The things we used to talk about! We had such good times."

There was something in Amanda's voice, something damply melancholic that Helena did not want to encourage. "That was when we were crazy students," she said. "Another life. I like to think *I've* matured since then."

"My first year of university," Amanda went on as though she had not noticed Helena's inference. "I was so impressed. You and Esther. My big sisters. And George a professor! And Ben a real live draft dodger! I admired him so much for his rebel stance. So like Reuben's when you think of it. You were all so sophisticated. The way you smoked and drank and used bad language."

"Don't remind me." Helena was attempting to jiggle the gear stick into reverse. An oversight at the rental agency had resulted in the car having a manual transmission.

"Aren't you going to do up your seat belt?"

Amanda's voice was soft, her delivery tentative. What Helena heard was criticism and instruction. "I never do up my seat belt," she snapped. "I don't like to be strapped into anything."

"If you saw the cases I used to see in Emergency, you'd do it up."

"I'd guess in overall statistics, smoking's a worse health hazard than not doing up one's seat belt." Why am I such a bitch, thought Helena. It's this head. It's not being able to see. "You wouldn't," she started to back up the car between a power pole and a garbage bin, "happen to have something for a headache?"

Amanda rummaged in her bag. The scrabbling sound made Helena think of gerbils in a cage. Amanda's horde of children kept gerbils as pets, along with three dogs and countless cats. Sometimes, the gerbils got out and were eaten by the dogs or cats.

"No. Sorry, dear. Nothing. I never get headaches. Oh, I so wanted everything to be nice this evening!" Amanda shut her bag and settled it on her lap with a plunking motion. "Your first visit in four years. I wanted you to have a good time. I wanted us to have a good time together."

"Look, it was great, okay? I had a great time. Apart from the smoke. And the beer." Helena's neck was twisted, her face strained, as she tried to see out the rear window. In the dim glow cast by dash lights and headlights, her hair stood out around her head like a black halo.

"You have lots of room on this side," Amanda called, her face turned away to look through the rain-splattered rear side window. Her fair hair was short, which had caused a volt of shock in Helena two days before at the ferry landing. She had scarcely recognized the clipped head. Amanda had always had long hair, below her shoulders the last time the sisters had seen each other. That had been nearly a year ago, when Amanda had visited Helena on the mainland. But in her visions of Amanda, Helena always saw her little sister with the waist-length hair of her flower-child days. She's put on weight, too, Helena had thought as they hugged. The weight had not been immediately apparent because of the loose long skirt and baggy top that Amanda had been wearing. Amanda had always worn those types of garments — smocks strung about with long strands of beads, sloppy rope sandals — the hippy uniform. Helena had always preferred clothes that did not interfere with brisk movement, like jeans and joggers. But, ah, yes, the face has scarcely changed at all, Helena had noted with approval when she'd stepped back and looked into her sister's clear grey eyes.

When they were safely into the alley, Helena shifted gears from reverse into first and looked forward. It wasn't until then that she became fully aware of the situation. Sheets of water lashed the windshield. The wipers, despite their frenzied whipping back and forth, were useless against the barrage, and the headlights could barely penetrate the dark tunnel ahead of them. "Jesus!" she said, pressing her right foot down gently on the gas pedal while raising her left foot carefully off the clutch. At the end of the alley she made a right turn into the street, then attempted second gear. The car jerked and threatened to stall. She stepped too strongly on the gas while letting her foot too suddenly off the clutch. The car jetted forward.

"Maybe you should let me drive."

That note again, what Helena thought of as passive aggressive, aggressively critical in its seemingly humble suggestion, which gave her reply a shortness she couldn't control. "I'm okay."

"I'm used to a manual."

"I said I'm okay."

"Are you sure?"

"Of course I'm sure. I rented the damn thing. I'll drive."

"I think we drank quite a lot."

"I didn't."

Through the sheeting rain, a hexagonal black shape on a

pole appeared abruptly at the corner of the road. Helena kept going. There wasn't time to stop before they were past it and, besides, she didn't want to go through all the clutch business again. No cars were coming, at least she couldn't see any headlights, the rain made it difficult to see much of anything. Just in case, as soon as she completed her turn onto the main street, she stepped on the gas and geared up into third.

Amanda let out her breath. "This rain is awful," she said "We should've stayed home. But I wanted you to meet my friends. They're such a good group. Extremely supportive."

Helena, too, had let out her breath, quietly, so Amanda would not know. She felt that she could now manage conversation. "That Trudy what's-her-name, the one I was sitting beside, she says you're a saint."

"Does she? She's been a good friend."

"She says she was ready to put her head in the oven. You talked her out of it."

"She's going through a bad time."

"She can sure toss them back."

"It's her husband. He drives her to drink."

"So she said. Seven times. I found myself counting them. God, I can't help myself," Helena sighed. "A walking stats compiler. That's what higher education does to you. But ... apparently he's seeing someone else."

"I know. Poor Trudy. It's someone he met at an AA meeting."

"It all sounds so *sordid,* but that's the flower child syndrome for you. So many of them failed to make any coherent sense of their lives."

"Sometimes I think they all ended up on this island."

"Lotus land, the land of milk and honey."

"I suppose that's the reason, one of the reasons, we came here. We were so idealistic. We were going to save the world. At least change it. Reuben with his protest songs. He never liked The Man telling him what to do. He had to do things his way."

"I've got a chapter in my thesis about that. Not Reuben specifically. But I address the possibility that the movement was an excuse for people who didn't want to accept responsibility, who bristled under any authority, perhaps relating back to parental authority. They weren't out to save the world so much as to find an excuse for self-indulgence. I found Trudy's description of her husband quite fascinating in view of that chapter."

"Reuben was quite willing to take responsibility. He just didn't want the government telling him what to do."

"Don't remind me, the way he used to go on about fascist states."

Both sides of the four-lane street were a wet blur of neon: *Harvey's, McDonald's, Esso, Chubby Chicken, Shell, The Captain's Fish & Chips, Landmark Insurance.* The strip, locals called this corridor of colourful lights, some flashing, some glowing steadily. It was also the main island highway running north/south.

Helena's face was close to the windshield. Her eyes narrowed as she tried to see through the water flaying the glass.

"Why won't you let me drive?" Amanda raised her voice to be heard above the clacking of the wipers. "I know the road."

"I'm okay."

"I'd know where we're going."

"Are you implying I don't?"

"I live here."

"I stay on the highway until your turn-off. I should be able to handle that."

"It's just that every road has certain dips and bumps and shadows. You get to know them after a while."

They had left the lights of the city behind and were driving along a lonely stretch of ocean embankment. A steel and cement barrier separated the highway from a steep drop that ended directly in the water. The road was slick and black. The headlights were on "low" because Helena couldn't find the "high" switch.

Suddenly, the car swerved.
"What was that?" gasped Amanda.
"I saw something."
"What?"
"Something. An animal maybe."
"We have lots of deer on the island. But I doubt they'd be out tonight."
"I should know what I saw."
"You're driving pretty fast," Amanda ventured.
"Do you think I don't know how to drive?"
"Of course you can drive. But you can't see."
"My vision is perfect."
"Since your operation, you can't see at night. Your eyes can't take glare. When headlights come up suddenly you're blind."
"Whose eyes are they anyway? I should know whether or not I can see."
"I'm just trying to be helpful. Why can't you accept help? I feel like crying for you. I cried the day they lasered your eyes."
"Your tears don't mean much. You cry all the time. Over the smallest thing. Dogs and horses in the movies."
"You never cry."
"Crying is a waste of time."
"I cry for what leaving Ben did to you."
"What do you mean by that crack?"
"You've gotten so hard."
"Not hard. Tough, maybe. You have to be to survive in this world."
"Do you still care for him?"
"Caring for a person doesn't mean you can live with him. God knows I tried."
"What did you try?"
"Everything. Getting angry, not getting angry, probing, leaving him alone. Nothing worked."
"Did you try loving him?"
"That remark just goes to show how little you understand.

You try living with a person who thinks we live a meaningless existence and where suicide is the only rational choice."

"That was his just his existential period. But in that idea was also the idea that we have to find an alternative to suicide."

"Whatever the theory, Ben is a person who can't receive love. Or give it, for that matter. Believe it or not, there are such people in this world. And those people are impossible to live with."

Amanda shook her head. "I don't believe it, not about Ben. Anyway, he's changed since four years ago. He's learned something from that experience."

"If he has, he hasn't let me know."

"But you're the one who left him. To go back to university."

"In the first place, I didn't leave him to go to university. He was impossible to live with. The two elements coincided. In the second place, he left me long before I left him. After that thing with his mother, he withdrew completely. He focused on his pain. He fell in love with it. It was like I had a rival. He didn't see me anymore. He didn't care about us; he didn't care about anything. I stay. I go. It was the same to him. He forced me to leave him. I stayed longer than most women would have. And I don't see him making any moves in my direction."

"Maybe it doesn't matter who makes the first move. So long as somebody does."

"Well, it isn't going to be me. Why should I? I didn't desert him. He deserted me. I wasn't the cause of his downfall. He'd fallen long before I left. Anyway, likely by now he's found another victim to torture with his mind games. There should be a clause in the divorce act for intellectual abuse."

"Are you still married to him?"

"Oh yes. Neither one of us can be bothered getting a divorce, I suppose. It takes time and money."

For a few moments the storm gained prominence of sound. Visibility was becoming more and more of a problem. Helena had to focus on the road ahead. When she was able to speak, her voice was a little less belligerent. "What makes you think he's changed?"

"What?"

"How do you know he's changed, that he's learned something?"

Amanda drew in a deep breath. "I saw Ben last summer." She exhaled slowly. "He came to see me."

"Why would he do that?"

"I don't know. He just showed up one day. Said he was in the neighbourhood."

"I suppose you talked about me."

"We didn't talk about you. But he still loves you. I could tell."

"Are you kidding? I told you, he doesn't know the meaning of the word. He believes in justice, not love."

"He finds it hard to love himself, because of what happened with his mother. That doesn't mean he doesn't love other people. How about his father? He loved his father in spite of their opposing opinions about the war."

"Well, if he'd loved his father more than his moral stance, he would have gone back and saved them all a lot of grief."

"I hope you didn't say that to him."

"Of course not. What do you take me for?"

"It's just that he's suffered so much for making that choice."

"Ben likes to suffer. It's as though he feels he was born to suffer."

"He might agree with you. The Jewish destiny."

"He doesn't believe in destiny, remember?"

For a few minutes, the sisters said nothing. Each seemed to be listening intently to the storm. But when Amanda broke the silence, it was obvious that her thoughts had been otherwise occupied. "I just wish you'd find someone to take care of you."

"I don't need anyone to take care of me. I can take care of myself."

"I mean emotionally. Everyone needs someone to take care of them emotionally."

"I *do* have friends."

"A bunch of intellectual snobs."

"That's preferable to having friends who are intellectually challenged."

"Your life is so sad."

"Leave my life alone."

"Maybe you need someone to talk to."

"I talk to lots of people."

"Cold, inhuman people."

Helena couldn't see the centre line of the highway. She could see the cement barrier only sporadically. She became aware of the tenseness of her body, of her hands gripping the wheel. She made a conscious effort to relax her muscles, one by one. "At least they're not a sociological phenomenon," she said. "Past the due date flower children. Although, I must say I find your friends *extremely* interesting in view of my subject. People who, maybe because they did too many drugs or something, I haven't finished my research on that part yet, but who, some of who, *have* turned out to be unmotivated and irresponsible, and these factors have spiralled them, some of them, down into a lower socio-economic class than they originally came from."

"So now my friends are low-class slobs. I'm a filthy slob. What else can you think of to criticize? My weight. I saw the way you looked when I had to loosen my seat belt. And how about my housekeeping? We haven't done my housekeeping yet. We always do my housekeeping."

Amanda's voice had risen during her speech. Helena kept hers low and even, which somehow smacked of mockery. "Your friends aren't *all* low class. And you're *not* filthy. You have a filthy habit, that's all."

"Oh thank you. Good. Great. That's a relief. The great Helena has pronounced that I'm not filthy after all."

"All I'm saying is you need to get a life, apart from that group of friends and dogs and cats and kids."

"And then there's the 'but' technique."

"What do you mean?"

"You're an expert at that."

"What?"

"My friends aren't exactly low class, but ... I'm not exactly filthy, but...."

"All I'm saying is, maybe you should widen your circle of friends. Women who do something besides sit around and smoke and expose their children to second-hand smoke and bitch about their husbands or the men who go in and out of their lives."

"Look, can we give it a rest? I admit to having slobs for friends. I admit to killing my family with my filthy habit. I admit that it's all my fault. Everything's my fault."

"I didn't say that. But you're a nurse. An ex-nurse. You know what second-hand smoke does to kids. And think of the expense."

Amanda sat up straight. "Stop the car and let me out! I don't want to listen to any more of this!"

"You can't get out."

"Stop the car!"

"I'm not going to stop the car. Be sensible."

"If you don't stop the car I'm going to jump out right here and now." Amanda reached for the door handle.

"You can't leave. It's raining too hard."

"I'm not going to sit here and listen to how I'm an inferior despicable person."

"You're not a despicable person."

"Thank you very much."

"I'm only trying to help you."

"How can you help me by thinking I'm inferior?"

"I don't think you're inferior." Helena's voice exuded patience, as though she were explaining the basics for the umpteenth time to an idiot. "All I'm saying is you haven't made the most of your life."

"What do you know about my life? You never come here to see me. In fact, you haven't been to see me for four years and you live just across the channel! Reuben is my life. But what would you know about that. You never did approve of him."

"That's not true. I always liked Reuben, his great sense of humour. I *did* wonder how the two of you would manage. Him, so ultra alternative and dragging you along with him."

"He didn't drag me along. I wanted to go with him. We've managed just fine. He deserves a lot of credit. It isn't easy making a living in the music business. It takes a lot of courage to even try. And he puts a lot of time into his market gardening business, too. He's worked hard for the kids and me."

"You didn't do *anything* with your degree."

"How about Esther? She didn't do anything with her degree, either. Oh, I suppose because she's married to a university professor and I'm married to a nearly-forty still-struggling musician, she's a success and I'm not."

"I know Mom and Dad wanted her to continue teaching. They put so much importance on education."

"Well, they were both teachers and they both died early of heart attacks. So much for the teaching career."

"You had beauty and intelligence. You got better marks in school than either Esther or me. You were so beautiful. And smart. Those Cave discussions, you didn't say much but then you'd come out with a remark that was so right on target it floored everyone. Mom and Dad had great hopes for you, that's all I'm saying."

"It's a good thing they're not here now to be disappointed in me. Is that it?"

"No. But you were the favourite."

"That's not true. I was the baby, that's all."

"It was hard on them, especially Mom, when you left with Reuben and came out here."

"There was no way I could *not* go along with Reuben. He was and still is my meaning in this life. I think Mom understood that."

"I only mean you're not making the most of your God-given gifts."

"You don't even believe in God."

"Just a manner of speaking. I could say genetically-derived traits."

"How could you believe in God when you think you *are* God."

"Don't be silly."

"You think you're better than everybody else."

"Not *everybody*."

"I'm scared for you. You're tempting fate. You're setting yourself up. For life to teach you a lesson."

"You'd like life to teach me a lesson, wouldn't you? You must hate me."

"I don't hate you. I love you." Amanda's voice returned to its characteristic gentle softness.

"Oh yes. More of your relentless Miss Goody."

"I pray for you."

"Praying is a waste of time."

"You were such a happy little girl. Saucy, it's true, but sunny and happy. You've lost that little girl. I pray you'll find her." Amanda put out her hand.

Helena lurched away from Amanda's touch. The car veered dangerously. "Don't touch me."

"Maybe you need someone to touch you."

"I said don't touch me!"

Through the torrent, sudden lights, a vehicle appeared to be heading directly toward them. Helena twisted the steering wheel away from the glare. The tires skidded on the wet pavement. She threw the wheel back the other way. The car righted itself but not before swerving across the highway into the oncoming lane.

For a moment the motor seemed very loud.

"I insist on driving." Amanda moved as if to undo her seat belt to shift places.

"Stay where you are."

"Why are you mad at me?"

I'm not mad at you, Helena wanted to say. Instead, she pressed her lips together in an ugly stubborn line.

"Why won't you let yourself feel my love?" Amanda pleaded.

"I said, don't touch me. How many times do I have to say that?"

"Watch out! You're going to drive us both into the chuck."

"Keep your hands to yourself then."

"Can't you recognize when someone loves you? Sometimes I feel like giving up on you." Amanda's voice finally broke. It threatened tears.

Helena became incensed. "How can you say that? Do you know what you're saying? That's a terrible thing to say."

"Watch your driving! Helena! Please! What are you doing? Oh my God!"

"Christ!"

An impact like a giant cosmic fist hit them before the car somersaulted over the cement barrier and nose-dived into the ocean. Helena felt that she was caught in a projectile. Then she was plunged into icy water. She was immersed in icy water. The water was all around her, outside of her and inside of her, inside her nose, her lungs. The frigid water was filling her lungs. Her limbs were paralyzed; her lungs were paralyzed. She couldn't breathe. She was breathing water.

Amanda! Amanda! She didn't know whether it was her last word or her last thought. Where is Amanda?

2. A Prairie City

"DARLING."
 "Here's to us."
"To us."
"What a wonderful idea to spend the evening at home alone."
"We're so lucky to have each other."
"So many people have no one."
"Some are alone even when they're with someone."
"Yes, we are lucky."
George Martin set his wine glass down on a low marble-topped coffee table and stood up. He stepped lightly in his black leather slippers to the fireplace where, with a faultlessly clean right hand, he picked up a heavy iron poker. On the third finger of his left hand, braced on his bent knee, was a wide gold band. He leaned forward to flip a smoldering log, sticking his rear end out rather comically. So thought his wife, who was watching him with loving eyes from the brocaded couch opposite.

Esther Martin was a plump, still-pretty, young middle-aged woman. Her brown eyes were still lively and her brown hair, untreated and as yet showing no sign of grey, was in large curls. She wore a floor-length at-home gown of rich blue velveteen and blue slippers embroidered with pink roses. Her fingernails were professionally squared and finished with peach polish. The hand that held aloft a wine glass displayed a set of rings, matched engagement and wedding, with fairly large diamonds. When she gestured with her hands, as she habitually did, they flashed and sparkled with reflected light.

While "Spring" of Vivaldi's *Four Seasons* filled the room with bird sounds and cheer, a sudden rattle of glass came from the tall windows that flanked the fireplace.

"Listen to that wind." Esther's voice, along with the rest of her, had retained a girlish quality.

George went to the window and pushed aside the sheer curtain hanging between heavy side drapes. "Can't see a thing," he reported. He turned and crossed the Axminster rug, picked up his glass, and sat back down beside his wife.

They were drinking champagne. The occasion was the completion of the first chapter, a long one, of George's book on extinct species.

"The radio said twelve centimetres of snow and wind chill to minus thirty." Even when discussing the weather George spoke in low mellifluous tones.

"Good grief! For this time of year," exclaimed Esther.

"I don't know when we've had such a November. Storms are creating havoc across the country."

"I hope Delores is all right." Esther's voice took on a shade of anxiety.

"Don't worry," George soothed. "We'd hear if she wasn't."

"I suppose you're right. She would phone."

"If there's anything higher education has taught our daughter it's how to use the long-distance telephone system."

"Now, dear, you wouldn't want it any other way. You like to hear from your little chick just as much as I do. What if she was one of those kids who never phone home?"

"Of course you're right. It's just that every time she phones it costs a helluva lot more than the long distance fee."

"Toronto is an expensive place to live. We knew that when she went there. You wanted her to have the best program."

George took a rather large sip of his champagne. "The six o'clock news showed snow in Vancouver. I wonder how Helena's managing."

"She may be missing it entirely. She's gone over to the Island."

"Really! She never goes to the Island. It makes her ill."

"She decided to try and face it. We spoke on the phone last Sunday. She sounded optimistic about the venture. It's only for a few days during reading week."

"What are those dear sisters of yours up to? Painting the town red?"

"They may be bailing water. Apparently, they're having a lot of rain out there. I hope things are going all right. Amanda was so looking forward to Helena's visit. She thinks Helena is mad at her."

"Did you explain?"

"It's not easy to explain."

"I suppose not, but likely Amanda would understand. She understands everything."

"It's not so much understanding as unawareness. She simply doesn't know what she does that so provokes Helena."

"I think she knows, but wonders why."

"Possibly. But I can't say to her, 'the way you live makes your sister physically ill.' Perhaps I'm a coward, but how can I say that? Her feelings would be terribly hurt."

"They're hurt anyway."

"I reminded Amanda how Helena always acts distant when she's preoccupied and how she's always been strong-headed in her pursuit of goals."

"Still, Helena *could* manage to get over to the Island more often."

"Helena simply cannot stand muddle."

George reached for the bottle of champagne on the table and poured them each another glass, one of which he graciously passed to his spouse, which his spouse graciously accepted with a smile.

"Especially emotional muddle," Esther continued. "That's why she went to the Coast. To get away from Ben. She always did need a quiet place where she could think, even in her teens.

She *chose* to finish her high school at a convent."

"Maybe she wanted to get away from sex. My parents sent my sisters to convents to avoid that confusion. If ever there was a synonym for human muddle it's sex. I've never understood why. Other species are able to manage it quite well."

"If so, she certainly reversed her attitude in university. She encouraged hordes of hopeful young men."

"All gonad driven."

"Spoken like a biologist. Don't you believe in romance?"

"The one she chose was intellectually driven."

Although Esther noticed her husband's skilful avoidance of her question, she decided not to pursue the subject in case it spoiled their perfect evening. "Yes, I do believe she fell in love with Ben's brain."

"The intellect can exert sexual power. Speaking of Ben, I saw him the other day."

"Our Benjamin? And you didn't tell me!"

"I suppose I didn't give it much thought. Anyway, he's hardly our Ben any more, if he ever was. Ben was always pretty much *his* Ben.

"As far as I'm concerned, he's still ours. After all, he and Helena are still married. Did you actually speak to him?"

"Only for a moment, we were both rushing off to classes."

"How is he doing?"

"Better, I think. They've given him one course."

"Now if he'll behave himself."

"Don't hold your breath."

"He's so principled. I don't know why he has to be that way. It puts people off."

"It's all right to be principled as long as you don't throw it in people's faces."

"I suppose he was wearing that old coat and jeans out at the knees. And that hair and beard that make him look like Jesus."

"He looked quite presentable, actually clean shaven and generally tidy."

"You're not going to tell me he's cut his hair!"

"Nothing so drastic as that. But he did have it gathered back. He was wearing a respectable looking parka, and I believe his jeans were clean and in one piece. I didn't look too closely. But he still has that hollow look around his eyes."

"Remember how I used to go over to his place after Helena left and try to clean it and him up, and met with total rejection." Esther's expression clouded for a moment, then, with an enthusiastic return to the present, "But, what did you find out? Is he seeing anyone?"

"I was not going to inquire into that. We talked shop, mostly."

"Does he still do that mission work? Hampers for the poor and such?"

"We didn't talk about it. But he once said that's where he feels at home. Among the dispossessed. I suppose that's how he regards himself."

"He dispossessed himself."

"That doesn't make him any less dispossessed."

"He always was a strange person. Remember when we first met him at university? Protesting the Vietnam war seemed like such a daring brave thing to do. I suppose that's why Helena fell for him."

"I don't know about brave but certainly daring. I always thought there were better ways of confronting the problem. Hospital work, office jobs, that sort of thing was available."

"But he was protesting his country's involvement in the war as a whole, so he couldn't morally have any part in it. Or so he used to say."

"Well, to each his own. He was so full of ideals, such a shame that he had to hit the ground of reality so hard."

"Still, we must help him."

"It's not easy to help Ben."

"We should invite him for a drink."

"He won't come."

"Maybe not. He thinks we've sold out to bourgeois materialism. Remember how he used to tease us? He had more sympathy for the efforts of Amanda and Reuben. I can still see the four of us waving them off when they left for the Coast in that old rattletrap car packed with all their worldly goods."

"Like so many of the flower children they didn't know what they were getting into. They had no experience with recreational gardening, let alone market gardening."

"They're not flower *children* any more," said Esther.

"Getting to be flower middle-agers. I wonder if Amanda had it to do over again if she would do the same."

"Oh I think so. She could never deny the existence of any of her children. She could never think, 'I have too many'. After all, which one would she dispose of? No, they're all precious in her sight. And she'd never deny her love for Reuben."

"But living on that scrabble farm and eking out a living. It can't be easy. Why didn't she go back to nursing?"

"She's always considered motherhood to be her career. She feels the world well lost for love."

"Amanda has a genuinely good heart." George tipped up his glass and noted that the bottle on the low table was empty.

"And Reuben is a dreamer."

"They've been true to the revolution."

"Unlike the rest of us."

"We grew up."

"Yes. I suppose saints and dreamers never do."

"Saints and dreamers have a tough go of it."

"But they've stuck together."

"That's something, in this day and age."

"They've been happy in spite of not having much."

"She always goes along with Reuben's crazy schemes and he supports her quilting and painting and beads and jam making and god knows what else she sells at the local fairs. In the end, they're a good match."

"So are we." A cloud arrived and settled momentarily on Esther's face. "Except for my lack of intellectuality."

"Don't be silly. We've had this conversation so many times. I keep telling you that not being an academic doesn't mean you're not an intellectual."

"Even when I can't understand half the things you talk about in your book? Oh, I suppose I have some intelligence, but I don't have a trained mind, not like you or Helena or Ben."

"And I keep telling you that you are exactly what I want in a wife. I encouraged you to stay at home and take care of the house and Delores, and me I might add. My mother wouldn't have dreamed of working outside the home. Being a housewife and mother is an important career on its own. You know I believe that. Is it that *you* wish now that you'd had more?"

"No, of course not."

"Well, then, let the matter drop. No need to go over it again."

"But in all honesty, I suspect it's been a little easier for our love to flourish in these surroundings. We live in paradise. A paradise you've provided for us."

"Thank you my dear. But a house is not a home until someone makes it so. Your interpretation of house mistress, cook, mother, is what has made this a home."

They kissed, briefly. George reached to the table. He picked up the empty champagne bottle and looked at it critically. He turned to Esther. "What do you think?"

"Do we dare?" she almost giggled.

"Why not?"

"First chapters don't get finished that often."

"A little indulgence once in a while won't hurt us."

George rose and, empty bottle in hand, moved through French doors that led into the dining room and from there through a swinging door into the kitchen. Esther watched him, her dark eyes aglow. She thoroughly approved of his still thick curly hair, only recently flecked with grey, an attractive iron grey, his trim build, his light step, his grey flannel trousers, his wool plaid vest. She bought all his clothes. Without defining it as such, she consistently tried for the country squire look and was consistently successful.

George returned to the living room with a new bottle. He made a bit of a ceremony of pushing up the cork with his thumbs until it popped satisfactorily, nearly striking the ceiling, landing on the carpet beyond the opposite end of the sofa. The champagne threatened to overflow; he held it over the marble top. Esther leaped to the rescue with paper napkins, patterned in a large floral print. They laughed together. George poured them each fresh glasses. They sat back down on the sofa, closer to each other than before. George put his arm around Esther's shoulder.

"Our shelter in the storm." Esther raised her glass to her husband. "To us. Who have made it happen." George raised his glass to his wife.

"Summer" was now shimmering to a close and George's looks at his wife were becoming suggestive, although after more than twenty years of marriage he knew there was no chance before dinner. Yet, he actually preferred adventures before dinner, before he had eaten and drunk too much. It was a small thing, a very small thing he told himself, and practically the only thing upon which he and Esther did not agree.

"And to our first chapter." Again, Esther raised her glass.

My first chapter, thought George. But it seemed churlish to nitpick the point. It was only Esther's way. She liked to feel part of everything he did. She was so fond of him, and also perhaps she did *not* have enough stimulation in her own world. "Let's hope it's not the last," he said for reply.

"Oh surely not."

"Of course not," said George. "My attempt at a joke."

"You're not worried are you?" The fine skin on Esther's brow furrowed slightly.

"No, no. It's just the old story. Preparation of lectures, classes, marking, committee meetings. Never enough hours in the day."

"Well, we're not going to think about those things this evening. This is our time."

"How was your day?" inquired George, happy to change the subject.

"Well, Louise dropped my Lady Anne but I've told you about that."

"Yes, when I first got home, but as I said, we can get another."

"We can't get that one. That one is irreplaceable. *She's* irreplaceable. No, I don't want another Lady Anne. She lived. She died. No other can take her place."

"I understand how you feel. Still, I must point out, she was only a piece of china."

"Yes, I know I'm being silly, but there it is. Louise felt dreadful, of course, but I don't know how many times I've told her not to dust this room, that I'll do it. Anyway, then I had lunch with Anna. She gave me the lowdown on the Arlinsons. They've split up."

"That's hardly news. You could see that coming for a while."

"But the thing is, James has left Gloria for another *man*. You'd think if he could tolerate the closet for twenty-five years he could manage a few more and go to his grave without upsetting the whole family."

"Please, no talk about the grave. He's only my age."

"Well, you *look* twenty years younger. Mmmm." Esther sipped and jiggled a loose slipper on her foot. "I do love champagne, those bubbles in my nose, like tiny balloons carrying me away."

"Are you getting drunk?" George teased.

"Not drunk. Tipsy." Esther put down her glass. She kicked off the loose slipper. With the flat of her hand she rubbed the back of George's neck where the hair was short and bristly. She looked up into his face, still handsome, though somewhat puffy, especially around the eyes. In reply, he looked down into the complacent face of his wife and gave her thigh a little squeeze. They beamed at each other. "And," she asked, "how was your day?"

"I did have a bit of a strange incident. After class, a student came to my office. Veronica something or other. One of those unpronounceable foreign names. She was distraught, on the verge of hysterics. She actually broke down and started crying."

"Poor thing. What was the problem?"

"Apparently, she's been in a relationship and the fellow wants to break it off."

"How sad. But why is she telling *you* this?"

"I think she just started talking and everything spilled out. She's alone here, without family, from the East. The reason she came to see me, of course, she wants an extension on a paper."

"The young," sighed Esther. "They're always in love with someone or other. It's as though they have to be. Still, it's hard on them. They're quite sincere in their broken hearts. Is there anything we can do to help her?"

"I don't think so. By this time next week, she'll have forgotten all about him."

"She must be about the same age as Delores. She shouldn't be alone. We must help her."

George was relieved from replying by Vivaldi's "Autumn," which took that moment to recover from its melancholy mood and reassert itself in a burst of sound. At the same moment, a blast of winter struck the house, causing a shuddering rattle from the windows. The lights flickered.

George remembered that he was hungry. "I'm hungry," he announced, setting his glass down, a little unsteadily since he had drunk the larger amount of champagne. He drew his arm from around his wife's shoulders.

Esther, too, sat up straight. "Oh, I forgot to serve the hors d'oeuvres," she said. "I bought an excellent expensive pate and a lovely piece of Camembert."

"I have an idea," said George, putting his hands on his knees. "Why don't I stoke up the fire and we'll have a picnic, right here on the rug. You bring out your pate and your cheese and I'll open a bottle of red."

"Will that be enough? I bought steaks."

"We'll have them tomorrow night. I don't feel like anything heavy tonight."

Gaily as two children setting off on a treasure hunt, they trooped off to the kitchen. Esther set a large teak tray, attractively, with plates and knives, cheeses and meats, fruits and crackers, a sliced baguette. George raided his wine cellar and brought up a good Bordeaux. Back in the living room, they set their hoard down on the coffee table. Esther went to fetch a cloth and George went back to the kitchen for salt and pepper. Esther spread the cloth on the rug and George put more wood on the fire. They set their lunch out and plunked themselves into the middle of it all. "I feel decadent," Esther trilled.

George poured the red wine.

Esther watched George pour. "Isn't it awful of us, two bottles of champagne and now on to a Chateau Bertinerie?"

"If we're the privileged class we may as well act the part." George raised his glass.

"Do you think we're hedonistic?"

"Only tonight."

"I do feel guilty about being so happy."

"It's the Catholic upbringing. Guilt and redemption."

"I fear I will have to pay for it sooner or later."

"Chuck 'em, those old superstitions."

"It isn't right that I'm luckier than my sisters. Helena with her broken marriage and no children. Amanda with husband and children but little else."

"Working hard, trying to live a good, a decent, life. It isn't luck when things turn out. It isn't as though we haven't earned what we have. Twenty years of marriage, raising a daughter, which was not always easy."

"You've convinced me. I hereby resolve not to feel guilty about being happy." Esther raised her glass.

They could hear the wind. Esther shivered. "I'm so glad we stayed in."

"We might even go to bed early." George put a warm hand on the side of Esther's neck and slid it down the warm skin at the back of her gown.

"Ummm."

"I have a better idea. We could take off our clothes right here. That's one of the privileges of people who've seen their only child off to college."

"I thought you were hungry!"

"At the moment, food is not what I'm hungry for."

"But we just got all the food spread out."

"We can unspread it. It will only take a moment." By now George had moved his hand from Esther's back to her front.

"Well..."

George stood up, a little stiffly, rising from the floor. They moved the food to the marble-topped table. Esther had her arms lifted to one side of her head to remove an earring. George had just finished reclosing the fire screen. They were stopped in their movements by the ringing of the phone, an extension on an end table near a wing chair.

"Don't answer it," George said.

Esther was torn. What if it was Delores? Needing them.

She reached out her perfectly manicured hand and picked up the receiver.

3. Across Town

"FUCK! DOES THIS MEAN we have to stay in?" Veronica held back a limp curtain provided by the landlord and peered through a frosted window into a sheet of snow driven horizontally by a howling wind.

Benjamin Levi was sitting in the halo cast by a desk lamp that he had screwed onto the edge of a vinyl-topped table. He was marking papers.

"Winter sucks!" With lips surprisingly full for such a narrow face, Veronica breathed a larger opening in the frost. She positioned one brown eye to the opening. Her nose nearly touched the glass.

"Why anyone would choose to live in this fucking country is more than I can understand! Anyone with brains would've dodged the draft in a warmer climate!" Her long mouth twisted down at the corners. "Goddamn fucking weather!" She flung back a thick strand of long blonde hair, her quick nervous fingers tucking it behind a delicate ear. "It's all over the world too. What a fucking planet. Only November. And look at it!

"And it's even worse in here." She looked across her shoulder, her sharp wary eyes darting around the room, as though she feared something dark and furry might fly out of the shadows. "It's fucking depressing in here.

"And you," her eyes lighted on Benjamin, "you're depressing. The way you sit there all the goddamn time marking those fucking papers. Do you think anybody cares?"

"Probably not."
"You could be a full prof with a TA doing that. You had every fucking opportunity…"
"How do you know?"
"You told me."
"When?"
"One night when you were drunk."
"Christ."
"You had all the advantages of rich parents…"
"They weren't rich."
"Compared to mine they sure as hell were. You had all the lessons, all the summer vacations at those expensive Jewish resorts, all the goddamn privileges that money can buy. You got all the scholarships, had the best teachers, and what have you done with your life? Just look at you! Forty years old and you can barely get one sessional course to teach. What sort of future do you have?"
"None."
"Why do I stay with you?"
"You mustn't stay. You must go."
"And the *time* you spend on those papers! Do you think anybody cares about your pearls of wisdom that you cast so generously before us swine in the form of witty margin comments? Do you think those students understand your subtle sense of humour? Do you think they have time to read your witticisms? Let me tell you, they're much more interested in who they're fucking at the moment or how they're going to make the payments on their new car. They're involved in *life*. *Life*! That's what makes the world go round, in case you've forgotten. They've got it figured out. You're the bird with its head stuck in the sand, which in your case is piles of musty old books, trying to figure out what happened in the past, trying to put a different spin on it, as if anybody gives a shit, deciding who was right and who was wrong, the French or the English, the Germans or the Americans, as if it really matters.

As if right and wrong weren't arbitrary."
"Give it a rest, Ronnie."
"Look at me! I'm a person!"
Without moving his head, Benjamin raised his winter sea eyes up from the essay he was reading and looked at Veronica over the tops of his glasses. With a small frown he lowered them again.

Benjamin's weary eyes were set into a weary face. Around that face, he had a great deal of brown curly hair that was drawn back by an elastic band. His complexion was sallow, like that of people in hospitals and prisons. His clothes were well worn but clean, which had not been the case as recently as a few months previous. On his feet were grey work socks with a red line around the top. On his chin was a growth of reddish stubble that he would dutifully scrape off on class day, once more into the breach, as he thought of it. When he looked at himself in the mirror, he sometimes thought how he would not have knuckled under like this ten years ago or even four years ago when Helena left. Let the fucks go fuck themselves. That's what he would have said of the establishment then. But since then life had taught him a thing or two. Since then he had touched bottom.

"You could cut your marking time in half! If you marked like most other profs."

"The sooner you shut up and let me get on with it, the sooner I'll be finished."

"Then can we get out of this hole? Go down to the Rose and Crown?"

"I can't go down to the Rose and Crown tonight," Benjamin mumbled, trying to concentrate on what he was reading.

He had cleared an island on the table for his work. Around this island, like jungle growth constantly threatening to take over, was the mess of his life: plates smeared with jam and peanut butter or ketchup and mustard, brown-stained cups, half empty potato chip bags, a miscellany of scissors, knives, cigarette packs, broken-leaded pencils, dried-up ball point pens, piles of books. Beyond, was more jungle: flaking paint, curled wallpaper, a cluttered mantel over a fireplace long devoid of its gas element. A lumpy armchair with torn upholstery and oozing padding was strewn about with newspapers and old magazines, its broad arms lined with overflowing ash trays, books, and empty drink cans. The only way out was through a badly scarred door into a dim corridor.

"Well, I can't stay in. No fucking way. I'm too depressed. I'd slit my throat."

"Don't talk such nonsense."

"It's not nonsense. Life is such shit." Veronica was back at the window. "What's the point of going on with this farce? You don't know how close I come at times."

Benjamin had just read the same sentence five times and still had no idea what point the student was trying to make. It was on the tip of his tongue to say, 'we all come close sometimes', but then he remembered the awful consequences of not paying attention, really paying attention, to what other people were saying. "Why don't you find something on the television?" he said instead.

"I can't focus on anything. Before I fell in love with you I could concentrate. Now I can't even watch a fucking sitcom on TV."

"Go to bed then. Before you know it, it'll be morning. You'll feel better in the morning."

"I'll go to bed if you'll come with me. You can mark papers in the morning."

"I can't mark sixty essays in one day. I have to pace myself."

"I can't stand this dump! I can make it down to the Crown. It's only a couple of blocks. I'm going stir crazy."

"Can't you see I'm trying to work?"

"I'm hungry." She turned her head toward the kitchen area of the room, which comprised a stove, a long counter with sink and cupboards and a fridge. The sink was piled with dirty dishes, the back of the counter was lined with empty beer bottles, the counter was littered with empty tins, jars and bottles. "What did you have for supper?"

"I can't remember." Benjamin looked over to the counter and spied the latest addition to the collection of pots that held a miscellany of dried up bits of food. "Kraft dinner. There might be some left."

"Kraft dinner! Gross! That's pitiful. A grown up person having Kraft dinner for dinner."

"Well, make yourself something else."

"What is there?"

"I don't know. Look in the fridge."

Veronica flicked her long thin body, which appeared even longer because of tight jeans and a close-fitting top, away from the window toward the fridge. She opened the fridge door and took a step back. "What're you growing in here?" She stretched a long arm into the interior and pulled out a plastic carton labelled cottage cheese. She pried open the lid and sniffed the contents. "Ugh, Crap!" She looked at the due date. "September 10th! Good Christ, that's more than two months ago!"

"Well, throw it out."

She pitched the container from where she was standing into an overflowing black garbage bag huddled like a sullen invertebrate near the sink. With the other hand she slammed the fridge door shut. "Oh, Jeez, there goes another nail." She straightened and examined the splayed fingers of her right hand. "My nails are in such bad shape, splitting and peeling. My body's a total mess. My body's falling to pieces."

"You have a lovely body."

"How would you know?" She moved to where he was sitting and placed her hands on his shoulders. She rubbed the back of his neck with her thumbs.

"Look, Ronnie..."

"You never look at it these days."

"I have to get these essays marked. And I'm tired."

She lifted her hands abruptly. "You're always tired. You make me sick with your fucking tiredness."

"You shouldn't have taken up with an old man."

"You're not old. You just act old." Veronica was rummaging on the table for a cigarette pack that wasn't empty. "Old and cold. You wouldn't recognize an emotion if it smacked you in the face. No wonder your wife left you."

"Leave my wife out of this."

"Oh, I suppose she's too good to be discussed by the likes of me."

"No. It's just..."

"It's men like you who've made me the way I am." She gave up on her search and turned away.

"There's no point..."

"If you're so hung up on her why did you let her go in the first place?"

"People, intelligent people, don't 'let each other go.' People are free agents, free to do as they please." Benjamin's voice, usually quiet, was raised. It had taken on a hard edge, as though he were speaking through gritted teeth. He pushed the student's essay away from him and a cup and saucer and plate went over the edge of the table with a crash. He looked at the pile of broken crockery on the floor. He took off his glasses and drew a thin hand down over his face, scooping in at the eye sockets, curving out and down the bony cheeks and bringing thumb and index finger together at the chin. "Why don't you watch something on television?" His voice was quiet again. "Give me another hour to get something done here."

"Then can we go down to the Crown? Where I can get some fries and a burger?"

"Maybe I could for half an hour. But I have to go to the Drop-In Centre tonight."

"You and your Christly Drop-In Centre!"

"Tonight will be a bad night down there. They'll be crowded. Volunteers might not make it in."

"Well, you can go to your fucking mission for all I care. I'm going to the Crown." She crossed the room to the front-door closet. "Maybe I'll pick up some mental case who'll drag me out to the back lane and murder me."

"Don't talk such rot."

"It's not rot. You think everything I say is rot."

"I don't think that."

"You didn't used to think it. At least, you pretended you didn't. You used to like me."

"I still like you."

"You don't want to sleep with me any more."

"I told you why not."

"Oh yeah, sure. Moral reasons. If you really wanted me you'd sleep with me, moral reasons or not."

"I don't want to take advantage of you."

"That's never stopped any man before."

"That's just it. You've been treated badly by men. I don't want to be another man who treats you badly." Benjamin's concentration was firmly broken. His head remained up from the table. "And we didn't really sleep together, ever," he said thoughtfully.

"I don't know what you'd call it then."

"We've had sex a number of times. And I admit the fault was mine. That should not have happened. But having sex is not sleeping together."

"What is it then?"

"It's a physical act which relieves tension."

"No, I mean the other. The sleeping together."

"Sleeping together involves trust and companionship. It involves giving solace and nurture to the other person."

"Well, it's all above stupid little me, I'm sure." Veronica slung a scarf around her neck and reached into the closet for her coat.

"You're not stupid. In fact, you're very bright."

"I am stupid. If I wasn't stupid, I'd walk out of here for

good. I'd forget you ever happened, just like you've already forgotten me."

"I haven't forgotten. I shouldn't forget. It happened. I was weak. I drink too much. I don't want it to happen again."

"Why don't you like me? What did I do?" In a sudden switch, Veronica's voice changed in tone, taking on a pleading quality.

"You didn't do anything. You're a perfectly charming attractive young woman. Much too good for me. That's why you should leave, find yourself a nice young man your own age."

"I don't like men my own age. They're all stupid."

"In any case, you should get out of here. You can do better with your life than waste it on me. You should meet some people your own age, of both sexes."

"You didn't say that two months ago when you asked me to come here and stay."

"You didn't seem to have any place else to go."

"Oh yeah, Mr. Saintly Motives. It didn't take you long to jump my bones."

"Of course I was attracted to your body. Who wouldn't be? But I also thought I could help you."

"And now you've given up on me."

"No. But I can't seem to help anybody. I can't even help myself. You need someone who's kind, who won't mistreat you even when you ask for it. You might learn to feel secure with such a person."

"Men are such a bunch of sleaze balls. And you're no better than the rest."

"It's so easy to treat you badly. You demand to be mistreated. And how do you think that makes the fellow feel? Not good about himself. Naturally, he wants to get out of the relationship. You demoralize your partner and you demoralize yourself. But we've talked about this before."

"I'm afraid all this psycho hype stuff is too deep for me. At least at the Crown I can hear some normal conversation. Even hockey scores are better than this." She bent to put on her boots.

Benjamin watched her zip up one boot and reach for the other. "I wish you wouldn't go."

"Surely I don't detect a note of concern."

"You know I'm concerned about you. God knows what trouble you'll get yourself into. I don't like you drinking too much with complete strangers."

"What does it matter? If you don't love me what does it *matter*?" She straightened and put on her coat. "I spoke to that relative of yours today."

"Who?"

"Dr. Martin. Oh, don't worry. I didn't tell him who I was, that is, that I know you. He's kind of cute."

"Cute?"

"Good looking."

"Is he? Perhaps. I suppose he is. He must be nearly fifty by now. I can't believe it. We're all getting old. But we're not related."

"You told me you were. When I was telling you about taking his course."

"Just by marriage."

"I wondered. He seems like a real nice guy."

"George? Yes, he is. His wife is very nice, too. She's totally devoted to George."

"Sounds like my pet spaniel."

Veronica wrenched open the door. She stopped a moment and looked back over her shoulder. Her face, framed by her ash blonde hair and a red woollen toque, with its sly fox-like evasion abandoned a moment, was open and vulnerable. "What would I want with old George," she said. "It's you I'm crazy about. Don't ask me why. You're not much of a prize." She banged the door shut behind her, leaving him finally in silence and peace.

He could no longer mark papers. His energy and motivation had been destroyed by the scene. He got up and went to the window, his movements tentative. Although he was of average height, he had a slim build and, besides, was so thin, he didn't seem to have much weight or substance behind him.

With the nail of his thumb he scraped ice from the glass and watched Veronica come out of the building and head down the street, into the storm. He turned back into the room and gathered up the student essays into a pile. He picked up the broken dishes and put them in the garbage bag. While he did these things, as so often happened, his thoughts drifted to images of Helena, the way she had looked bent over the sink washing dishes or before the bathroom mirror brushing her hair, or the particular way she used to step into her bath, lowering herself slowly into the water. Sternly, he cleared his mind. Such thoughts were against the rules of survival.

He looked at his watch. He may as well go.

He arrived at the Centre to find his predictions correct. Only one other volunteer was there. Victor, who was applying for graduate school in the social work program and needed volunteer hours to add to his resume, was sitting at a table with one of the regulars playing checkers. The usual assortment of street people lay about on couches, sat in armchairs or at tables, smoking, drinking coffee, reading newspapers, staring into space.

Benjamin pulled up a chair beside Victor. He looked over the group. "Where's Bruno?" he asked.

"You know Bruno," said Victor. "He won't come in unless he has to."

"A night like tonight, you'd think he'd have to."

"He's probably curled up in his cardboard box over his vent."

"There's Sammy," said Benjamin. "If Sammy's here, Bruno should be here."

Benjamin went over to where Sammy was sitting, smoking and working his moist lips loosely over bare gums. Low growls and mutterings came out of his throat as his damaged brain transported him to another space where he fought apparitions. Regarding him, Benjamin knew that there was no point in questioning Sammy about his roommate's whereabouts.

He got his parka and returned to Victor. "I'm going out to have a look," he said. "The old guy's over seventy. It's only two blocks to his place."

From a half block away, he could see the cardboard structure. As he got closer, he could make out the dark shape of Bruno huddled over the heat vented from the system of an office building.

"Hey, Bruno, you can't stay out here on a night like this." He took a step closer. "Bruno." He bent closer still. "Hey, man." He shook his shoulder. Bruno fell over sideways. In the street light, Benjamin could see that the old man's beard was stiff and white with frost. Patches of white blossomed on the skin of his cheeks, thin skin, all that stood between blood trying to pump and the brutal night. "Hey," Benjamin knelt in the snow. He pulled Bruno up and held him in his arms. Bruno's head fell back against Benjamin's shoulder. The eyes opened. A vapour of breath escaped his mouth. Bruno motioned to Ben to put his ear close. Benjamin heard a faint, hoarse whisper, "I'm sorry. I'm sorry."

"For what? What're you sorry for, man?" Benjamin attempted to keep the other man talking but the head fell loosely to one side. Benjamin stared as the white vapour stopped. He felt for a pulse. His own hands were so cold it was difficult to feel anything.

"Hey Ben, Ben, are you there?" Victor's voice called through the dark.

"Here." He heard the crunch of Victor's footsteps and felt his presence behind his shoulder. "What are you doing out here? You're gonna freeze your ass off." His voice was a little angry. He felt both sad and angry, sad at Bruno's senseless death and even more senseless life, angry at a god who dispatched his victims so callously.

"Someone wants you on the phone."

"Couldn't you take a number?"

"She insisted on holding. She's darn near hysterical."

She. Ronnie then. What sort of trouble had she gotten herself into now? He turned back to the man in his arms. "Here, give me a hand."

"Bruno?"

"Yeah, silly old bugger has frozen himself to death."

II.
What Happened After

1. A Winter Morning

I. HELENA

HELENA WAS SUFFOCATING. Water filled her mouth, her nostrils, all the cavities of her head. Her lungs were about to burst. Then she felt herself rising to the surface, face up. If she could only hang on a moment longer, one more moment. She broke the surface. She gulped, taking in great draughts of air. She knew that she must move her legs and arms. She knew that she must swim. It was the only way she could save herself. But when she tried to move, an arm, a leg, something restricted her movements. And the air was not right. It was not cold, fresh, salty. It was warm, too warm.

She opened her eyes. A black wall slapped her in the face. But it was not water. She was dry. She was warm. She was between dry, warm flannel sheets. It was only a dream. A nightmare. Amanda was not dead. She had not killed her sister. Thank God. She made a vow right then and there to be nicer to Amanda and to visit her more often.

But she was in a strange place. Where? She hoped that she was not at some man's apartment, some fellow whom she could not remember. Had she drunk a lot last night? She couldn't remember. But she sometimes did. One thing she did know, one thing in the here and now, was that she was too warm. No wonder she had dreamed that she was suffocating. Her hands could feel layers of blankets, a quilt. The sheets were cloying. She brought her left hand out from under the sheet and held the back of it close to her face. It was too dark to see. She hoisted herself up onto her elbows and looked around. Ahhh, there we go, red, on the night table. 4:10. She thought a moment: morning or afternoon? Winter or summer? If summer, it would be lighter. Winter then. Or possibly spring. Or fall. Early spring. Late fall. She slid herself across the sheets and felt around on the night table for a lamp. A switch. Good. She clicked the switch. The light came on in a subdued glow. She looked around her. Drapes hung in folds across the window; a dresser sat across the end wall and another stood to the right of the bed. She lay back down, her head squarely on the pillow and closed her eyes. She breathed in a remembered smell of scented bed sheets, lemon furniture polish. She knew where she was. Esther's. In the guest bedroom. She had surfaced into the house of her sister.

From somewhere came the sound of water, a sudden gush, a toilet flushing. Someone was up and using the toilet. She, too, should get up and go to the bathroom. But it seemed too big a thing to do. She heard water running from a tap, then the tap turned off. Was someone getting a drink? Getting an aspirin, a sleeping pill, a shot of whiskey? Whatever it took to get them through the night.

She must have dozed off. Now she heard different sounds, the clinking of dishes, the shutting of a cupboard door, again, water from a tap. Someone was in the kitchen. She turned her head: 5:20.

Her mind was alert now. She would not be able to soothe it back into a comatose state. She sat up, threw back the covers and swung herself onto the edge of the bed. Her head spun. She closed her eyes. Something hurt, a pain came from some part of her body but she could not identify the spot. She felt bruised all over. She looked down to where white lace and forearm met, but there was nothing visible there to help her identify the source. A stab of pain sliced through her right eye, sliced through the other pains and through the indefinite floating pain that for two years had enveloped her every conscious moment. She realized two things: she would have to find a pain killer and she would have to find a toilet.

She made a firm resolve to stand up. She raised her head and saw the dresser. She reached out her arms and with both hands grasped the smooth wood of the edge. Supporting her weight on her hands, she stood. She took a step and her foot came into contact with something. A suitcase lay open on the floor, a suitcase piled high with neatly folded clothing. On the flapped-open lid was a small mound of something dark and shapeless — the outfit she had worn yesterday, a skirt and jacket, stripped off in a hurry and discarded. She remembered last evening, the airport terminal, the chrome and glass, the stark whiteness like an operating theatre, the emptiness because of the late hour, the voice on the intercom predicting snow, and then Esther rushing at her, furs, scarves and curls bouncing. She remembered Esther's hands gripping the steering wheel as she manoeuvred the car through falling snow and slushy streets. She remembered the *pah dah pah dah* of the windshield wipers.

Suddenly, everything, everything, washed over Helena like a gigantic black tidal wave. The nightmare was a reality. The car had flown into the ocean. She, Helena, had been released into icy wet blackness. She had floated up just in time to see a dark shape like a small whale, its sheeny back glistening, pause a moment before descending, almost gracefully, and slowly disappearing into the black water and the storm-lashed night. Amanda had been trapped inside that dark shape while some twisted ironic force had flung her free, leaving her to surface into coldness so intense, so harsh, so bitter, no human being could survive it for long.

Amanda was dead. She had killed Amanda. She had killed her sister. But that was years ago. Two years and three months. Soon it would be two years and four months. Then two years and five months, and six months, and seven months. And no relief. No relief from the workings of her brain.

She remembered why she had come home to Esther.

She lurched to the bathroom. The vinyl on the floor sent a shock of cold through her feet and up through her body. She flipped the light switch, made it to the toilet and sat down. She put her head down on her knees. She remembered that the month was February. She hated February.

She pulled open the mirror door to a cabinet, careful not to look in the mirror. Esther must have something for a headache. Didn't everyone have something on hand for pain? She found some extra-strength Tylenol and shook several into the palm of her hand. How many would it take for this particular headache? She looked down at the white oblongs. They seemed to grow in dimension, as if calling to her, offering their particular solution of oblivion. But she had something better in her handbag, something better for sleep. Where was her handbag? Her head snapped up, her hand dropped the pills. Her heart started to race and she couldn't breathe. Where had she left her handbag last night? She turned and bolted, slamming her side and her head first against the bathroom doorjamb then, bouncing off that, against the bedroom doorway. Where? Where? Frantically she looked around. There. On the bureau. She rushed to it, snatched it up, felt in the special pocket. Yes. She had not lost it. No one had found it and taken it away from her. The bottle was still there. She unscrewed the cap and shook one small blue tablet into her hand just to make sure. But these were not for now. These were for later. These were for after she had found Ben. It was not quite time to sleep. First she had to find Ben. Then she would be out of this hell. Otherwise, she would go to another hell, an eternal hell. She had seen hell; she didn't want to spend eternity there.

Back in the bathroom, with shaking hands she retrieved the white oblongs from the sink, swallowed two with tap water and returned the rest to the container. Hanging on to the door frame and walls, she made her way down the hall to the kitchen. She knew this house well. She had been here often. She had lived here one summer, when she had been young, happy, a long time ago, when she had been blissfully unaware of what life had in store.

The hall runner was thick and springy beneath her feet. She made no sound. The radio in the kitchen was playing softly … *You don't have to say you love me, just be close at hand*.…

George stood at the kitchen counter. He was wearing red jogging pants, a long-sleeved sweatshirt, and a blue denim vest. He was measuring beans into a coffee grinder.

"Good morning," she whispered.

He turned quickly, his face breaking into a smile. She hadn't seen him since Amanda's funeral and her first impression was that he looked well, even better than then. He had good strong features and thick hair, the sort of looks that aged well.

"Good morning," he said in a normal voice, advancing toward her. "It's all right. You don't have to worry about waking Esther. You could drop a bomb beside the bed."

He was going to embrace her. She held up her hand. "Please," she said. "I'm such a fright in the morning." She evaded him further by dropping herself into a chair, then attempted to fill the awkward gap. "I remember that, Esther's talent for sleeping."

"She doesn't worry about things." George returned to the cupboard and took down a coffee filter. "That's the secret."

Helena noted the familiar table and chairs, heavy oak, the chairs softened by back and seat cushions quilted in cheerful floral patterns. On the table were place mats in a similar country cottage design. The fabric items were new, or maybe not so new. When had she been here last? Since she couldn't do the calculations necessary to figure it out, she abandoned the question. She hugged her shoulders and stared at Janus, the two-faced god who adorned George's back.

You don't have to stay forever, just try and understand… It was a woman's voice. George switched it off.

"Nice vest," she said, feeling that the situation called for an attempt at social decorum, especially after her rebuff.

"A gift from my students," he said, over his shoulder. "Christmas. They took me out for a drink."

"They must like you."

"I didn't know if I should accept it, the vest, that is. But then I decided their feelings would be hurt if I didn't."

"Colourful design." It was a square stitched onto the denim. The left side of the picture was dark, subdued purples and blues, the right side bright, pinks and greens. In the centre of the square was a flaming sun and in its centre a circle of two faces, one light, one dark, fitted into each other.

"Janus," George said.

"I believe he was the Roman god of the rising and setting of the sun."

"Yes. Also doorways, beginnings. One face looks forward, the other back."

He stopped talking to buzz the grinder. Helena looked around the kitchen. The fridge was new; it had vertical doors with freezer space on one side. The stove, across from the fridge, was the same as when she had lived here, It must be fifteen years ago now. The counter, a U-shape, was spanking clean and tidy as usual. The window above the sink, at the bottom of the U, was a square of grey light. The floor was polished tile.

"Everything looks so bright and clean," she said when the grinding stopped. "Have you had the place painted recently?"

"Not recently." George whisked the ground coffee into the paper filter. "But maybe since you were here last. Esther does it. She likes doing that sort of thing."

"Yes, I remember. I've been living in such dumps. Normal tidy households seem positively compulsive."

"I thought your apartment was quite comfortable."

"I gave that up when I went to England. Lately, I've been up the coast."

"That's right. Esther told me. Prince Rupert, wasn't it?"

Prince Rupert, land of the sado-macho wierdos, she thought. "Yes," she said. Likely he knew the whole gruesome tale of what she'd been doing the last couple of years. She suspected that Esther told George everything. Although even Esther did not know the half of it.

Through the square of window behind George, Helena could see black branches against a dark sky. What hour did it become light this time of year? "Esther said you're into morning jogging."

George plucked a steaming kettle up from the stove and poured slowly over the coffee grounds. "Still, I could have picked you up last night. It wouldn't have been a problem. I hope Esther explained that to you. She said she wanted to pick you up."

"Oh yes, she said you offered. But she told you to go to bed ... she's up half the night anyway..."

"We joke about that. She goes to bed about the time I'm getting up."

"She always was a night owl."

"The thing is, she doesn't like to drive when the road conditions are bad."

"She did fine. Everything went smoothly. My luggage even arrived on the same plane I did. But the roads *were* bad. You can still go jogging?"

"Addicts can jog in any kind of weather. But actually, it's a great morning. Thermometer shows," he stuck his head close to the window, to the left of the sink, "plus five. Sidewalks are likely clear already."

"Yes. It was a wet snow. Almost rain."

"I've found it's good to exercise first thing in the morning. Gets the old system up and running."

"You're looking good."

"I feel good. I come home, shower, then I'm set for a good day's work."

"Do you have early classes this semester?"

"Not terribly early. But I try to get something done on my book before all the interruptions start."

Helena just about said, 'you're still working on that?' She said, instead, "That's the one about…"

"Extinct species."

"Right."

"It should have been done by now. But I'm afraid I've hit a block. I finished the first chapter more than two years ago. Then I discovered that someone in California is into the same mother lode, which has to do with the failure of the gene to assert itself under certain conditions, and so I've had to revise my material and I must admit the whole thing has gone stale on me." George finished his pouring and set the kettle back on the stove.

"Sounds like me and my dissertation. I've lost interest, totally."

"It's not too late to finish your doctorate though, is it?"

"I have a couple of years before the limit is up. But I just can't seem to put my mind to it. I can't seem to take control of it, of the material, I feel so … powerless. I think to do a doctorate one needs to have a sense of self. I seem to have lost myself, any assertive power I did have."

"Maybe you'll get it back, your assertive power."

"I doubt it. It doesn't seem important any more. The world does not need yet another bad thesis."

"What makes you think it would be bad?"

"Even if it wasn't. Who cares what the flower children are doing now?"

"A lot of people, would be my guess. But it sounds like you're soured on the project so nothing anyone could say will change your mind. You're the one who has to be fired up." George reached up to a cupboard and brought down two cups. "This is about ready."

"Mmmm, smells good." Helena stood and immediately slumped back down.

"Are you all right?"

"Just got up too fast."

"You stay there." He poured coffee into the cups and brought one to the table.

Helena watched his hands set down the cup. She noticed the wide gold band. Wide bands had been the fashion that year.

"I can't remember," George was saying, "do you take cream? Sugar?"

"Just cream, please. Or milk. That is, if you have it. I don't need it."

"I know we have cream here, some place."

"Are you still instructing labs?"

"Not many." His voice echoed from inside a cold clear space. "I seem to spend more time with paperwork and committees than I do in any scientific endeavour."

"You don't sound too pleased about that."

He straightened and turned, shutting the fridge door behind him. "Oh well, to get along in life, we all must compromise to some extent. But I like to take on one lab component myself each semester to keep in touch. The graduate students keep me young, keep me on my toes." He was back at the table. "I hope I didn't wake you up with my kitchen clatter."

"No." She poured cream, holding the carton with both hands. She picked up the mug with two hands, carefully raising the porcelain rim to her lips. "Good," she said, and, setting the mug back down on the table, "Good." She put her hands in her lap. She squeezed the right one with the left. "No, my dream woke me up." She looked up and around the kitchen. "I don't suppose you have a cigarette?"

George, too, looked around. "I'm afraid not. It's years since I gave up the habit. And, of course, Esther never indulged."

"I remember you quit shortly after your wedding. Just hoped you might have a stray."

"I thought you quit."

"I did." She had taken it up again after the accident, taken it up with a vengeance, not caring if it gave her lung cancer, hoping it would. But the main thing, it brought Amanda closer. When they had been very young they used to sit on the porch steps in the middle of the night, both home from late night parties, having a last smoke and sharing gossip, dreams and stories about boyfriends. "I started again."

"I'm sorry…" George looked around again. He seemed perplexed.

"It's okay. I have some in my bag. I'll get one in a minute." I can't get one now, she thought. I can't stand up. I can't walk. What were we talking about?

George came to her rescue. "Your dream," he said. "The one that woke you up." He had returned to the counter where he stood, leaning against it, to drink his coffee. "What was it about?"

"I don't remember," she said. "You know how dreams are."

"No," he said. "I never dream."

"Really?" She was truly astounded. To sleep and dream no more, was that from Shakespeare? At any rate, that was her goal.

"Of course I realize that everyone dreams, I simply don't remember them."

"Lucky you. I dream more, or remember them more often, since the accident."

"I'm not surprised. It must have been quite a shock. The jolt. The water." George glanced down at her then quickly away, sideways to the table top.

His eyes have grown lighter, she thought. George used to have such intense dark brown eyes. Age is bleaching us all out. Again, she took a chance with her shaking hands and the coffee. Again, she set down the cup. "How's Esther? I mean, has she gotten over … Amanda?"

"I suppose some things you never get over entirely." George's eyes shifted to a side window near the back door. "But Esther's very good at accepting things. Of course, it's easier for her."

"Yes. She didn't cause the death."

"I meant she has her faith."

"Can she still believe all that stuff?"

"About the hereafter and seeing loved ones again? Oh yes, and especially since Amanda's death. She's become a regular at the church. No harm in it, I suppose, although you might think it laughable."

"Believe me, I'm not laughing. Whatever gets you through. I wish I could do it."

"She doesn't question too closely."

"And you? How do you get by?"

"Routine. In the end, nothing saves us like routine."

"I wonder if any of us ever gets over anything. It's strange the way things hibernate, but they're always there, waiting, in the subconscious."

"I'm afraid I don't have much patience with the subconscious."

"Don't you believe in it?"

"Oh yes, one must believe in it. But one doesn't have to encourage it. One doesn't have to keep probing it like a sore tooth. In my opinion, it's better left alone. The primal scream, all that. That's what mankind has been trying to overcome ever since stepping out of the mud. To my mind, progress means replacing the subconscious with the conscious, replacing it with reason. Sometimes it seems we're travelling backwards."

"But surely in order to understand the conscious, we have to understand the subconscious."

"Cause and effect. A causes B. And if you can't go back and change A, you may as well learn to live with B. What I'm saying is, past behaviour doesn't matter so much as present behaviour."

As George spoke, Helena watched his face intently, which was easy to do because he did not look at her directly. It must be the accident or the life she had been living since then. He must know that she had been sleeping around, that she habitually drank herself into a state of oblivion. He must feel embarrassed for her, uncomfortable with her disgusting life.

She saw upon closer scrutiny that he did look older than in

the old days. The skin around his eyes was puffy, his eyelids had begun to droop. His hair was greying, his mouth a thinner line. But aging suited him; he was now the experienced man of the world, the distinguished professor. Even though he was wearing jogging clothes and sipping coffee in his kitchen, she could sense power of intellect and position. And that voice! Soft, husky, syllables rolled off his tongue. Italian had been his first language. His father had been a landed immigrant in Montreal who had great success in the restaurant business. A woman could fall in love with that voice, she thought. When they were students, she had been half in love with George herself. Now, in middle age, he was still a sexy man.

He had stopped talking. She became conscious of a silence between them. "What time *does* Esther get up these days?"

"I don't know. I'm usually out jogging. What are you two up to today?"

"Not much, I hope. But likely Esther has an agenda."

"You don't sound terribly enthusiastic."

What would he do if she suddenly blurted out, 'If only I didn't find everything so meaningless! Nothing seems worth doing — working, shopping, eating.' She was suddenly curious about him. Here was a man who had life by the throat, who seemed happy and content with his lot. How did he, anyone, do it? He had his work, of course. George had always been deeply involved in his work. And he had Esther. Anyone who had Esther could not help but be among the blessed. Still, it must be more than that. Happy people must think a certain way. George had never needed the idea of a deeper meaning to life; he didn't need to make a connection between the ordinary and the profound. He didn't need the profound. An image of the Cave flashed through Helena's mind: the dim interior, the smoke haze, the disc jockey on Fridays, with his stroboscopic lights casting brilliant flashes of purple and chartreuse and coral on the walls around them against which the figures at the tables were outlined as shadows. "I remember from our

Cave days, you believed in free will and freedom of choice and that people should act as they pleased without worrying about repercussions from a higher being."

"Did I say that? One talks so much nonsense when one is young."

"The arguments we had!"

"The beer we consumed!"

"But you must have a personal philosophy?"

George furrowed his brow. He looked out the window into the back yard. "No…" he said. "Not really. Just the usual. You know, trying to do one's best work."

"Ben was stuck with his stern Jewish God whom he tried to believe was dead. But his sense of a moral universe wouldn't go away. Only now it was man's responsibility. What a burden! I wonder if he still thinks that way."

"It's all so gloomy. The moral good, the terrible burden of choice, the responsibility of defining one's own nature, etcetera. I don't think it matters much. We try to do the best we can, of course, not to hurt people and so on, but quite simply, we are born and we die and that's the end of it. Driven, compelled, of course, by our reproductive forces. The thing is to try and have a pleasant journey through."

"So you don't feel the need to save your immortal soul."

"As a scientist, I can't believe in a soul. The eyes are the window to the soul, the poet says. I'm afraid I see only eyes, molecules, genetic material. Well, a woman's eyes, that's different."

"I wish I was that way. For me, if life doesn't have some deeper meaning, then why bother to do anything?"

"Can't you just do the thing for its own sake? But I suspect you're one of those people who *need* to believe there's a deeper meaning."

"Maybe. I don't want to believe that Amanda's life was nothing more than her existence as a biped on this planet for thirty-eight years. But, also, when you think of it, life has to be more than meaningless. It's too perverse to be meaningless."

"I suppose I believe the meaning of life is just that, what we experience while we're alive on this planet, and I try to see to it that my experiences are happy."

"But what about suffering?"

George shrugged. "I suppose my philosophy, if we want to glorify my shoddy ideas with such a grand term, is that as individuals we must try not to suffer. I might even say we have a duty not to suffer. Our job is to pass on genetic material. An evolved position would be to pass on the best genetic material possible. I realize that sounds like the cold-blooded scientist. But we're not likely to attain that goal any time soon. Presently, human beings tend to pass on genetic material in a haphazard chaotic manner that totally lacks any intellectual component."

"But what if you're the sort of person who can't help yourself suffering?" asked Helena who was not interested in genetic material, but was certainly interested in suffering.

"That's it. Some people can't help themselves. I happen to be able to help myself. So I do."

"It sounds like a nice philosophy. Comfortable anyway."

"Yes, I do believe in comfort. Why not? Why be uncomfortable if you don't need to be?"

"Ben would say that being uncomfortable is the meaning of life. That through being uncomfortable we might learn to be good. So we should ask ourselves questions that make us feel uncomfortable." Helena smiled without humour. "What a grim pair we must have made. Except in those days, the first years of our marriage, we hadn't come up against any real discomfort. We didn't know what was lurking around the corner. Ben's mother…"

"There you go. You have to stop that. There was nothing lurking around the corner. Things simply happened. People do get sick and die. Ben's mother got cancer and died. Why invest it with more meaning than that? You and Ben are people who invest moments with meaning and out of those moments create a mythology."

"But you do believe that we can make choices?"

"Oh yes. For instance, I chose to take on more administration responsibilities."

"And the effect of that is that you become an administrator rather than a scientist."

"And then one simply has to live with that. Or change it back if you want to or if you can."

"But what if that was the wrong choice?"

"Well, in this case, I could probably reverse my decision to some extent. But I tend to believe there are no wrong choices. Only different choices. And then you get onto a different path, which may be equally good. Or bad."

"I guess my mind can't get over the idea that there are wrong choices." And I made one, she thought. And the world doesn't forgive wrong choices. In fact, it seems to delight in them, takes pleasure in turning the screw. We live in a malevolent universe. She didn't mean to say the word "evil" out loud. It sounded positively fundamentalist. But it slipped out. "Evil surrounds us. It gets inside of us."

George did seem somewhat dismayed by that. "Oh ... I wouldn't say..."

"I used to think evil was an idea dreamed up by witch doctors and such. But now, I don't know."

"Nonsense."

"Maybe you can contact evil like you do the flu."

"Now you *are* fantasizing."

"Maybe an exorcist makes sense."

"I'm afraid I'm not up on exorcists. Do they have to be saints or something?"

"Not saints. I think they're special people who are somehow given the power."

"Power?"

"Of goodness. They can draw evil out of a person and take

it upon themselves and then, ideally, destroy it with their goodness. Some people do have that power within them. Their goodness is stronger than evil."

"Have you told Esther? About the evil part and the exorcist business?"

"No."

"I'm not sure you should. She's very impressionable."

"No, I won't say that to her. I don't really believe it myself," she lied. She didn't want to alarm him into thinking he had a crackpot under his roof. "I've simply come home to see my big sister." She's part of the process I need to go through, she thought. The process of dying. But she had no intention of letting Esther know that, let alone George.

"Yes, I think it was a good idea to come home."

"And Ben. Do you ever see Ben around the university?" For Benjamin, too, was part of the process.

George looked down as though he were studying his empty coffee cup. "Occasionally."

Helena kept her eyes steady on George's face. "How is he?"

"He seems fine. We don't talk much. Just to say hello. He's been reinstated. Only as a sessional. But he has three courses this semester."

"They started him out with one, on a trial basis."

George seemed surprised. "You've talked with him then?"

"He came to see me in the hospital. After the accident."

George was silent. He seemed to be waiting for her to either pursue the topic or not, as she wished. When she did not, he straightened and set his cup down on the counter. "I hope you'll be comfortable here. You know I don't mind if you're a fright in the morning." He smiled at her across the room, his eyes on her chin, as if he found something fascinating there. "We haven't had a house guest for some time."

"Esther said in the car last night that Delores didn't come home last Christmas. She has a new beau and they went to his family in Hamilton."

"Yes, she seems quite taken with this one."

"Esther said they're living together. What do you think of that? Are you a modern father?"

"Oh yes, what else can you be? All you can do these days is go with the flow. If I voiced disapproval she'd go ahead and do what she wanted anyway."

"Well, I'm no expert. I certainly don't know anything about raising children. What does Esther think?"

"Oh, Esther wants Delores to get married. She wants to throw the big shindig. She wants Delores to be safe, secure, and happy."

"That's Esther for you," said Helena. "To think that marriage and children automatically result in safety, security, and happiness." But why wouldn't she think that? she thought. That's been her experience.

George looked at his watch. "I should be off. Do you mind?"

"Of course not. I wouldn't want to interfere with anyone's fitness regime."

George moved to the door. "There's more coffee. And of course, help yourself to anything you can find. There's cereal in the pantry, bread here in the box for toast…"

"Thanks. I can't face food in the morning."

"I usually breakfast when I get back." He took down a jacket from a shelf and put his arms into the sleeves. He bent over to change his slippers for runners, then straightened, slightly red-faced. Hand on door handle he paused, staring ahead through the glass. "What I'd say is that usually we act in a way that best ensures our own survival." He opened the door. "At least the survivors do." He closed the door behind him.

Through the early morning half light Helena watched George make his way along the walk. At the end of it, he slipped on a patch of ice, flung out his arms, righted himself, and disappeared around the garage into the lane.

The snow was almost gone. The wide verandah, the barbecue against the house, hooded for winter, the curved walk out to the garden and lane, were bare, while the patchy snow on the lawn either side of the walk was crusted. Last night the snow had come down in large wet flakes. Helena saw windshield wipers. The image regurgitated, became bile in her mouth, mixed with the taste of bitter coffee — last night, Esther navigating the small car, slipping and sliding along the bleak treeless streets, windshield wipers scraping splats of icy water, windshield wipers whipping sheets of rain. No, she must not think of windshield wipers.

Instead she thought of the bottle of pills in her purse. She thought of these with longing, as an exhausted person thinks of bed and sleep, or a starving person food, or an alcoholic the next drink. But first she had to talk to Ben.

The last time she had woken up on a ratty couch in an abysmal room with the latest man she had found to abuse her, the last time she had faced herself in a brown clouded mirror over a rusted sink and dripping drainpipes, the last time she had observed fresh bruises on her jaw and around the socket of an eye, Amanda had intervened. Amanda's flesh superimposed itself on her bones, covering purple bruises with her own unmarked skin, and at the eyes, covering anguish with grey clarity. "Ben came to see me last summer." Amanda's voice, Amanda's gentle voice, had come out of the face in the mirror. She had to find Ben and make him tell her what Amanda had said.

As some people are visited by saints, she had been visited by Amanda, and Amanda had directed her to Ben. Helena had to know what had happened between Ben and Amanda during their visit. She had convinced herself that there was significance in it. It was just too strange, Ben going to see Amanda. It was not the sort of thing he would do. He never imposed on people that way. He hated driving. He had never owned a car. Something must have directed him to Amanda. Amanda must have said something to him, something about her, something that she could decipher as a message of forgiveness. Helena hung on to this conviction. Without that message she could not die. To die in the state she was in would be to spend eternity in a black vacuum of torture. Amanda, through Ben, was her only chance.

II. VERONICA

"NO FUCKING WAY!"

"Esther..."

"Don't say that name to me. I hate that name. I can't stand that name."

"How can we discuss..."

"There is no discussion. I'm going to phone Esther today."

"You'll do nothing of the sort."

"Won't I?"

"It'll destroy Esther."

"Why the fuck should I care what happens to Esther? Esther is a fat sloth hanging upside down from a dead tree."

"Veronica, please..."

George and Veronica were in bed in her room in what had once been a grand old house near the university. Long ago it had been partitioned into rooms that were rented out to students — it reminded George of a rabbit warren. Veronica's room was better than some. It was on the second storey and opened onto a balcony overlooking a street lined with old poplars. In summer it was surrounded by bowers of branches, the leaves reaching from the street into the balcony, giving George the impression that he was floating in a green airy glade. In winter, he seemed to be floating in a white fairy tale wonderland. Was this why, when he was here with Veronica, he felt that he was experiencing freedom? It was the same feeling he'd had as a young man not yet caught in the stream that would decide his life for him. It was the feeling of being young and behind the wheel of a new sports convertible, driving with the top down on a summer evening with your best love of the moment by your side.

In other ways, however, his relationship with Veronica placed him firmly into a dungeon, a conspiracy of deceit that weighed heavily on his shoulders. He longed to be free of the murkiness that surrounded him. He longed to be reborn into the clean, clear, innocent light of day. He shifted his body into a more comfortable position on the sagging mattress. Sometimes, they had a good laugh about the mattress, but not today. "I'll have to think of something," he said as much to himself as to Veronica.

"It'd better be soon. This has been going on long enough."

"Do you have to yell? Don't you have a normal tone of voice?"

"Screaming's the only thing that works with you."

"Can't we be reasonable human beings?"

"No."

"Why not?"

"Because you always win. When we have a rational discussion, you twist things so you always win."

"I'm telling you, I need more time. What's twisting in that? It's a simple request."

"I can't stand this one more day!"

"Shhh. My God, the neighbours. They'll think I'm killing you."

"That's what you'd like to do. Destroy the evidence."

"Don't be crazy."

"You drive me crazy. I'm going crazy here in this room!"

"You should go out more. Go out with your friends."

"Pass me off on my friends, so you can be rid of me. You don't want to be with me any more. You don't think I'm fun any more."

"Fighting isn't fun. Can't we be kind to each other?"

"At least when I'm fighting I know I'm alive. Not just being someone's doormat."

"I'm tired of fighting."

"You've had your fun and now you want out."

"I don't want out."

"Then why are you looking at your watch? I'm *tired* of you looking at your watch. I'm *tired* of you saying that you've got to go. I'm *tired* of being Dr. Martin's affair."

"Don't overdramatize. You have a life."

"Some life. Being grateful for the dregs of your life."

"Esther and I..."

"I told you I don't want to hear about Esther. For me, Esther doesn't exist."

"You're right, she doesn't exist. Not here in our world. But Esther and I have been together a long time."

"Time for a change."

"A person can't just toss out twenty-two years."

"Why not? People do it all the time. They toss out thirty and forty years."

"You don't understand. You've never had a relationship which lasted longer than a few months."

"So now I'm promiscuous."

"It's true, isn't it?"

"It's true because I didn't find the right person until you."

How can I be doing this? wondered George in amazement. How can I be here in this squalid room with this woman half my age? He had the impression of being shifted sideways, of being displaced from himself and deposited in an alien and unknown space. Amanda, thought George. It's her fault. Well, of course, it's not really her fault. But yes, it *is* really her fault. Amanda, the underlying cause of the inevitable effect. Her senseless death the cause, Veronica the effect. He had always been extremely fond of Amanda. When they were young and he was already streamed into a world that could be studied, measured, rationalized, she had appeared to him an anomaly. He had no patience for anything beyond reason and yet there was Amanda, living proof of something that might be called a force of goodness. That this force, that someone so worthwhile, could so easily, so unfairly, be erased; that someone so young, a good deal younger than he, could be wiped off the slate, so quickly and finally, had shocked him.

If he was being honest with himself, however, as he sometimes was, George had to admit that his malaise, his feeling that he was sinking into a grey predictable region where he was doomed to exist for the remainder of his years, had begun before Amanda's death. Likely, it had been coming on him gradually, but one day, shortly after Delores had left for the east, he woke up to the fact that nothing astonished him any more. He no longer enjoyed his teaching or his students. He was doing administration instead of research. He had ceased reading anything that was not necessary to his work, had ceased thinking beyond his work. And even his work, the mainstay of his life, was going sour on him. The whole business of life had fallen into a sort of unremitting gloom. This soul sickness, or what might be termed as such by someone who believed in souls, infiltrated everything, the smallest details of George's life. He became so bored with small rituals such as making his morning coffee, getting himself dressed, walking to the office, that he could scarcely lift the coffee pot, button a shirt, put one foot before the other on the well-worn path. He could not stand himself. His physical being, his flesh, his smell, sickened him. He would catch himself staring at the skin on his soft belly thinking how it was like some hairy white grub. The little toe on his left foot had always been slightly curled under the next one. One morning he sat on the toilet staring at this toe and thinking how ugly it was, all his toes were for that matter. Toes were really a very ugly part of the human anatomy. Human beings were ugly, perhaps the ugliest of all creatures. Sometimes he could scarcely eat; the whole cycle of lifting food to his mouth, chewing, swallowing, digesting, eliminating seemed insanely grotesque. He would catch himself sucking his teeth and be revolted.

Amanda chose that time of George's life to be killed, an event that startled him into thinking of mortality in general and of Amanda in particular. He recalled the youthful Amanda of those far away fervent student days. How enthusiastic she had been! How loving! How caring! How dedicated to humanity! The discussions they had had. She felt so deeply for the wrongs of the world. She, even more than the others, wanted to save it. She joined all the causes —deforestation of the jungles, pollution of the environment. He recalled how she had stopped using detergent because of what it was doing to rivers, how she was shocked to learn that he and Esther used spray deodorant. She had been, they all had been, so alive, so involved. Then she was dead. As a scientist he was used to death of living organisms. What could be more natural than death? Things die. He would die. But he had never before truly considered his death. Amanda's death served to remind him of his own, which would be, relatively speaking, soon. And what had he accomplished? What had he even enjoyed of this life?

Esther knew nothing of this mental state, no one did. He went about his work, his daily round acting like the same old George. He was not the sort of man to expose his inner self to others and, in fact, his inner self up to then had been in pretty good shape. On that November evening two and a half years earlier when Veronica had come to his house, he had not been looking for diversion of that sort. He knew that he had to pull himself up out of whatever funk he was in. He had to finish the book, although given his lack of motivation he did not know how he was going to tackle a project that took so much creative energy. Perhaps he could get back on track by leaving it for a time, putting his interest into something entirely different. He had always had a faint urge to join one of the biological research teams bound for South America. Or perhaps travel to distant exotic places with Esther would be more appropriate. Or taking up a hobby, photography perhaps, might do the trick. Likely, he did not need to do anything so drastic as uprooting himself. He had always thought that he would like to try sky diving at least once. Then again, perhaps it was already a little late for that.

Was it any wonder that Veronica's arrival into his life seemed fortuitous, like the successful joining of cells toward new growth? Was it any wonder that as some men turn to God, he turned to Veronica? During those first weeks, it was difficult for him not to believe in heaven and that she was a miracle from that exalted place dropped into his ordinary existence. Later, he sometimes wondered if she were more properly a demon from hell sent to test him, to entice and ruin him. Whatever the case, if he had been a religious man, he would have been ready to damn himself to hell for eternity for what she offered him. Since he didn't believe in heaven or hell and their inhabitants, he had to be satisfied to be ready to damn himself to this planet for the duration of his existence on it. Even now, in their close moments, the game seemed worth the candle, for when he was with Veronica he felt connected to his animal self. With her he knew who he was, the being distinct and separate from his social self. But he also knew that life with her would be outside society and, while it was all very well for Ben and Reuben to take that stance, it was not right for him. He had never wished to define himself in their terms and, in any case, he was too old to take the position of an outsider.

Certainly, Veronica had restored his faith in life and in himself. He *could* work, he *would* finish the book, he *would* yet make an important discovery. She had given him a reason to live. He would always be grateful to her for that. But he could not imagine dismantling his life, a life so routine, so settled, so written in stone. It was *his life*. What matter that he had found something with Veronica he had thought lost forever? That with her he felt he was a vital human being, not an old man dragging his feet to the grave? Such thoughts were immature when measured against the structure of what he had built as his life.

"I have to go," he said, looking away from her. He didn't like to see her face when he made that announcement.

"You don't have to go. You could stay if you wanted. You don't have a class today until three."

"I have to work on my book."

"That's another laugh."

"What do you mean by that remark?"

"That book is another thing you keep putting off. You'll never finish it."

"Thanks for your confidence. How can I finish it when my mind is exhausted by this constant fighting?"

"How about me? What do you think it does to my mind? Do you think I like it any better than you do?"

"Yes, I think you like to fight."

"That's not true. But I'll fight if I have to. I'm not going to lie back and take it."

"Take what?"

"Your injustice."

"I do the best I can."

"It's not enough."

"Look, please, I have to go to work."

"Work he calls it. Coming on to all the cute little undergraduate bouncy tits and bums."

"Don't be silly."

"Don't forget, I was your student. I know your techniques."

"Please, Veronica."

"And how about *my* work? I won't get any work done today. I'm too upset. Maybe I should find someone else."

"Don't do that." The idea caused a sort of plunge inside George, as though his blood pressure had suddenly dropped to dangerously low levels.

"Someone who won't beat me to an emotional pulp."

"Oh come now. It's not as bad as that."
"I can't put up with this any more!"
"Shhh, shhh, calm down."
George put his right arm under her shoulders. He slid his left between the sheet and her warm body. He held her tightly, pressing her face into his chest. He knew that she liked his chest. She liked its feel of solidity and security. She liked its warm hairy fuzziness. She, who had never had a proper home, could sink into his chest and feel at home there. She had told him that. He ran his fingers through her long pale hair, combing it back from her high brow. Blue veins pulsed beneath her white skin. Her smooth bare shoulder felt like silk to his fingers.

He could not give her up. Sometimes with her he felt such joy, pure joy. Without her his life would slump back into the grey lifeless mechanical round it had been before she arrived. *He* would slump back into his soft, lethargic, heap of self. He needed her to fire him up. He was too young for his life to be over.

There was something else, too, something about her that was a mystery. It was as though he knew her from somewhere else, another place, another time. And that knowledge allowed him transcendence beyond the confines of earth to a place where he could glimpse something larger, something more expansive. The experience affected him profoundly. It was uncanny. He was a man with his feet on the ground. He could not remember ever having the experience before, certainly not with Esther. But he loved Esther; he did love her. He had never said that he didn't. It is possible to love two people at the same time, he thought. The middle-aged professor, the good neighbour, the family man, the serious, reliable citizen loved Esther. But the primitive man inside, that creature he hadn't realized was there until two and a half years ago, loved Veronica.

He was still stroking her skin. "We'll work something out. If you love me…"

"I may love you but I don't trust you." Veronica's voice was muffled, but he could tell it was somewhat mollified.

He made his voice as soothing as possible. "Just be patient a little longer."

"You've been saying that for the past year." Veronica turned her face up so that he could hear her more clearly.

From one of the other rooms came the sound of a radio, the cheerful patter of an upbeat morning show, pleasant voices speaking in a friendly way to people who lived normal blameless lives, who listened to the Top Forty.

"You don't understand," he said.

"I understand perfectly. You're a coward. You can't face pain. Not even discomfort." Her tone was almost resigned.

"Things like this take time."

"You've had enough time." Her voice threatened to rise again. She flung herself onto her back, out of his arms. She stretched the length of the bed.

"I have to tell Esther gradually, work up to it so it isn't too much of a shock for her."

"I don't give a shit about Esther!"

"Shhh!"

"Don't you see? You keep putting Esther before me. Esther has everything. I have nothing."

"You have me."

"Big deal. So does Esther."

"Not in the same way."

"That's what you tell me. You probably tell her a pack of lies, too. It wouldn't surprise me if you ditched the both of us and went merrily off with a pair of those bouncy tits. You can't trust a liar."

"I'm not a liar."

"What do you call what you've been doing for the past two and a half years?"

"I didn't used to lie."

"You've been lying like a trouper all your life, Georgie. You lie to yourself."

George was suddenly aware of the evil-smelling sheets, the flat hard pillow, the stains on the ceiling. He swung himself into a sitting position on the edge of the bed, his feet landing on his pile of clothes on the floor. Elbows on knees, he stared at the red jogging pants on the shadowy flowers of the worn carpet, at the hooded pullover. Those aren't my clothes. The thought crossed his mind. This isn't me here in this room. This isn't me doing these things. "And yet you talk about us having a life together," he said. "How can we have a life together when that's your opinion of me?"

"I know *you* and I love you. That's real love," Veronica said to his back.

"And yet you want to ruin me. What kind of love is that?"

"I want as much consideration as Esther. I deserve it. I'm as important as Esther. I'm a person!"

"Shhh. I know. But this is a world-shattering step. Do you realize how many lives such an action of mine will disrupt?"

"Maybe they need disrupting."

"It will be the end. The end of me."

"Oh come off it. All that will happen is that a wife will learn the truth about her husband. It happens every day. You'll be surprised how few people care."

"Esther will care. Think how she'll feel. Don't you have any empathy for Esther?"

"You can't be complacent in this life. You can't sit back and think you've got it made. You've got to keep your eyes and ears open at the water hole. That's the law of the jungle."

"I know you've had a rough time of it. Does that mean everyone has to have a rough time? After all, it's not Esther's fault."

"It's not my fault, either. But I've never been able to avoid facing reality. I've never had that luxury. Unlike Esther, I've always had to deal with life in the real world. And as for you, you've never had to leave your ivory tower. Anyway, Esther has what she wants, her smug genteel existence."

She'd be shattered, thought George, looking up, weary of

the arguments. His gaze swung in a semicircle. Near the door was a dresser, the top cluttered with bottles of makeup, jars of face creams, tubes of mousse and gel, canisters of sprays, trays of eye shadow, containers of lipsticks and nail polishes in various shades, hair combs, clips and curlers, curling iron and hair dryer. The mirror had lost much of its silver backing. The resulting black patches caused gaps in reflection, blotting out parts of the room. Its edge was stuck around with snapshots and business cards and greeting cards. On the other side of the door, a card table was set up with a word processor and stacks of books and printer paper arranged in neat piles. Across the room, near the balcony window, a wooden stand held a CD player that he had bought for her last Christmas. On a shelf, was a row of CDs, mostly pop and rock.

Behind the surface atmosphere of the room, the cluttered paraphernalia of modern young-womanhood, was an old-fashioned quality: the style of the dresser, with its hinged and bevelled mirror, the faded carpet, the wide baseboards, the large-flowered brittle wallpaper. To George, the place had an aura of ghosts. He had been sincere when he had told Helena that he strove to live on the conscious level. Yet, in spite of himself, he recognized that there was something in this room, something he could not name, which drew him like a magnet. It was as though the room contained him, his past, not only in the way it was similar to his family home in Montreal, although that home was much grander and continually refurbished and repaired, but beyond that, to European roots which he had never personally experienced. There was something indescribably compelling about those roots and that lost time. It was this intangible phenomenon as well as the magnet of sex that bonded him so strongly to this perverse goddess. *She* contained something of him, something he could not name. He couldn't figure it out. It was a muddle in his brain.

His eyes lighted on the kitchen component of the room, a counter along one wall fitted with cupboards, a hot plate, and a microwave. A communal fridge and a regular stove were in a downstairs kitchen.

"Do you have any food around here?" he said.

"There's some cookies over there some place," Veronica informed in a distracted voice before returning to her immediate focus, which, George knew, she would hang on to like a pit bull. "She should know her husband is a cheat."

George stood up.

"I'm tired of being treated like a tramp. You sneak around, fit me in at your pleasure."

He crossed the room.

"When I think of how stupid I've been. What I've put up with. What I've done for you because I loved you. No wonder you think you can treat me like dirt. Well, you're fucking wrong!"

"Do you think I like it any better than you do?" George was rummaging through the cupboards. Ahh, there they were, cookies and crackers. He chose the cookies, Dad's with chocolate coating, his favourite. Veronica must have bought them especially for him.

"Change it then. You can change it."

"Maybe I can't." George turned with a cookie in his teeth.

"If you don't, I will. I'll go to the house."

"Don't go to the house."

"Why not? Is that sacred ground?"

Yes, thought George, Yes, it is. Aloud, he said, "Why do you hate Esther? She's never done you any harm."

"She has what belongs to me. And she got it without even trying. "

George stood in the grey morning light before the curtainless window. This time of year, the branches of the tree were a thick matted network of gnarled and twisted arms. They seemed to be reaching out for him, probing his flesh like long sharp witch's fingers. Instinctively, he looked down to see that the windows were closed. Almost immediately, he lifted his eyes, berating himself for his foolish thought.

"The semester will soon be over," he said. "Then I'll have time to think straight."

"You go back to your nice house and your position and I'm stuck in this crummy room. I don't even have friends any more. To have friends you have to be involved in similar interests. My pastime is screwing a married man."

"Shhh. You have your studies." George moved back to the bed with the box of cookies in hand. He swung his feet up, cushioned a pillow behind his head, and started working his way through the package. Veronica lay beside him, stretched full length on top of the covers. She was almost as long as the bed. When standing, she was nearly as tall as he. He liked that about her. He thought that they made a nice-looking couple. The few times they had appeared in restaurants or other public places he had noted that they looked well together, a stunning contrast. She was so blonde, he so dark, she so willowy, he solid as an oak. But their strides fit, their styles coincided. She *had* style, in spite of growing up in an atmosphere of ignorance, subsidized housing, alcoholic parents. How that had happened, he did not know. Education must be a factor, but determination must have also played a part.

"I haven't done anything on my thesis for a month," she said. "I can't concentrate. All I can think about is you."

"You must get back to it. Put thoughts of me aside. You want to be finished this spring." The crunch of the cookies between his teeth sounded loud in the quiet room.

"How can I concentrate on anything, let alone nurture deprivation of rats when you have me in a constant state of turmoil."

"You have yourself in a constant state of turmoil."

"I wouldn't be like this if you'd do something."

"What, exactly, do you want me to do?"

"I want you to jog along home and tell wifey all about me and how you're going to leave her and live with me."

"Don't be ludicrous."

"What's ludicrous about that?"

"Shhh. Don't shriek. It's simply not thinkable."

"I don't have any trouble thinking about it. Can't you see things from my point of view for once? You said your marriage was over. That you don't have sex with your wife any more. Which, by the way, I'm sure is also a lie. Your one child is grown up and on her own. You said all that and I believed you and I fell in love with you. Now I want you to live with me. Why is that unreasonable?"

"You're like an angry resentful child. You want to smash something. You want to smash my marriage, my life."

"Why shouldn't I want to smash your life when you compare it to what I have?"

George looked around the shabby mean room, bleak in the grey light of late winter. "This is the life you made for yourself before I met you," he said. "Your life isn't my fault. I didn't seduce you any more than you seduced me."

"Oh Georgie, you're pitiful. Grow up. Things happen. You take the next logical step. That's all. Besides, I'm doing you a favour. Your marriage was dead on the rocks. You were like a fish thrown up onto the beach and dehydrating in the sun. Well, I've come along to flip you back into the sea. You should be grateful to me, instead of treating me like dirt. You should be grateful that I'm giving you a way out of your boring conventional set-up."

"Has it been that bad, knowing me?" He put aside the empty cookie package and reached over to curl a strand of her hair around his thick finger. Just touching her hair caused the fire to start. He would never, could never, get enough of her. That was the plain simple truth of his life. She was the plain simple truth of his life. Esther was the complication. Esther involved property, community standing, family loyalties, professional status. It was as though he and Esther were a corporation. But he could not toss out a whole way of life. He could not toss out Esther. The two women were entirely different, entirely separate. They existed in two distinct compartments of his brain and these two parts could not be brought together. There was no solution. He was caught in a problem without a solution.

"Don't start that." George realized that his fingers had travelled from her hair down to her breast, her nipple. "You're just trying to soften me up. I know your tricks." But her voice had altered. "Don't you see why I'm fighting like I am? I fight for what I want. I want you and I'll fight to get you."

"You have me."

"I want us to live together, like a real couple, to have a home, friends over, rent videos and make popcorn, like other married couples."

"I never said we could live like that together. I never said I'd leave Esther. I made no promises."

"Oh no, you've been very careful. Always the careful one. You told me you don't love her any more. Was that a lie too?"

"I don't love her the way I love you, but Esther and I are ... friends."

"Then, she should want you to be happy."

"It's not as easy as that." George's voice was thoughtful. "She may love *me*."

"So what else is new? Half the population is suffering from unrequited love."

"But Esther's love is pretty overwhelming."

"So is mine. I'll match her in battle any day."

"Do we have to speak of battles? We're supposed to be speaking of love."

"I'm tired of seeing you in the morning. I'm not a morning person. I want to see you in the evening."

"I do the best I can. Sometimes I come in the evening. We went to that conference at Jasper."

"I want *us* to go to the fucking opera. I want *us* to have season's tickets to the theatre."

"You know that's impossible."

"Why?"

"Everyone we know goes to the opera. I'm a married man."

"Well, for Christ's sake, get unmarried. Everybody else does. Don't you see? It's not impossible. Anything's possible."

George swung himself off the bed and picked up his clothes. Her voice followed him. "You told me you loved me. Or do you deny that, too."

"I do love you."

"I know. It's all sex with you."

"Sex is extremely important."

"Fucking animal."

"And why not. Should we be different than other animals? The instinct to mate is the strongest instinct in the animal world. Why should I be different?"

"God bless you. Yes. Well, off you go, jog back to wifey. Tell her a pack of lies, just like you tell me."

George bent and kissed Veronica full on the lips. He would not let her mouth go until he got the response he desired, until she clung to him with arms lifted around his neck and shoulders, until she lifted her body up to his, pressed herself up towards him. It took all his willpower but he loosened her arms and straightened. He went to the door and turned. She was lying on her side, elbow braced on the pillow, head resting on her hand, legs crooked slightly at the knee. Her hair cascaded down around her shoulder, across one breast. Half hidden by her hair, her sharp shrewd eyes were ready to attack or retreat, whichever would best help her get her own way. George let himself gaze a moment at that body, pale and mysterious. Even at rest it contained an energy ready to spring into action. He may be despicable, he may be condemned for it, but he would come again. "Do you think this is easy for me?" he said.

"Well it's sure as hell easier for you than it is me."

"You're not betraying anyone. You don't have to tell lies. I'm the one who has taken the responsibility of telling lies. For you. I've done these things for you." He opened the door.

"For yourself more likely. For a good lay." She swung herself up into a sitting position on the edge of the bed. "Shut the door a moment." She leaned forward, hands on the edge of the mattress, hair falling forward on her shoulders. She was looking at him in her singular direct yet slanted manner. "I have something to tell you."

There was a long silence. George could almost hear the shifts of her brain. Across the space he could sense her cunning thoughts. Something in her voice, a careful tone, sent a thrill of fear along his spine.

III. ESTHER

ABOUT THE TIME THAT George was saying goodbye to Veronica, on the other side of the campus Esther was entering her kitchen in a neighbourhood of well-kept middle-class homes inhabited by professors, doctors, accountants, and moderately successful lawyers. She padded into the room like a tabby roused from sleep declining to accept a world that would impose its reality into her drowsy comfort. She was wearing a pink velour robe over a frilly nightgown. Her face, swollen from sleep, had a red curving line where her skin had been crunched against her pillow.

"Dear," she said and hugged Helena's shoulders.

Helena was still sitting at the kitchen table. Beside her on the table was a cup of cold coffee, a full ashtray, and a scattered newspaper. She shrugged herself out from under Esther's soft pink fuzziness by standing and taking her cup to the microwave.

Esther followed, giving her a hug around the waist and taking up her limp left hand. The timer beeped.

With the excuse of reaching into the microwave for her cup, Helena pulled her hand away. She managed to extricate herself from Esther's embrace and took her coffee to the table. Again, Esther followed, trailing a cloud of scent that Helena found suffocating. When Helena was seated, she bent and gave her another hug around the shoulders. She kissed the top of Helena's head.

"How are you this morning dear?" Esther's voice was slow, tentative, her morning voice. "Did you have a good night? How did you sleep?"

"Good. Did you want coffee? I'm afraid I took the last of what George made." As Helena spoke she shrugged Esther's hands off her shoulders and shifted perceptibly away.

Esther straightened and stood before Helena like a rebuked child. Her hands, folded in front of her, seemed lost if they could not be putting themselves on someone. Helena, seeing those hands against the pink fabric, noticed how they were no longer young hands. A sudden flood of feeling for her sister washed through her. For God's sake, she told herself. After what happened with Amanda, how can you dare be so snippy to Esther? Besides, you're the one who made the call. You're the one who reached out your hand and picked up the phone. You dialled the number. Esther didn't ask for a derelict on her doorstep. The least you can do is be civil. "I always sleep well in that bed," she smiled up at her sister. "It was wonderful to wake up and find myself in your house."

Tears flooded into Esther's eyes, giving them the appearance of glossy mahogany. She stepped close to Helena and took her head in her arms. She pressed Helena's face against her warm pink bosom. "That's right dear. You're home. You should have come here ages ago. You must stay as long as you like. Until you feel better."

Esther's body felt like a soft cushion. It *was* comfortable. It *was* reassuring. But Helena had set herself against comfort and reassurance. "I won't stay long. I just seem to be in the most awful confusion. I can't seem to get my head turned around."

"No wonder. What you've been through." Esther squeezed Helena's shoulders, kneaded her shoulder blades through the light cotton of her nightgown. "You're so thin, dear. Are you eating?"

"Oh yes. I don't seem to have much interest in food, that's all."
"We must try and put a little meat on those bones. Your hair is so short." Esther ran her fingers through Helena's hair, pushing up the bristly hairs on the back of her neck. "You used to have such lovely long hair."
"I can't be bothered with hair. Or makeup. It all seems so superficial."
"I almost missed you at the airport last night. I scarcely recognized my own sister."
"I know. I look so haggard."
Esther stepped back and sat down in one of the other wooden chairs. "You do look a little tired, dear."
She hasn't changed her hairstyle since we were teens, thought Helena. And that myopic squint because she refuses to wear her glasses has become permanent. "You look great," she said. "The cat who licked up the cream. You have scarcely a line or a wrinkle."
"That's because I've gotten so plump."
"It suits you. George, too. He's put on a bit of weight, still he looks good. You've gotten to be a comfortable middle-aged couple."
"Don't sound so disapproving."
"I don't mean to. I might have at one time. Now I think it's wonderful. I wish I could find such peace of mind."
"Maybe you will, here. You must stay until you get yourself sorted out. That seems only sensible. But you didn't mention in your call anything about your plans."
"I have none. I have no direction. I seem to be turning in blind circles. I don't even have coherent thoughts. And at the moment I have a headache."
"Oh I'm not thinking. Do you want breakfast?"
"No, no. Coffee is all I ever have."
"Do you want something for the headache? We must have something around here. George must have something. Esther was looking around at the cupboards in a bewildered manner.

"It's much better than it was. I found something in the bathroom. But, would you mind if I lay down?"

"Of course not. You must rest. That's what you need. Lots of rest. I'm so glad you've come home. It wasn't good for you to stay away so long. Here, do you want your coffee with you?"

"No. I've been drinking coffee for the last two hours." Helena stood up.

"Oh, I should have gotten up earlier."

"No, no. I didn't mean to imply that. Believe me, I'm quite used to early mornings with pots of coffee. Sometimes I wake up at three or four and can't get back to sleep. I have to fill the hours with something. Smokes and coffee." She decided not to mention whiskey.

"Come and lie down." Esther directed her into the hallway leading from kitchen to bedroom. "Here, I'll help you."

"I don't need help." Again, Helena was aware of the brusqueness in her voice. And Esther's eyes were starting to look weepy again. "Do you want to come with me?" she relented.

Helena moved slowly down the hall, holding herself carefully, Esther anxious at her elbow. When they arrived at the guest room, Helena lowered herself to the crumpled bedding, slowly and stiffly, as though her body were covered with bruises. She lay on her back and stared straight up at the white ceiling.

Esther busied herself with opening drapes and straightening bedclothes before sitting herself down on the edge of the bed. She put her hand on Helena's shoulder.

"Don't touch me." Helena's voice was flat and harsh.

Esther retracted her hand.

Damn, thought Helena. "Sorry," she said. "But I can't stand being touched right now."

"Sorry dear. Maybe I should go away and let you sleep."

"No. Don't leave me alone. I don't like being alone." She thought of the procession of men she'd hooked up with. Even they were better than being alone.

"What do you want me to do?"

"Just sit there." Helena recalled the words of the song on the radio. "Stay close. I need to know you're there."

"Can I get you anything? A sedative? Oh no, you said you had taken something. Water? A blanket?"

"Stop fussing Esther!"

"Sorry."

"Sorry, I can't think straight when you fuss." Helena lay very still, her hands crossed, as though she were already in her coffin. Only her mouth, a pale thin line, moved. "Sometimes I think I'm going crazy."

"Things take time. That ... experience ... must have been so hard on you physically, if nothing else. You were in the hospital for nearly a month."

"The hospital was easy. The hard part was going home."

"I should have stayed with you longer."

"I would have only dragged you down with me. There was no sense in us both going under."

"I thought you were going to be all right. But now I wonder if I was being selfish in wanting to get back to George."

"No, you did the right thing. Can you imagine the two of us moping around that small apartment? Feeding each other's misery?"

"Did you ever attend a meeting of that bereavement group?"

"I didn't go. I convinced myself that it would be a waste of time. And my time was so precious. I was so busy thinking about my agony, I had no time for anything else. I realize now that I didn't want to share my grief. Sharing it might have thinned it, even trivialized it. No, I wanted to hold it close and vivid forever. If I lost my pain, I would truly have lost Amanda."

"You need the *right* person to share grief with. I was so lucky to have George."

"Yes, George has turned out to be a satisfactory Prince Charming."

"But what *did* you do then? After I left."

She had sat in a room and stared into space. She had slept.

She would sink into sleep the way a person sinks into a coma. And still she was tired all the time. When she couldn't sleep, she would become panicky. And yet she couldn't take drugs. She was afraid of having an anonymous overwhelming darkness take hold of her. Her mind was a dark space. When she could not blot out her mind with sleep, she filled it with sickening nightmarish stuff she found in books. One book was about a serial killer who cut off people's eyelids while they were still alive. It was unqualifiedly horrible and it suited her mood at the time. She read dozens of books in the same vein. She would finish one and immediately pick up another. She would trek to the local library and bring home yet another pile of them. The gruesome violent world they conveyed became her reality. She could relate to it. She felt at home there, enclosed in a space of horror that corresponded to the horror inside herself. She thought she would go mad in that space but she didn't want to get out of it. She had panic attacks, she couldn't breathe. She would run out of her room to a Shopper's Drug Mart or a Dominion, both within a few blocks of her apartment. She would take a bus and wander around shopping malls, endlessly, aimlessly. Sometimes, she would come out of a trance and wonder which mall she was in and how she had gotten there. The faces of strangers calmed her somewhat. To know that there were ordinary people in the world, to know that there was a more or less normal world allowed her to get through another day.

During the first weeks after the accident, her mind was in the excruciating pain of the present. She did not think of the past in any but a superficial way. She could not fathom ensuing days. That phase was bad enough but when she came out of that first state of shock and remembered the horror of her past, the horror of herself, her wickedness in thought and deed, especially in thought, and realized that there would be more days, years of days, she knew that she was in real trouble.

"I went to Europe soon after." Helena turned her eyes toward

Esther who sat slumped, looking like a large pink fluffy pillow tossed carelessly on the edge of the bed.

As children and as young women, the two sisters had been close. Helena had been born into a world in which Esther existed. From Helena's beginning they had shared nearly every waking moment. When they went to school, they walked together. They had other friends, but they always returned to each other. In their teen years, they swam together, learned to cook together, went to movies together, even dated together. When they married, they visited back and forth, both as couples and singly. They went on shopping sprees and had their teacups read. Helena was as fond of Delores as she might have been of her own child. When Helena went to the Coast, she took strength from the fact that Esther was in the world, not terribly far away, that she could see her sister in a few hours if she absolutely needed to, that she could speak to her by picking up the telephone.

Amanda had been born into a world in which the close relationship of Helena and Esther was established. While she had attached herself to both sisters, it was Helena, as the one closest in age, with whom Amanda had the stronger connection. A sensitive nature to begin with, Amanda was especially susceptible to Helena's tyranny, her dictatorial pronouncements on what was and was not acceptable in the matter of dress, hairstyles, deportment. Helena did not acknowledge her own imperious disparaging nature, and since she, herself, was perfect, it was her duty to set the world right. She simply could not help herself. Not only did she want the people she loved to be efficient and competent, she wanted them to be without flaw. It caused her real pain to see Amanda leave for the Coast with Reuben, two hillbillies, as she saw it, with their worldly belongings tied onto a trailer like a tin can to a dog's tail.

Thoughts of Amanda were always with Helena. They had become the background fabric of her mental life. She saw Amanda in a variety of poses and actions, but the vision that most often appeared was of a girl sitting over homework at the kitchen table in the house in which they had grown up, her long golden hair falling about her shoulders like a shining cape, the fine skin of her brow furrowed with concentration.

"Amanda was so beautiful," Helena murmured, her thoughts breaking through her silence. "So intelligent, so full of promise."

"Yes, dear."

"I said that to her in the car that terrible night. She thought I was criticizing her for not doing more with her life."

Esther was silent.

"Maybe I was. Why oh why oh why was I so hard on Amanda?"

"You're being too hard on yourself now."

Helena looked toward Esther. "How about you? After you got home. How did you manage?"

"At first it was terrible. Terrible. I couldn't believe it. My mind simply could not comprehend that Amanda was no longer here. She was proof that there was goodness in the world. She cast a sort of net of blessing out into the world. Then goodness was gone. Her blessing was gone. But then it came to me. She's still here, I'm not sure how. But I feel her presence, her blessing all around me."

"It's wonderful. Belief."

"I haven't told George all this, not in detail. I'm not sure he'd approve. But he was quite relieved when I stopped crying so much."

"You and Amanda, with your tears."

"Amanda was worse than me. She cried as only the saints can cry. She offered up her sorrow for the world."

"I didn't cry much. Even now, I can't seem to cry. That was something Amanda said to me in the car that night, how I never cry. She was right. I won't let life have the satisfaction of drawing tears out of me."

"Perhaps crying would help. Perhaps tears would be a release."

"Perhaps, but you can't force tears."

"Mine seem to come without me willing them at all. But Amanda's death seems to have entered another place in my mind now. In the back of my mind. It's not immediate any more. It's gone into the past. It's become a dull ache, rather than the sharp pain it was at the beginning. Reuben feels the same."

"You've heard from Reuben?"

"I phone him from time to time."

"And they're managing?"

"Oh yes. I believe Reuben has a new friend."

"So soon?"

"It's been two and a half years."

"Still, you'd think he might have waited a while longer. He and Amanda had such a good marriage. They were so *involved* with each other."

"It's *because* they had a good marriage that he's able to have a relationship with someone else. He has so much love to give, of course he would find someone to give it to."

"I'm afraid I can't be as evolved as you. I'm just a lowly homo sapien full of the base emotions of malevolence, jealousy, rage. I can't believe Reuben has forgotten so soon."

"He hasn't forgotten. He has the children to think about. He must go on, whether he wants to or not. He needs to create a life for the children. The little one is only four. He needs help, and she seems willing to help. The children like her."

"Maybe you're right. At the funeral, he looked so lost. 'We were kids together,' he said. He looked at me with those clear blue eyes of his. 'What am I going to do without her?' he said. Seems that he's found a solution to that question."

"I only hope she's competent. Reuben and Amanda lived in such confusion, on the edge, financially, emotionally, physically on their little scrabble acreage. They felt too deeply, about the world, about each other. Maybe the friend will help ease the confusion. He says Amanda is still there for him, supporting him, advising him. He actually talks to her. I'm sure he's discussed the new friend with Amanda. Maybe the new friend was her suggestion. She wouldn't want him to be lonely. She would want him to be happy. Likely the friend helps ease the pain."

"Well, I'm afraid it's still a sharp pain for me. And likely always will be. My dream won't let me forget. It keeps it all so vividly before me."

"That's the same dream you told me about when I stayed with you?"

"I keep reliving the accident. It's more real than when it happened. When it happened, it was like a dream. A nightmare. Now the nightmare is real life. Whenever I have that dream, I wake up wasted, with no resources to get me through the day. Then I have to start all over again, building strength and energy. Sometimes," she said, tentatively, as though testing Esther's reaction, "I wonder if it's worth it."

"Of course it's worth it," Esther cried, stretching out her hand. She stopped it in time, so that it did not drop to Helena's shoulder but hung suspended over the prone figure as though pronouncing a benediction. "It has to be worth it," she went on. "Maybe you'll stop having that dream here. Here, where you're safe and loved. You've come through the storm. You can start over. Think of this as a beginning."

How could she tell Esther that she didn't have the strength for another beginning, that once she found Ben, once he released her, she would be quite ready to leave this planet? She couldn't tell her. But it did not seem right to keep it from her, either. To partake of Esther and George's hospitality, their generosity, while all the time planning to wound them, seemed another betrayal. "I shouldn't have come here," she turned her head away.

"Of course you should have. Where else would you have gone?" When Helena said nothing, she went on. "I don't know much about your life, I mean what you've been doing these past two and a half years."

The man in the bar, thought Helena. Going up to his room when she was flat broke. Hitchhiking to some place on the

Mediterranean with another man, one she had met in France. "I thought I was beginning a new life when I started travelling," she said. "Then I met a man in Europe. I'll tell you about him sometime. I thought *he* was a beginning. But then that didn't work out and I went back to the Coast to begin again. And then I met Keith. Now *that* was a beginning all right, the beginning of a nightmare. You see what I mean. I don't know if I can take another beginning." Her lips felt cold. "I seem to have lost myself."

"I lost you, too, these last few years. When you were a student, I could visualize you going to class, lecturing, writing, perhaps doing research in the library. I could see you having friends over in the evening, making dinner for friends or going skiing. But when I didn't know what you were doing, where you were, I couldn't *see* you. I didn't have a picture."

"Neither did I. I still can't envision myself doing anything, accomplishing anything. I can't see myself with any coherency. For a few months after I came out of the hospital, I couldn't even cook myself a meal. I couldn't see myself doing it, therefore I couldn't do it. When I think of the last few years, I can feel myself bouncing off walls, reeling from one catastrophe to another, but all I can see is a confused blur."

"You must get back the picture of yourself. You must stay here. And not go away again. For a while anyway. This is the best place for your search. This is where you started. I'm so glad you've come home. You and I must find each other again, too. You must tell me how I can make you comfortable. What do you *do* all day? Have you gotten back to any sort of routine? Do you read? How are your eyes? After that surgery, you had trouble with blurred vision." While she spoke, Esther's right hand kept lifting out of her lap, half reaching toward Helena and withdrawing.

Helena put out her hand and caught her sister's in midair, bringing both their hands down to the bedcover. "You're so good to me." She made a conscious effort to look directly at her sister. Strange how, unless she forced herself to see the real present Esther, she always saw the sister of their youth. Which Esther does George see? she wondered. "Are George's eyes giving him trouble?" she asked. "They seem to bother him."

"I know what you mean, the way they blink and shift. I keep telling him he must go for a check-up. He says he hasn't time."

Helena closed her eyes and listened to the rhythmic throb of a vein in her right temple. "Everything here is in such order," she said. "You have no idea how wonderful it is to come upon peace and order in this world. Your home is so lovely. You've created a paradise for George and Delores. And this bed! A real antique isn't it? Victorian. And these cushions, you always liked rich brocade. Those Royal Doulton figurines on the dresser. They look so much like you."

"I wish I were that trim."

"It's the manner. Elegant. You are every inch a lady."

"That word, I'm afraid, has fallen into disrepute."

"It shouldn't have. What other word do we have for an exquisitely gentle woman? And even a crocheted cover on the tissue box on the dresser! I do believe it matches the crocheted toilet seat cover in the bathroom."

"Now you're teasing. You always did make fun of what you called our bourgeois existence. I suppose that was Ben's influence." Esther hesitated a moment. "Are you going to see him while you're here?"

"I don't know." Liar, she thought.

"Do you ever hear from him?"

"I used to. Before I gave up the apartment. He'd phone. Leave a message on the machine. I never returned his calls."

"Maybe you should have."

"I was absolutely incapable of picking up a telephone receiver and choosing numbers. It seemed too big a thing to do, too large an action to take. How about you? Have you heard from him?"

"No. I keep meaning to have him over for a drink. But you

know Ben. He's so prickly about what he calls superficial social situations. He seems to feel uncomfortable when form and decorum are called for. Whereas George rather likes them. He likes putting on the cap and gown and marching solemnly down the aisle and taking his position on the..."

"So he doesn't know I'm in town?"

"I don't think so. Unless George told him you were coming. They see each other once in a while at the university."

"I wonder if he's happy. But, then, was Ben ever happy?"

"George says he thinks too much."

"Yes. Ben was always processing something, even in the old Cave days."

"He had a brilliant future. Everyone said so."

"Which he destroyed. Going to class all doped up. Ranting like a maniac."

"He's back there, as a sessional, but I believe it's fairly steady."

"I hope he doesn't make things difficult for himself this time."

"I certainly wish him all good things. I feel he's still part of the family."

"He doesn't want to belong to an institution, including marriage and family, and it would be against his principles to be successful in the worldly sense."

"George says he seems quieter, almost subdued. Likely he needs the money."

"Lack of money never seemed to bother him."

"But he must need *some* money."

"Ben took everything so seriously. We were all wild with questions of morality, but for him it wasn't just talk and ideas. He tried to *live* the moral good. He set such high standards for himself."

"He sounds so grim. No wonder you left him."

"That isn't why I left him."

"No, of course not dear."

"We were students with a capital S. How foolish we were."

"Yes, I could actually see you and Ben lobbing bombs at

the establishment. Along with Reuben. I do believe Amanda quieted him down."

"They were true flower children. And now one wonders if any of it mattered. None of it seems to have made a lasting impression. Make love not war. What's happened to that idea? And yet we were so fired up with ideas. Reuben and Amanda were so together on that. He was a good partner for her. And yet that was another thing I criticized, her choice of husband."

Helena was silent a moment, thinking. "At Amanda's funeral, he wore a suit, not a particularly good one, a little shiny, but he wore one."

"Reuben?"

"Ben. I'd never seen him in a suit before."

"It was good of him to go. Of course, he was there for you. He hadn't seen Amanda in years."

"He went to see her the summer before ... her last summer? Did you know that?"

"No."

"He did. She told me."

"I wonder why? You two had been separated for years."

"Apparently, he was in the neighbourhood and dropped in."

"That doesn't sound like Ben."

"That's what I thought, too. Does he have a woman friend?"

"George hasn't said anything but, then, likely he wouldn't know."

"Who'd put up with him? At the end, he never spoke to me, he just sat around the house reading and smoking pot, lost in a haze."

"But wasn't he going through a sort of trauma at the time? Because of his mother?"

"That's no excuse. That's just the time he should have communicated. If you choose to live with another person, then you choose to take on the responsibility of sharing."

"Yes, communication is the most important thing, according to all the articles. That *is* one thing, George and I are totally open and honest with each other. I can read his mind like an open book. Perhaps you and Ben were both too intellectual. With George and me only one of us is."

"Does that still bother you?"

"No..." Esther's reply was tentative.

"Whatever you are, dear Esther, it appears that you are exactly what George desires in a wife."

"Yes ... I suppose. I just hope he doesn't feel that he's compromised his life because of me."

"Why would he feel that? He seems to have the life he wants."

"Yes ... He might have done more research, less administration."

"I don't imagine he's compromised any more than anyone else." Helena's voice was brisk.

"No, but I'd rather he hadn't compromised at all."

"That's being unrealistic. Haven't you compromised?"

Esther thought a moment. "No. No, I don't think I have. I don't think I've had to. I'm the luckiest of the luckiest. Of course, we would have liked to have had more children, one more at least, but that wasn't compromise, that was a medical problem, part of God's plan for me."

Helena thought it wise to remain silent.

Esther's tone brightened. "How about Ben? What are you going to do about him?"

"Do I have to do something about him?"

"This can't go on forever. You two being married."

"Why not?"

"I don't know. It just seems ... abnormal. And what if you find someone else?"

"That's not likely to happen. I don't care if I never have another relationship with a man."

"Are you serious? I know you've had some bad experiences, but I can't imagine you without a man in your life."

"Dear Esther, you're so happy with George and the married state you can't conceive of any other life for a woman."

"Would you ever go back to him? Ben, I mean."

"What makes you think he wants me back?"

"He hasn't asked for a divorce. He must want you back."

"It doesn't necessarily follow. He's such a peculiar person."

"Do you still love him?"

"It goes beyond love. You must know that. You must feel that way about George. Love isn't in question. You get so intertwined, so grown into each other. Ben went to see Amanda. He went and I didn't. I hadn't been to the Island for such a long time before ... that last trip. Amanda actually thought I was mad at her. She told me that in the car that night. It tears me apart, that for the last few years of her life she thought I was mad at her." Helena turned her head away. "Why didn't I go to see her more often? Spend time with her? I ask myself that question a hundred times a day."

"It made you ill. Her life made you ill. Her life was always in such turmoil. You can't stand chaos. Especially emotional chaos. That's why you left Ben and went to the Coast. Remember?"

"Yes. I'd forgotten. That is why, isn't it?"

"You have a mind that demands clarity."

"A terrible character flaw, to need clarity in this world. It makes one recoil from becoming involved with other people."

"Perhaps you need to be that way to survive."

"Yes, well, the irony is Amanda's death has thrown me into total chaos. Which I deserve. Maybe I won't survive."

"Don't talk like that, dear. You only need time. And I'm here to help you through. You must talk to me. Get it all out of your system."

"To become involved in other people's pain, to have the strength to endure it, that's true goodness. That's you Esther. You went often to see Amanda."

"It didn't make me ill. If it had, perhaps I wouldn't have wanted to go, either. I've had such a regular life. I've never had to face adversity, not like Amanda, or you. Perhaps if I had, if I were tested ... perhaps it would be a different story. Anyway, you're through with all that. You're here. You're home. It's a new life dawning for you."

There was silence in the room. Helena closed her eyes and felt a familiar coldness start to creep along her veins. That was the way she went to sleep now, a coldness like death taking hold of her body.

The furnace came on with a thump. Warm air hummed through the vents. "You were always so good to Amanda," Helena murmured. "Not like me."

"Shhhh."

"You're so good and I'm so bad."

"Even if that was true, which it isn't ...sometimes God loves most the ones who deserve it least. Perhaps because often those are the ones who need love the most."

"Don't change, Esther," Helena mumbled. She clutched her sister's hand. It was a strong capable hand, the sort of hand you could put yourself into and feel reassurance. "The world needs people like you."

Helena was sinking into the dark, accompanied by her usual silent cries. If only we had stayed home that night. If only, if only. I should have let Amanda drive. I should not have drank so much. I should have ... I should not have....

Through the dark shroud surrounding her she could feel Esther's hand stroking her hair, her forehead. Her last sensation was Esther's cooing, "That's right dear. Sleep. You've had enough for now. We'll take this up again tomorrow. You need to sleep. And rest. Rest your brain. That's what you need. Lots of rest. And time to think things through. I'm so glad you've come home. It wasn't good for you to stay out there so long."

IV. GEORGE

MAYBE SHE'S RIGHT, thought George as he was jogging away from Veronica. He was conscientious about actually jogging during these escapades, although sometimes he did allow himself to slow it to a brisk walk on the way home. He had to.

As a rule, George did not think about his situation. He had made that rule for himself at the beginning. He had decided to suspend thought, to go with the flow, to simply enjoy whatever happened, enjoy Veronica. He knew that if he thought about what he was doing, the enormity of it, if he thought about Esther, about his standing in the community, he would spoil the experience for himself. However, on this particular stark morning George realized that he had to do something, one way or another. If he did not, Veronica would. It was only a matter of time before she contacted Esther.

How George longed to return to innocence. If only he could wipe out the last two and a half years. If only he could go back to that happier time. True, he had been having some sort of middle-age crisis, but he would have worked it through. With Esther's help he would have emerged triumphant on the other side. Instead, he had gotten himself into an unsolvable muddle. If only he could return to the place in his life where he had been that evening before the telephone rang and changed all of their lives forever.

"We're so lucky." Had he said that or had Esther? It didn't matter who had said it, they thought as one. Lucky. Lucky. The word reverberated now in George's head. Yes, they, he, had been lucky. He had not known how lucky he was.

"Don't answer it," George distinctly remembered saying.

If only ... thought George.

Esther had flown to the Coast that very night. He had followed a few days later for the funeral but had returned almost immediately because of his classes. Esther had stayed on, and Veronica had entered his life. In fact, he consoled himself, if Esther had not stayed so long at the Coast, Veronica would not have happened.

George knew what it seemed like, the older man seducing the young woman, professor seducing student. But it had not been like that at all. It had started so innocently — at home, in *his* home. He had answered the door one evening when Esther was away to find Veronica standing on the step. At first he did not know who she was. Then, through the bulky winter coat, the red scarf and toque, he recognized in the pale narrow face, the thin straight nose sloping down from a high forehead, the long narrow reddish-brown eyes and wide mouth, the student who had waited for him after class a couple of weeks previous, the one he had quite openly discussed with Esther.

"She's not much older than Delores," Esther had said. "We must help her. She shouldn't be alone."

George's breath was coming in short ragged spurts. Time to walk. His path had taken him along the edge of a ravine that dropped down to a river. The world was black and white, white snow, black tree branches, white sky. A narrow passage of open water in the river snaked black through the still landscape.

He had given her an extension on her paper, and that evening, that fateful evening when Esther was away, she had come with the excuse of dropping it off. Naturally, he had invited her to step in out of the cold. What was unnatural, at least for him, the staid, stolid Dr. Martin, was that he found himself saying, "Look, why don't you come in for a drink. I was just having one. My wife's away visiting her sister and I hate to drink alone."

He had taken her coat and hung it in the front closet. He still remembered his first smell of her, the subtly sweet smell of her body as she shrugged out of her coat, the clean smell of her hair as she took off her toque and tossed it on the hall bench, and something else, faintly fresh and minty, something like spearmint gum. He had watched her slide long leather boots from her thin legs. She was wearing tight jeans and a long-sleeved shirt almost the exact colour of her eyes. As she walked in front of him through French doors into the living room he could not help but notice her buttocks, firm, yet a little fleshy and pendant, like two ripe plums either side the deep crease of her jeans. Immediately, he corrected his vision.

She sat down on the sofa and folded her hands on her knees. Her face was more delicate than he remembered. He noticed how her hair fell across her forehead and how her eyes peeked out from behind it like a small animal's watching from behind a hedgerow.

A brisk fire was crackling on the grate. The cold weather had set in early that year and then had persisted, indeed, would persist all that long and dreary winter.

"Are you warm enough?" he asked. "Would you like to sit closer to the fire?"

"This is fine." Her voice was quick, nervous, chittery. It made him think of the birds that flocked to the feeder that Esther was careful to keep replenished, especially during cold spells. "How do they manage to stay alive?" Esther was fond of saying, gazing through the window at them pecking away on the back deck railing. "With just that little bit of fluff between their beating hearts and the brutal weather."

"What would you like to drink?" inquired George. "I was having whiskey." Then it occurred to him that she was a child. "And pop, we have pop around some place. Or juice, tea, coffee?"

"Wine? Do you have wine?"

"White or red?"

When he came back with the wine, he saw that she had shifted position slightly. She was sitting now with one leg and foot up underneath her. He set a glass, one of Esther's good crystal goblets, on the low coffee table and uncorked the wine in front of her. "I'm afraid this hasn't breathed," he said.

"It'll be fine." Her wide, generous smile softened the brittle intensity of her face.

He was going to pour a taster's amount but then had the thought that she might not know what to do with it so he poured the glass half full and set the bottle on the table. He picked up his tumbler of whiskey.

"Cheers," he said. They raised glasses. He turned to one of the wing chairs near the fire and sat down. "Such an early winter this year," he commented.

"Benjamin told me about the accident. Is that why your wife is at the Coast?"

He must have looked startled. "You know Ben?"

"Yes. I met him at university. I believe his wife and your wife are sisters."

"Yes." George looked into the fire. "A terrible thing, terrible."

"Ben told me how he sat with his wife in the hospital. He held her hand. At first she didn't even know he was there."

"Yes, she was having a bad time of it."

"He went right away. To the Coast. That night. He took a plane in the middle of the night."

"Yes. He and my wife were on the same flight."

"They've been separated for so long. Still, he went, the minute she needed him."

"I suppose so."

"What's she like? Helena, I mean."

"Oh, she's ... intelligent," he said and then wondered at how that was the first word that came to mind. "Yes, she's very intelligent. That may be her problem. She doesn't suffer fools gladly. Unlike Esther." He added the last to himself and was surprised when Veronica's response indicated that he had spoken out loud.

"Esther? Your wife."

"Yes." He suddenly realized that he should not be telling this stranger, this student, family secrets. He also realized that he was on his third tumbler of whiskey. He set it on the mantle, clasped his hands loosely and turned toward his guest.

"How are you?" he asked pointedly.

"Fine."

"Getting things sorted out?"

"Yes. I'd like to thank you for listening to me that day. Likely I was overreacting, but at the time things looked pretty bleak."

"No problem. That's the way with most things, give them time..."

"I'm already over it."

Youth, he marvelled. She was ready to take the bridge over a man and now, two weeks later, she seemed a different person.

It was only later she told him that the man had been Ben. Then, as he put it together, he realized that her real purpose in visiting him that evening was to get information about Ben, more specifically about Ben and Helena. Later, she openly admitted it. Later still, she told him that that was before she had fallen madly and inescapably in love with him, that what she had felt for Ben had been a pale facsimile of what she then felt for him. Ben had become a vague and distant memory, she said.

He noticed that her glass was empty. He rose, poured her another, this one a little fuller than the last, and returned to his chair.

"I haven't found anyone else," she volunteered. "I don't want to jump into another relationship right away."

Relationships. That's what they called them nowadays. In his day they had said "going together" or "dating" or "having a thing." Young people nowadays were so advanced in their articulation, in their ability to define life. It was quite frightening. "That's smart," he said. "Give yourself time to get your mind straightened around."

"And emotions."

"Emotions?"

"Get my emotions back on track. Settled down."

"Yes, of course. It's good to get out with friends. Don't become too much of an introvert." He felt that he was giving advice to his own daughter, he found himself using the same tone of voice. He said as much. "I have a daughter about your age."

"Is that her?" Veronica was looking toward the piano.

He got up and crossed in front of the fireplace to the piano. From its top, he picked up a framed photo and looked at it. Delores smiled up at him. She was so like her mother, with that glowing quality, an inner light that turned an ordinary pert and pretty face into a beautiful one. "Yes, and that's Esther, my wife, with her. We had it taken just before Delores left for university. Four months ago now. She's in Toronto." He passed the photo along to Veronica. Then he picked up a second one. "Here's another of Esther. As she was when I first met her."

"She was very beautiful."

"Styles were different then, of course. Hairstyles. The short curly look was in."

"She looks so ... interested."

"Yes, I suppose she was. Still is, for that matter."

Looking at that old photo, he thought how Esther had kept that germ of wonderment alive in herself all those years, how her life seemed to be one long series of exciting happenings, the neighbour's new baby, the old Chinese woman at the supermarket, the boy who carried out her groceries and wanted to marry his sweetheart but couldn't afford to. How was it that Esther who went through her life half asleep until noon should get more out of it than he who each morning went forth into the jungle to face students, faculty, the bureaucracy, to study and define life, cells, organisms? Did he have no basic understanding of his subject, which was life itself? Esther decided that it was because he did not involve himself. He said he thought he did. She said she meant his deeper self. He said he involved all of the self that he knew about.

George suspected Esther of still being religious. How else could life be such an object of reverence and mystery. When they were first married, he had hoped that her religion would gradually disappear. That it hadn't had not been a problem. She kept her own counsel on the subject, never foisted it on other people, did not attempt to influence him. She had not even insisted that Delores be raised in the Church. She knew how adamant George was about all that he called "hoodoo voodoo." However, George suspected that her spirituality, if not her Roman Catholicism, was still there, perhaps even stronger than ever, as was so much repressed material in the human species.

By now George had brought out the album from where Esther kept it in a sideboard. He sat beside Veronica on the sofa, quite close. You can't show another person photos from across the room. Veronica slid her foot out from under her and placed that leg across the other. Her knee accidentally touched his thigh. He felt that he had been burned on that spot of his skin, a burn that travelled through his veins to include his entire body.

"This is Esther again," he said. "We were at a football game. I suppose those hats and pennants look a little ridiculous now. Do they still do that?"

"I don't know," she said. "I don't go to football games."

"Ahhh, here we are. In the Cave. That's what we called the smoking room. It was downstairs in the Arts Building and a thoroughly unhealthy place. You could cut the smoke with a knife. Of course, we all smoked in those days. We didn't know we weren't supposed to. And coffee! We'd sit all afternoon and drink cup after cup. Or beer. We put away a lot of beer.

And we'd argue. Politics, economics, literature, the meaning of life. Oh, we were full of ideas."

"Ideas?"

"Ben was a wild-eyed radical. Look at him. A young Lenin, although his politics were quite different. He believed strongly in the democratic process, but he felt that his country had betrayed that process, that that process in his country, in the States, had been drastically demoralized. That was during the Vietnam business."

"And that's why he came here," she said. It was a statement, not a question. Later, he realized that she knew Ben better than he did.

"Yes. Ben was an unusual person. He had a sense of self. Even then, when he was so young. Some might have thought him cocky, but he had something to be cocky about. He aced every course he ever attempted. He had a creative mind. Perhaps that was his downfall." The last was said more to himself than to her, but she was quick to pick up on it.

"What happened to him?"

"Oh, a lot of things. But the long and short of it, to my mind, he lost confidence in his ability to make good decisions. He started questioning his decisions and therefore himself."

"You mean about escaping the draft?"

"Amongst other things. And there's Helena, sitting next to him. She was a radical too. Everyone said they were well suited. I think she saw herself a bit as an Anais Nin."

"Anais Who?"

"Nin. She was a freethinker. Lived as she pleased. According to her own code. In Europe. She hung out with the likes of Henry Miller. Oh, she couldn't be that wild, Helena I mean, being a Canadian, but she liked to think of herself as a free spirit. I doubt she ever indulged in free love, but she liked to think she could. Even then she was too smart for her own good. And there's Esther. And there's me, the good-looking fellow in the middle."

He meant it as a joke, but she took him up on it. "You *were* good looking," she said. He resented the surprise in her voice. But looking at the photo more carefully, it struck him a soft blow but a blow nevertheless. His skin was not as tight as it once had been and, while he could never be described as balding, his hair was certainly thinner, especially at the temples.

"Were Benjamin and Helena married then?" she asked.

"No. I suppose they were engaged, unofficially, that is. Nothing formal. They eloped eventually. Which didn't surprise anyone. Ben wouldn't have stood for much pomp and circumstance and Helena wasn't the type, either. Sometimes a woman wants a big splash. Esther and I had a huge affair with everyone there but the Pope. We'd been married a few years when this photo was taken. The wedding pictures are in another album. Esther has it all organized."

Veronica had held the album close to her face and stared with narrowed eyes. He had wondered if there was something wrong with her vision, but he learned later that she had very good vision. She had been studying the pictures of Ben and Helena.

"You were all together," she said, lowering the album. He thought he detected a wistful tone in her voice.

"The six of us. We even got Amanda and Reuben in this one."

"Amanda. That's the one who died?"

"Yes. She went into nursing. But at one point the three sisters were all at university together. That must have been the year Esther was finishing up. And that's Reuben there, with the crooked grin and twinkly eyes."

"He has a nice face. He looks like he'd be a nice person."

"He was. Or I should say, is. He was a farm boy from Saskatchewan. A bit naive, but weren't we all? He thought he could actually live his dream. To be a folk music star. Another Bob Dylan. Influence a whole generation."

"So what happened? To Reuben, I mean."

"He hasn't become a star but he's still a musician. He still has a band."

"So he has lived his dream."

"Yes, I suppose so."

"And Amanda stuck with him?"

"Oh yes, she stuck with him all right. It wasn't an easy life."

"I'll bet she didn't mind. I'll bet she didn't mind at all. Not if she loved him."

"You're right. And that was the measure of Amanda. They were what we called flower children. Make love not war, live off the land, protect the environment, all that sort of thing. They went to the West Coast. I suppose it was easier to live off the land there. I remember when they left, in a bucket of bolts, dragging all their worldly belongings in a trailer behind them, piled high, tied around with rope so the pots and pans wouldn't fall out. Brave souls or foolish, I couldn't decide which. We waved them off at the crack of dawn. We'd partied all night, a warm summer night. Their going-away party. Four in the morning and already light. Esther made Amanda promise to call her the minute they arrived some place, any place."

George was silent a moment, remembering, his head twisted sideways, staring at the photograph in the album on Veronica's lap. He suddenly felt sad. "We were going to change the world."

"What happened?"

"The world resisted, I suppose. Or perhaps we got tired." He realized that he was sinking into nostalgia. He supposed he was in his cups. "It was all so long ago." He took the album from Veronica and snapped it shut. "But we managed to have some good times along the way."

"I mean to your gang."

"It broke up, as gangs do. Amanda and Reuben left, Helena and Ben's marriage turned sour, Esther and I were settled in with Delores. Life became serious."

"Still, you belonged to something, to the university, to each other. It must have been nice."

George nodded. "The university was much smaller then. Everyone knew everyone else."

"It's different now. Impersonal." Veronica uncrossed her legs.
"Still, you must have friends there."
"Oh yes." She took a swallow of wine and set down her glass.
"And what are your aims?"
"Get this degree, then I'm outa there. I've had it up to here with academia. I want to live a little."

Later it was he who had talked her into going to graduate school. Her first response to that had been, "No fucking way." She was older than he had first thought — twenty-eight and registered as a "mature student." Coming out of a dysfunctional family set-up — father abusive, mother shrewish, both alcoholic — she had left school at a young age and for several years taken a variety of jobs. A disastrous relationship changed her life. The young man came from an educated professional family. He was a student; she worked at Wal-Mart. He was her first real love and he dumped her. She enrolled at university — perhaps to regain her self-esteem, perhaps to be part of the world to which he belonged, George could only guess at reasons. She did very well. And why not? She was quick and smart.

He had encouraged her to go on in psychology. She had a natural aptitude for studying people and a keen interest in statistics dealing with aberrational behaviour. He taught a course that was a requirement for psychology students in the science faculty whose work would include conducting experiments with animals. He told her about grants and assistantships and her marks were such that she was successful in her applications. The great thing was, as he had explained to her, it allowed them to be more accessible to each other. It kept her at the university, close to him, even in some of his classes. It made their meetings convenient. They could have coffees, even lunches upon occasion, although they were always discreet. George knew how gossip could get started and whip through the department like bush fire. But even to brush elbows in a lab or murmur greetings in a corridor would fill him with an exhilaration, an expectancy of life, which he had thought gone forever and which had been kindled that first evening.

"And how about lovers?" George put the albums aside and felt a small thrill of daring. Was he, George Martin, actually flirting with a student? He must be, as they used to say, three sheets to the wind, whatever the hell that meant.

She seemed disturbed by the question. She leaned forward to pick up her glass, her hand caught it sideways and sent it flying off the table onto the floor where it hit a chair leg and smashed, sending bits of crystal and droplets of wine all over Esther's immaculate carpet.

She sprang up. "Oh f… my God, look what I've done. And that was good crystal, too, I could tell. I'll buy you another. Just tell me where to get it. And look at the rug. Oh, I'm so sorry." She went down on her knees and started picking up bits of glass. She jumped up and ran in the direction of the kitchen. She came back with a cloth and again flung herself on her knees. She started dabbing at the beads of red. Fortunately, not much wine had been in the glass.

During all of this, George was ineffectively swaying from leg to leg, protesting, "that's all right, don't worry about it … please … it's not a problem." When she dashed into the kitchen, he half followed but met her on her way back. Because of the sudden violence, the sudden movement, the sound of breaking glass shattering the quiet composure of only seconds before, he was in a state of confusion.

Then he pulled himself together, bent down and grabbed the hand that was busy dabbing wine into the rug. "Don't do this." He pulled her to her feet. He spoke in low soothing tones. "Really, it doesn't matter. I'll get the rug cleaned tomorrow." He was holding her wrist. Her bones felt so fragile. He looked into her eyes. They seemed to flicker with tiny flames. Then he noticed blood. On his hand, her blood had trickled from a cut on her finger. He pulled her hand to his mouth and put his mouth around the cut. His nerves jumped like an electrical current. He felt an exquisite agony, so sharp he almost cried out. He led her back to the sofa, sat down and pulled her down onto his knee. They stared at each other. It was in that moment, some minute point of time within that short intense moment, that George made the irrevocable decision to let himself go with the feeling. He had both his arms around her, then he put his legs up on the sofa at the same time lowering himself until he was stretched full length, taking her with him. As they lowered, her legs straightened. He turned her full against him and they lay like that for what seemed to George a long time. He could hear loud thumpings of his heart. Then with half-closed eyes he fumbled for her lips. They kissed slowly and long. The kiss was mingled with the taste of her blood. It drove him into a frenzy.

He fumbled with the top button on her shirt, his mind already busy wondering how he would deal with bra clasps, the bugbear of his youth as he remembered. Much to his relief, she was wearing nothing under the shirt. He enclosed one breast, firm and smooth, with his hot hand. The heat inside his body accelerated. I'm going to burn up, he thought. I shall become a black cinder.

She must have felt his heat through his clothes. "Fire. Fire," she murmured.

He tried to take off her jeans but that was impossible. However, she cooperated by jumping off the sofa and slithering out of them. He sat up. Her shirt and panties dropped to the floor. She stood before him, tall and slim, yet with full breasts and hips. He heaved out a great shuddering sigh and gathered her to him and pressed his face into her belly. He breathed in her female smell. He pulled her down until she knelt between his knees. Her hands were in his hair. Now his mouth was against her neck. He pressed himself against her, at the same time pressing her to him, feeling her breasts through the fabric of his shirt. "You have to take this off," she said, starting to undo buttons.

Realizing that the sofa would be inadequate for their needs, he took her hand and led her to the carpet before the fire. At the periphery of his mind, Esther's shadow threatened but with one master stroke he obliterated it. As he pulled Veronica down with him, as he felt her silken cheek with his rough one, as he tightened his arms around her, a dizzy physical joy washed over him. He put all thought out of his mind, firmly, and for a short time he let himself exist only in the world of sensation. He could not have stopped this thing that was happening, not if he would be killed for it, not if he would be hung and quartered, not if he would have to suffer the torments of hell for eternity. This is all there is, he thought.

Lying naked in Veronica's arms, her sweat mingling with his and drying into a salty crust on his skin, George felt that if he died that moment, he could directly enter heaven. He had been purified. He was in the state of grace that Esther used to talk about.

He forgot that he did not believe in Esther's state of grace. He forgot that he did not believe in heaven.

They were on their backs, stretched out and recovering. "You were pretty energetic," she said.

"For an old man."

"You're not old."

He had a sudden thought. "Don't be angry with me."

"I'm not angry with you. That was wonderful."

And she did seem to think he was wonderful. She seemed to have genuinely enjoyed the experience, to have enjoyed him. He made an attempt to bring reality in the form of the mundane into their ludicrous and futureless situation. "I'm afraid I've put on a bit of weight around the middle," he ventured.

"I like that in a man," she said, putting her hand on his hairy mid-section. "I like a man to have substance. My very own cuddly bear."

He could not believe it, those first days, weeks, months.

Lazarus raised from the dead. That was the simple truth of it. He did not *intend* to deceive Esther. But what could a man do who had been dead and then given a second chance at life? It was a miracle. Veronica was a miracle. He was grateful. To Veronica. To life. He had not expected this.

They still found joy in each other. He was pleasantly surprised that they could come new to each other each time, that with her he could still know ecstasy and that he could still please her so. When they were not quarrelling, they had good times together. Not so long ago she had said, "Loving you makes my life worthwhile. At first maybe I got into it for fun but now it's what my life is all about. You're my destiny and you can't change destiny. A love like ours was meant to be. It can't stop ever. Can it? Can it?"

"No," he had said.

"I live for you. To hell with the thesis, I don't care about the thesis, all I care about is you. You feel the same way. Don't you?"

"Yes, yes, yes," he had said.

George was returned to the immediate world by someone passing on the walk. He was on the campus, crossing from the jogging path along the top of the river embankment to his residential area. He was winding his way around the various buildings: biological sciences, chemistry, physics. Then he was on the walkway fronting the famous old halls: Assiniboia, Athabasca, Pembina. George loved this part of the campus, the old part, with its huge trees and old brick and stone buildings. This was his turf. These were his people. He nodded to several students, to one colleague who was wearing jeans and had long white hair and a youthful face, to another in a dark suit who had short iron-grey hair and a pouch face. Then he was crossing a large parking lot, then a newer section of campus, then a thoroughfare, busy at that time of morning with rush hour traffic. He had to stop and wait for a red light to change. Then he was on the familiar streets of his neighbourhood. There was the small park where he used to take Delores in the warm evenings and push her on the swing. There was the corner store.

The area between his home and the university, George thought of as his. He had walked this sidewalk for so many years. He was not unaware of the irony in the fact that Veronica lived on the other side, the student side, of the campus. He had thought before about the difference between the two areas, one upholding the status quo of solid professionals, the other inhabited by transients living erratic, unstable, financially insecure existences. How had he managed to cross that barrier? How had he managed to live in two such different worlds? How had he, a faithful family man, a respected man in his community, admired at the university, how had he cold-bloodedly divided his mind in two, as he might have divided an amoeba in the lab, and built a solid wall between the parts?

George had always been able to focus without distraction on the immediate. By the time he turned the corner onto his street, he had put Veronica on a back burner in his mind and engaged his thought fully with the idea of Esther. Far down where the street curved he could see his house, two-storey, white, with gable windows and green trim. His eyes travelled the street itself, the sidewalks, the houses of his neighbours and friends. Together, they had planted saplings, laid sod, raised families. He could not give this up, that was the long and the short of it.

He'd had his fun. Two and a half years of it. Now the shit had hit the fan, as they used to say. Fifteen minutes ago, when Veronica had said, "shut the door," the party had ended.

"What is it?" His heart had beat rapidly. He knew she was going to tell him something unpleasant. "Are you going away?" She had talked about this, about applying for jobs once she had her degree and that the jobs of preference were in the East. He felt sick to his stomach. He vowed to never again eat another chocolate-coated oatmeal cookie. "Have you gotten a job?"

"How could I have a job when I don't have the degree yet."

"They're conducting job interviews for potential graduates.

Right now. On campus. They're already looking at the fall."
George scarcely knew what he was saying. He was thinking, if she gets a job somewhere else, I'll have to follow her.

"I haven't applied for any of those jobs. I'm not interested in those jobs."

"What is it?" he said.

"Shut the door and I'll tell you."

"What is it?"

He heard a noise behind him in the corridor. Someone came along the hall and went into the communal bathroom. He stepped quickly back into the room and shut the door. "What is it?" he said again.

Veronica looked him full in the face out of the sides of her eyes. Her eyes were measuring him, challenging him. "First, I want to ask you something."

George braced himself as though getting ready to take a blow. "What?"

"I want you to promise that you'll give me an honest answer."

George's eyes darted. His mind shifted as though it were slithering sideways in his skull.

"You're already wondering how you can get out from under an honest answer, aren't you? Your mind is setting itself up to spew out the response that will evade the issue rather than the one that is straight. Georgie, you would have made a great politician."

George turned to leave. "There's no point in me staying here and being insulted."

"Calm down. Just try and give an honest response for once in your life. For once in your life don't sift through the options until you come up with the most personally advantageous answer. Do you think you can do that?"

He said nothing. He willed his face to be blank, impassive. He was dealing with a different Veronica, one who had collected herself, who was able to collect herself. He felt like a father who suddenly realizes his child has grown up.

"It's not that difficult. Don't think before you answer. Say the first thing that comes into your head. Pretend it's a game. You like games. You're good at games."

His chest felt very tight. Maybe he'd have a heart attack right here on the threadbare carpet, she'd have to call an ambulance. Serve her right.

"Ready?" her voice was cold, level, as though she were conducting an experiment and he was her subject.

He would not dignify this ludicrous scene by speaking, but he did look her squarely, if somewhat balefully, in the eye.

"Remember, don't think." She paused. Then she spoke quickly, all in a rush. Her face did not move, her lips scarcely opened. "Do you love me? Tell me, yes or no."

His eyes lowered briefly to her body. They rose again to her face. "Yes," he said. "You know I adore you."

She breathed out. "Well, then," she said, "you may as well know. I'm pregnant."

It took George's mind a moment to make the turn. It was as though she had spoken in a foreign language that his brain had to translate word by word, then form the disparate words into a comprehensible whole. But what she was saying was not possible. "This isn't possible," he said. "You've been taking the pill."

"I know. I don't know what happened. They say, the doctor said, that every once in a while it happens."

"You must have missed a day."

"No."

"You're lying. You're not pregnant. You're saying this to get me to stay."

"In the first place, unlike you, I don't tell lies. In the second place, I wouldn't lower myself to that sort of subterfuge to get any man to stay. In the third place, I've been to a doctor. I've had the tests."

"You've done this on purpose."

"Actually, I didn't do it on purpose. But now that it's happened, maybe it's fate."

"Don't be stupid. There's no such thing as fate. Let's at least keep this on an intelligent level."

She shrugged a beautiful shoulder. "Suit yourself."

He stared into her taut face. "This doesn't change anything." He hesitated, even in his distraught state, he could not be crudely blunt. "There are procedures for unwanted pregnancies."

"True. But it just so happens that this one isn't unwanted. Oh, at first I thought of it. But the idea of killing our child, something we made together, you and me, doesn't appeal to me. So then it occurred to me, other men support their wives and children. Why can't you?"

"How can I support you? I have a wife and family. I have a house to keep up. Professors don't make much money."

"It's zero hour, Georgie. Time to grow up. Time to leave your ivory tower. Time to face reality."

"Why did you do this thing to me? This terrible thing?"

"I didn't do it on purpose. Believe me, I was more than a little surprised when I heard the news. But now I'm thrilled, if you want to know the truth. Just think, I'll be a mum. When I was a little girl my ambition was to be a mum. I was so lonely, I'd sit in a corner alone and rock my doll and pretend I was a mum. I'm finally realizing my ambition. And you know what? I think I'm going to be a very good mum. There's no way that I'm going to let anything interfere with the little bugger having a decent life if I have anything to do with it."

"And how about me?" George found his position totally incomprehensible "I could be a grandfather. How can I be a father? Couldn't you have had a little consideration for me?"

2. A Morning in Early Spring

V. BENJAMIN

HOW COULD SHE DO IT? She couldn't do it. But it had taken her so long to get this far. All she had to do now was walk down this street. Towards Ben. She couldn't do it.

She took a step backward, towards Esther's car parked at the curb. She looked up at black branches etched across a grey sky and felt the chill of fear shiver down her spine.

Helena didn't like being afraid of things. Once upon a time, in another lifetime, she had made a point of facing her fears. But back then, as she told herself, she had been strong, and if you're strong it's easier to be brave.

What exactly are you afraid of? she asked herself. Ben? But that's nonsense. What is there about Ben to be afraid of?

What if he knew the truth about her? What if he found out that she had let herself be picked up by pure sleaze, that she had picked up pure sleaze, that she'd gone home with sleazy strangers. It was a wonder she wasn't murdered. Maybe she had hoped someone *would* murder her. Sometimes she would meet a nice fellow, one who was kind to her, one who seemed to care for her. She wanted nothing to do with him. She wanted only men who would mistreat her, betray her, cheat, lie and steal from her. And she did her share back. And she learned to drink. Drink took away the pain for a while. Oblivion — that was what she needed. Drugs, drugs helped too. But you had to be careful with drugs. Sometimes they magnified the monsters.

What if he found out that she had always had it in her heart to kill Amanda. That maybe it had not been an accident, that she had deliberately lost control of the car, deliberately skidded and swerved the car into the ocean. When they were children everyone had liked dear little Amanda better than they had the scowling stubborn uncooperative Helena. The injustice of this, for Helena had thought herself at least equally as good as Amanda, had shadowed her into adult life, had had the power to infuriate her and put her in a belligerent mood. Was it that mood that had caused the accident?

Sometimes she remembered her parents bringing the newly born Amanda home from the hospital and placing her carefully in a frilly bassinet. Sometimes she could see the scene so vividly — the quiet nursery, the crib, the baby with rosebud mouth and chubby flushed cheeks sleeping, the older sister stealthily opening the door. Perhaps the adults were sitting chatting on the front porch of a Sunday afternoon and she, the intruder, tiptoed across the carpet, picked up a lace-fringed pillow and placed it squarely over the baby's face.

She told herself this story over and over again until it became true.

If Ben knew these things, he would hate her. He would despise her, which would be worse. He must already be disgusted with her. For killing her sister. For bringing devastation to so many people, including Reuben and Amanda's children. How could he not despise her? She despised herself.

She looked at the car and thought about getting back into it and driving away, back to her sister, back to sleeping and moving food around on her plate and being dragged out to shopping and lunches. But, no. She couldn't do that, either. She couldn't prolong her own misery or Esther's. It was time to relieve them both of the burden of her mortality.

She looked down the street. The distance threatened. Something sinister lurked between the trees, behind the fences. She should have parked directly in front of Ben's. Then she would not have time to waver. But what if he saw her through the window? The thought was unsettling, that he might be watching her, that he might see her before she saw him.

She directed her mind to why she had come. What had she hoped to gain by seeing Ben? To get the blackness out of her mind. To replace it with light. Or some kind of light. Whatever is in your mind when you die will be with you for eternity. She believed that. She had seen a vision of eternity, a dark vision. Ben was the only one who could help her. Amanda through Ben.

Helena saw Amanda's face, she heard Amanda's voice: "Ben came to see me last summer." During her travels, her disastrous wanderings and seekings, Helena kept thinking about that visit until it had taken on immense proportions. In her mind, Ben's journey became a pilgrimage. There was *something* about it. There *must* be something about it. As some people when dying reach out to God, Helena reached out to an idea. The idea had brought her here, to this place, to this point. But now doubt imposed itself. What if there was nothing significant about Ben's journey after all? What if Ben was not a connection between her and Amanda? What if Amanda had not left her a message?

What if she had? She took a step forward. You have to face him, she told herself. Unless you do, you'll never know. You have to know, one way or another. Before you can die, you have to know.

She started walking. The trick was to keep walking and think of something else. Spring is so long in coming here, she thought. It could still snow, the sky looked threatening enough — threatening and grey and uninspiring, offering no help to her own grey mentality.

The neighbourhood was old and had once been a fashionable district. But fashion had moved west, leaving this area to be designated the east end, a derelict district of shabby hotels, suspect bars, seedy nightclubs. This was Ben's terrain, where life had set him down, where he had a mission. This was where he felt he belonged, rather than in the faculty club lounge or at suburban cocktail parties or summer backyard barbecues hosted by colleagues. Because of what had happened to him, he felt at home with the lonely confused sinners of the world.

I know so much about him, thought Helena.

From time to time, she glanced from a piece of paper in her hand up to the numbers on the houses. The inhabitants of the street seemed to be a mix of old couples hanging on to the family home — trimming lawns, planting flower borders, repainting and reroofing — and renters whose landlords had no other interest than collecting rent which, more often than not, would be a cheque from social services. These were the houses that invariably had sagging verandahs and curtainless windows and stacks of beer bottles on front porches.

But it would not be a house. The telephone directory had given an apartment number. It must be the building at the end of the street. She hoped he'd be home. She had not been able to bring herself to call him. The thought of doing so had filled her with such nervous agitation, she had actually felt ill. How would she face him, then? She didn't know.

Driving here, it seemed strange to her that she had never seen where her husband lived. Seven years ago she had left their small apartment near the university, which they had furnished and decorated while in the euphoric and optimistic state of the newly wed. What they lacked in funds and expertise they made up for in enthusiasm and ingenuity. They made expeditions to lumber yards and building supply marts and clearance sales. They eagerly looked forward to each new edition of *The Bargain Finder*. Off they would go to garage sales and obscure addresses. They painted bricks and boards for book-helves. They restuffed and recovered a friend's discarded couch. They sewed curtains and cushions. They brought home a ball of tumbleweed and stuck it in a piece of pottery. Helena ransacked Esther's storage cupboards for suitable items, part of her sister's overflow wedding gift cache. They had thought their little apartment exceedingly attractive, and it was. They laughed with friends and declared their decor "bargain bohemian." They had been very happy there for a while, before things, before Ben, started falling apart. That was the place she had walked out of. She had left with one huge suitcase, she had climbed into a taxi, she had gotten onto an airplane. She had done these things alone. She had not wanted even Esther to accompany her. If Esther had been there, she might have changed her mind.

She knew that Ben had lived on this street for quite some time. The Volunteer Centre was only a few blocks away. She couldn't be sure when he had started at the Centre. She couldn't map his exact movements during these past years. At first, he used to phone her. Before she changed apartments and told the department and Esther not to give out her new number, he would phone her in the middle of the night when he was out of his mind and couldn't sleep. She could not deal with those calls. Ben had always been so strong and self-sufficient. She could not deal with a pitiful, vulnerable, needy Ben. She did not want to be drawn in to that. She did not want to be coerced into returning to him. She did not want him to drag her down. Then they would both be doomed. They would both be pulled under the fragile barrier between the ordinary, cheerful world and the dark swampy mental regions of the damned, where she had ended up, anyway. The irony was not lost on her.

Ben's building was an old apartment block faced with false brick. Various shades of red were patched here and there with yellow. False balcony railings of black iron fronted some of the windows. One end of the structure was sinking into the ground.

She turned in at the broken gate. She tripped on a crack in the sidewalk. She mounted the sagging front steps and reached toward the door. Her hand was trembling.

Would he invite her in? Leave her standing at the door? What was the worst that could happen? He might slam the door in her face. No, he was not likely to do that. But there would be an awkwardness. Is that what she was afraid of? What exactly was she afraid of? That he would not recognize her. Two years of dissipation had added ten years to her face. But he had sat with her in the hospital. At one time they had been lovers. They had been best friends. They were still married, for that matter. As she steadied her hand on the door handle, it occurred to her to wonder what *she* might do, what *she* might feel. What part of herself would be recalled by this meeting with her past life, her past self? Her stomach heaved. Why hadn't she thought to eat something?

She braced herself. She pulled the door open.

A foul odour assailed her. Mould? Rotting vegetation? She looked for an apartment listing but there didn't seem to be one. She started up a half flight of stairs, changed her mind and started down a half flight, changed her mind again and went up. Four doors, numbered from 5 to 8, were positioned at four corners of a square hall. Number 9 was what the directory had listed. She started up another flight. Now she could smell old smoke and stale beer, or was it rubbing alcohol, along with the rot and decay. She tried not to breathe.

It was a Thursday, just after ten in the morning. The building was quiet. Her steps were quiet. The door to Number 9 was half open. She stepped sideways through.

At first, she could see nothing but light and shadow, then the darker patches became shapes, table, chairs, a bureau of some sort. As her eyes adjusted, she could see that a rectangle of stark white light across the room was causing a glare that interfered with her vision. Then she could see that one of the shapes was Ben.

He was sitting in front of the window, sideways to her, his head bent to a stack of papers on the table before him. The light glinted on the metal rims of his eyeglasses. For a few moments she watched him, this person she had lived with, she had been happy with.

He might have seen a movement, he might have sensed her presence. He looked up. "Helena," he said, rising from the table. "Helena," he repeated, his tone surprised and pleased. He came quickly to the door. "I heard you were back." His voice cracked, as though his throat was parched.

"Who told you? George? It must have been George." She did not look at him. She let him lead her into the room.

"I hoped you would come."

"Why didn't you call then, if you wanted to see me?"

"I didn't know if you ... here, have a chair." He scooped up an armload of something — books, magazines, laundry — from off a large chair.

She tried to say something in the nature of a joke, something light and amusing, but she was unable to speak. She felt her throat swell and her chest tighten. Tears welled up behind her eyes. In a moment she would break down into uncontrollable sobs. Abruptly, she walked to the window and looked down to the street. She swallowed several times. She blinked her eyes. She set her lips tightly.

He simply stood, giving them both time to recover.

She turned slightly and looked down to the table. "You're marking papers."

"So what else is new?" What she took to be an attempt to laugh came out of his mouth as a strangled croak.

"Yes. You were always working. You never knew what to do with yourself when you had a day off...." She became aware that she was babbling. She stopped herself.

He dropped his armload back into the chair. He cleared his throat. "How about a coffee? Instant, I'm afraid."

"That would be fine."

What Helena really wanted was a shot of whiskey, but she didn't want to ask for that. Besides, Ben had never been a whiskey drinker. If he had anything on hand it would likely be beer. She certainly didn't want beer.

Anyway, the coffee was just an excuse to give them time to

reassemble themselves. Ben was very good with things like that, with making situations easier for people. She remembered that about him.

He busied himself at the kitchen counter. She needed to sit down. She sank into the chair he had just vacated. "I suppose I should have let you know I was coming," she said.

"It doesn't matter."

Her back was to him. She could hear him rattling the kettle lid, turning on the tap. She kept her eyes steadily before her on a student's paper. Her eyes fastened on the words: *By starving people, the government forced them to sign ... band members weakened by illness, hunger and the death of their chief ... Qu'Appelle Valley ... 1907.* "You're teaching this stuff now?" Her voice was lower, steadier. Good. "Your field was American."

"They needed somebody at the last minute. Hayes, you wouldn't remember him, but he died suddenly of a heart attack. He was the Canadian man. Actually, I'm enjoying the course very much. A lot of prep, but it expands my knowledge. I'm learning as much as my students. And I am a Canadian now."

"You are?" She was truly surprised. "You loved your country so much."

He made a great noise clattering something. "I decided to stop looking backward. The point of life is to move forward."

"You always talked about going home."

"Father died a few years ago."

"I didn't know." She turned her head toward him.

He was wearing limp brownish trousers, a colourless shirt with sleeves rolled up to the elbow, a shapeless knitted vest. On his feet were down-at-the-heel slippers over grey wool work socks. He seemed smaller than she remembered.

"His death was a consideration in my decision." He was rummaging around on the counter. His hands were trembling. They always had when he was nervous. As though to steady them, he clutched the edge of the counter with both hands.

"To let all that go."

"You were able to *decide* to let it go and then do it? That's amazing. But you always could do what your mind told you to do."

"Not always." He paused a moment, then went on. "At some point I realized that I tend to create mythologies about my life, the draft dodger, the radical intellectual, the misunderstood outsider. I had to learn to replace fiction with fact."

"It's funny you should say that." She spoke quickly so that there would be no blank spaces, uncomfortable gaps. "About mythologies. That's what George said to me, the first day I arrived, you and I are the sort of people who create mythologies. I suppose what he meant was, we make too much of things. We over-interpret ordinary events."

"Yes, well, I try not to do that any more. I try to live in the real world." He was turned toward her now, the palms of his hands supported by the counter behind him. "It's liberating … no longer letting yourself be controlled and manipulated by illusions."

He feels better, she thought. Speaking had always helped him order his mind and assume a voice of authority. "Besides," he went on, "I thought it pretentious of me to raise my life to the level of myth." He gestured toward her with his hands. They were steady now. "If we're to have clean cups," he said, "I'll have to wash dishes."

"Let me help." Glad of something to do, Helena stood up and took off her coat, a navy blue raincoat, which she draped over the back of a chair.

"Can you collect those cups on the table?" He had turned to the sink. Hot water was gushing from the tap. "They're my total supply."

"Which you don't wash until you run out."

"Don't complain. My housekeeping has improved a hundred per cent from what it used to be." By adding water to the dregs of a plastic bottle of detergent, he had enough for one more job.

"I can't imagine what it used to be."

"Living alone, a person gets into sloppy habits."

He's alone, she thought.

Helena brought the cups to the sink. "You like being alone." Her voice was coming stronger now. And Ben, busy with his housekeeping, seemed more comfortable. Maybe things would be all right after all.

He cleared off the drain tray, a rubber mat and rack. "You always said I'd make a good monk."

She began washing the cups. "But who ever heard of a Jewish monk?" She turned. "Where's your tea towel?"

"Tea towel?"

"Don't you have a tea towel?"

"There may be one…" He looked around in some confusion.

"How about paper towels?"

"Uhhh…"

"No? Kleenex? Don't answer. We'll have to let them air dry."

"Just put some coffee in these cups. And hand me those plates. I may as well do a complete swamp-up while we have these great suds. Ahhh. There's something so comforting and reassuring about hot soapy water."

Helena put coffee and boiling water into two cups. She kept stirring after the granules were dissolved. She couldn't think beyond the brown liquid swirling around the spoon.

"I don't have milk or cream." He was scraping a pot, looking toward her. "You like cream."

"It doesn't matter. I can drink it black."

She carried both cups to the table. Benjamin followed, giving his hands a quick wipe on the sides of his trousers. He pulled forward another chair and sat down. He foraged amongst the stack of student papers. His hand emerged with a pack of cigarettes. He shook one up and held it out to Helena, then tossed another up from the packet into his own mouth. He found a wooden match in his shirt pocket, lit it on his thumbnail, held it out to her. While his head was bent to light his cigarette, she finally dared to look closely at his face. He looked older. Well, of course he was older; they were both older. He no longer had a beard, the lines on his face were evident. His skin looked pasty. It always did this time of year, until he got a summer tan. He still had a great deal of brown curly hair. It used to be drawn back by an elastic band, but it was too short for that now. "You've cut your hair," she said.

He looked up suddenly and caught her with his eyes. She could not bear those eyes. At one time they had been so certain, so clear with a straightforward purpose. Now they were bewildered, questioning, containing a pain that she suspected was never totally absent. She looked down at her coffee.

"On my fortieth birthday," he said. "I thought it was time."

"I liked your ponytail." She flicked her eyes up briefly.

"I'll grow it back."

They both looked down. How easily, how unthinkingly, they had fallen into their old camaraderie. That they were comfortable together had been one of their strengths as a couple.

She took a sip of scalding liquid and winced. She looked around the room.

Ben had never been the materialistic type, but this was ridiculous. Hanging from the brown-spotted ceiling was a jagged piece of plaster that looked like it could at the merest jarring come down on someone's head.

Her survey stopped when it came around to his face. He had removed his glasses. He was looking at her. She recalled the intense look his eyes took on when he was wild with a new idea. When she first saw him, around a table in the Cave, he was spouting a theory, punctuating it with his hands. She had noticed his hands, even then imagining what they would be like touching her. Mid-sentence, he looked her way. The world stopped, simply stopped. The others around the table faded into a hazy background. She watched his mouth open and close; she had no idea what he was saying.

The silence was becoming uncomfortable. She must break

it. "In the hospital, for two days you sat and watched me drift in and out of consciousness. Then you left without giving me a chance to thank you."

"You were in pretty bad shape."

"Yes."

"How are you now?"

"Some days I'm okay."

She had lowered her eyes to her coffee cup but she could feel his eyes still upon her.

"I've never seen you with such short hair."

"No."

"You're thin."

"Esther's been trying to fatten me up for the last two months. But I'm afraid I'm a lost cause."

"I heard you were travelling. I didn't hear where."

"Oh, all over." She picked up her cup.

A wave of exhaustion surged up within Helena's body, deep in the core. For the past hour she had been battling her nerves. She had tried to hold herself strong. Now, it struck her — where she was and who she was with. She started to tremble, her legs jumped, her skin crawled. She drank from her mug. She set it down. "Ugh, Ben, this is terrible coffee. I don't suppose you have any whiskey around here?"

"I may have." He went to the cupboards and opened and closed several doors. "I can run out and get some." He banged another door shut. "There's an ALCB store on the corner."

"No, no, don't do that," she said. Yes, you'll have to, she thought.

"Ah." He was at the far cupboard, next to the wall. "Success." He took down a brown bottle and found a couple of clean tumblers in the drying rack. He went to the fridge and looked in the freezer compartment. "I'm afraid I don't have any ice," he said.

"That's all right. I don't want ice."

He returned and poured them each an inch of whiskey and set

the uncapped bottle on the table between them. He produced two more cigarettes from the packet and went to the stove in search of another match.

Helena picked up her glass, took a large sip, held it in her mouth a moment and swallowed. She could feel the liquid burning through her, warming her, bracing her. She could feel her strength returning. She stared at a spot on the table as though her life depended on her memorizing some detail of it. "You may as well know," she said, "I've lived a rather dissolute life the last few years."

"You don't have to tell me." Unable to find a match, Benjamin was bent to the gas flame of the stove top.

Why should he be interested in anything about me or my life? she thought. We're separated in the true sense of the word. "Maybe I want to tell someone," she said. "I haven't been a very nice person."

He came back to the table. He held his cigarette toward her so that she could light hers from his. "We never were nice people, you and me. We always wanted our own way. We thought we knew it all."

"Thanks," she said, drily.

"Two intellectual supercilious snots, that was us."

But you've changed, she thought. How did you manage to change?

"How about Esther?" he said. "Do you talk to her? I remember her as being a very sympathetic person."

"Esther's so naive. She thinks everyone is a dear soul. One of her favourite expressions. It's amazing. She can't assign selfish or malicious motives to anyone. She's lived such a sheltered life with George. She's the one who's a dear soul. But she does want to help me straighten myself out."

"Are you going to let her?"

No, she thought. "I don't think she can," she said. "Esther lives on the surface. While I seem banished to the depths. She's in the charmed circle of humanity. I've been cast out. When you do something opposed to life, you are cast out."

"Now you *are* making up mythologies."

"Maybe. I don't think so. There are lots of precedents. People who become lost souls and must wander the earth and never be at home. Your street people must be like that."

"Mostly, they're schizophrenic. Certifiably ill."

"How do you know I'm not?"

"I don't think so." He looked steadily at her.

She could not meet his eyes. "Anyway, Esther can't conceive of anyone being bad. She finds the good in everyone."

"Maybe you should let her find it in you."

"She'd have a long job ahead of her."

"Still, maybe you should let her try and help you. She loves you. You'd be doing her a favour."

He doesn't want to help me, she thought. He doesn't want to have anything to do with me. He's unloading me on Esther.

"Maybe that's why you came back, so she could help you," Ben went on.

Helena shifted impatiently. She didn't want to be told how to live. She wanted to be told how to die. "Maybe I came back to see you," she said. Shit, she had not meant it to come out of her mouth quite like that. She looked at him. He seemed to have stopped breathing, his typical reaction to an emotion thrown in his face. "You went to see Amanda," she went on, brusquely, relieving him of the wrong idea. "The summer before the accident. She told me, that night in the car. The picture I keep seeing of Amanda is one of her face just before we hit the barrier. Shock and terror is what I see. I need to have another picture of her in my mind. Can you give me another picture?"

Benjamin let out a long sigh. He poured Helena another inch of whiskey and upended his glass. He threw back his head and closed his eyes. "The summer my father died, I had to get away. I rented a car and started driving. I found myself on her island. I stopped in to see her. She gave me a cup of tea, herbal tea. She had an herb garden. She showed me all the tender small plants. Reuben was away some place. I didn't see him. Or the kids. I only stayed an hour."

"What was she like? I mean, what picture of her do *you* have in your mind?"

"'Serenity' is the word. She seemed at peace. She had lived, was still living, the ideals of the revolution, although I don't think she thought of it that way. The "make love not war" slogan was simply part of her personality. We sat in the sunshine, in a little grassy spot. She brought out a tea pot and cups, on a tray, and set it on a tree stump. We sat on logs around the stump. She was wearing one of those long shapeless dresses she always wore. Her hair was shorter, but you know how it was always so wispy around her face. She looked very young. I had the impression that I'd walked into a Beatrix Potter scenario."

"She was able to stay a flower child to the end."

"Yes, and a true flower child, not one of the pseudo types. She was a person who would look to find a reason to believe. A beautiful person."

"Which I erased from this world. Can you see the enormity of what I did? A good person gone, a bad person left."

"I don't like the expression 'bad'. We're all simply at different stages of our journey. And what makes you think you're bad?"

"I was so horrid to Amanda. I was so busy finding fault. Poor Amanda was hopelessly incompetent. She never seemed to know how much she could manage. Instead of getting down to some serious organization and then following through on it, she was always taking up projects. She always had bits and pieces of things lying about, embroidery, crocheting, knitting, silk flowers. She tried everything in every craft book. But nothing was ever properly finished. The same with her people projects. She was always taking in the halt and the maimed and the drugged-out. She was always head of this or that committee for the old or the young or the under-privileged or the misbegotten or the sick or insane. She kept herself so busy, everything was always in a confused mess. It all bothered me so, I'm afraid I lectured her on it. That's one of my last memories of her, my harping on her case."

"You always were hard on people who can't cope."

"I know. I could never understand that some people simply can't do it. I always thought they weren't trying. If they would only get up a little backbone, they too could conquer their trials and tribulations. And now I've got it back in my face."

Benjamin sat silent, his hands folded quietly in his lap.

"Oh, I miss her so," Helena burst out. She was sitting with elbows on the table, hands up and clasped. She put her head against her hands. "I so depended on Amanda. Even though I didn't see her often, I knew she was there. I felt positive vibrations coming to me from her. I knew that I was in her head, in her thoughts, in a good way. I felt safe in that place. Then that place was gone."

"I've had that thought, too. That we were all part of a narrative in her mind. When she died we were no longer part of a coherent narrative."

"We were thrown out of paradise. I no longer feel at home in this world."

"When we lose our place, we have to try and find it or find another. Sometimes we have to find a new meaning for home. A new idea for home."

"I suppose that's what you try and do with your street people. Provide a new meaning for home. But I don't think I can find a new meaning."

"Have you tried?"

Oh, yes." She searched her mind. She doubted that men and booze qualified. "I went to a bereavement group." It's not a lie, she thought, although, again, she had doubts, this time as to whether one meeting would qualify as an attempt. "They said it would pass, the grief. I lost interest when it didn't."

"It doesn't pass without effort. You have to make a decision to get rid of it."

"I can't make rational decisions about emotions the way you

can. Anyway, it comes to me when I'm asleep. I keep having a dream, where the accident happens over and over again. I don't want to live if I keep having that dream. But I'm afraid to die because what if it's true, what they told us in Sunday School, that there is life after death and if you're bad you'll be tortured in the fires of hell for eternity. For me that would be an endless eternity of having that dream. I wish I would stop having that dream."

"Maybe you never will stop having it. Maybe you'll have to learn to live with it."

"That's impossible. I can't do it."

"That's because you haven't found the way yet. It takes time."

I don't have time, she thought. "Time is the enemy," she said. "I don't want time."

"Time is your friend." Benjamin spoke slowly, emphatically, in low even tones. He's used to this, she thought, used to talking people into handing over the gun or the pills. "As long as you're alive, you have time to try and set things right."

But is it worth it? she wanted to say. Why *not* give up? Why *not* choose death? But she didn't want to reveal too much. He might try and stop her.

"Death takes away all possibilities for setting things right," he said.

Helena sighed. "I get so *tired* of it." What? she asked herself. Suffering, she answered herself.

He seemed to know. "There's good suffering and bad suffering. You have to replace bad with good."

She found herself looking at Benjamin's hand where it was now resting on the table. It was a good strong hand. She almost reached out and covered it with hers, but she did not want to start something. She saw that she had finished her whiskey. She must go. It was either more whiskey and oblivion, in which case she would have to stay too long, or leave now, while she could still drive. She stood up and gathered her coat from the chair back.

At the door, she turned. Around Benjamin's shoulder, she could see into his bedroom. Across the bed, on a night table piled with books and magazines and an overflowing ashtray, was their wedding picture. Ben had such a pleased expression on his face, as though he had just swept up the princess and carried her off on a white charger. Her own face was unbelievably soft, unrecognizably malleable. Her eyes were full of dreams. Quickly, quickly, she looked away.

"What happened to us Ben?" She kept her eyes on a brown stain on the wallpaper. "And not only us. What happened to the revolution? All our protesting, did it do any good at all?"

"We were going to change the world. We were all so hopeful. Did we even think of the future?"

"We thought we'd all get wonderful jobs, have infinitely good health, conduct our experiments, discover the cure for cancer, discover a highway to the moon, to Mars, write our novels, our history, do good."

"We started out with such hope, such strength, such power. Was life simply too much for us?"

"We can't blame life."

"We are to blame then."

"'Blame' falls into the category of bad thoughts." They were silent a moment. Then, "Would you want to come back?" His eyes were steady on her face, as though he had resolved to keep them so. "I mean ... would that be of any help to you?"

Helena felt his male presence. She wanted him to put his arms around her. She took a step backward. "Would you want me back?" She felt a lump grow in her throat.

"Yes."

Helena swallowed the lump. It seemed to get caught in her chest. "It's never seemed to me to be a viable solution. I'd scarcely fit in to your life." She half turned, waving her hand at the singularity of his existence. "Nor you in mine."

"What is your life at the moment? I mean, is there anyone else?"

"No. What I mean is, I have no life."

"Maybe we can make a life together. Maybe out of our non-lives we can make a life. We could find a place. Buy some real furniture. There are some low cost condos near the university."

Helena's mouth twisted. "Somehow I don't see you in a housing development."

"Maybe you're right. But there are other places to live. Other people like us live, people who don't fit in. People do manage to live together."

"Yes, some people do."

He held out his hands, palms upward. "What can I do to help you?"

She had not yet found out what she needed to know. She could not leave without finding out. Here was her chance. An opening. She took a breath. "Tell me about Amanda," she said.

He dropped his arms back to his sides. "We walked down through an orchard, down to a creek. We talked about the garden, the day, the sunshine. We walked back up the hill. I got in my car and left. She called me a Christian Jew."

Helena braced herself. "Did she say anything about me?"

"I'm afraid we talked about me. Selfish of me, when I think of it now. But I seemed compelled to talk."

"What did you talk about?"

"Oh, you know, my old problem, my guilt, my confusion. I was still carrying that. I needed to talk and she let me."

Helena couldn't let the idea go. Amanda had left her a message — for months now she had carried that in her mind, a seed at first, growing into a reality. "Are you sure she didn't mention me?" she asked.

His face was perplexed. She knew that expression. It was the one his face got when he was thinking how best to say something that might disturb the other person, when he was trying to find the right words, the best words, the least hurtful words. "She might have ... I don't remember anything specific."

Helena felt that she had been delivered a blow to the mid-section. She turned to the door so that he would not see.

"My arms are open," he said, behind her. "If you change your mind."

She was able to compose herself and turn her head. She looked into his face. It was a good face, scrunched up with the effort of trying to save the world. She wanted to hold that face a moment in her mind. Before she let it go forever. "You've beaten your addiction to self-destruction," she said. "You're one of the lucky ones." Again, she turned to the door.

"Remember," he said. "I'm here."

"I'd only make you unhappy," she said without turning.

"That's okay. I'm one of that so-called chosen race not meant for happiness."

Those were the last words she heard him say before she stepped through the door and closed it behind her.

VI: AMANDA

THROUGH GLASS DARKLY SMEARED with urban grime, Benjamin watched Helena, a small black figure, disappearing into a network of budding poplar branches. His brow was marked with two small vertical cuts. Why had she come?
 He had no illusions that she actually wanted to see *him*. Well, it didn't matter. She had come. That was the main thing. He had been so pleased to see her, he had not let himself wonder. Now, he did.
 She wanted something. He didn't mind. He wanted to give to her. But what did he have to give? Amanda, information about Amanda. That was what she had been leading up to from the moment she stepped through his door. His visit to Amanda, the details. She wanted something she could live by, something she could hang onto.
 But was there anything to hang on to? Was there any sense to it all? He thought of his street people. He thought of Bruno. Because he and Amanda had died the same night, both, it seemed, victims of a malevolent god, he often thought of them together. Their deaths had been equally bizarre, one freezing to death without proper shelter in the middle of an affluent society, the other drowning in a metal box she couldn't get out of. Bruno had started out with an ordinary life and had ended up in a cardboard shelter over a heat vent. Amanda

had been the promising younger sister in a trio of intelligent accomplished women and had ended up scratching for a living on a run-down acreage in a self-imposed exile. How did such things happen? But maybe that was not a valid question. Maybe we are simply a collection of molecules. Maybe we are simply animals, involved in the equivalent of grazing, digesting, sleeping, chasing down prey. How about George's cause and effect theory? But the same cause could have different effects. Was it all chance or was there an underlying pattern?

Helena seemed to be asking these kinds of questions. He thought it a positive sign. She had arrived at the place where she was looking for meaning. When a terrible blow first comes, people are too stunned to think about meaning. They walk around as the living dead, zombies to shock and disorientation. When they get to the stage where they look for meaning, that is a sign that they are coming to life.

She had not been reluctant to talk. That was another good thing. He knew from his crisis counselling at the centre that when people can talk, it's usually a good sign. Not always, though. Sometimes people talk just fine then a few days later you find them dead.

She was delusional, he was sure of that. Like some of his derelicts seeing pictures in their minds, she was probably imagining things that had not happened. On the other hand, she *had* been driving the car in which Amanda had been killed. That was a fact, one she had to somehow work through. She had come to him for help in working it through and he had failed her.

How often had he sat with people raving on drugs, delirious through illness, whispering through despair? How often had he listened to their confessions, found the words to soothe them? But he had not been able to find the right words for this person who meant so much to him. All the things he might have said — replace negative thoughts with positive thoughts, Amanda would want you to forgive yourself —

sounded pompous and tired. Yet those things were true. He supposed that was why clichés became clichés. They spoke everybody's truth.

He had not been able to supply her with a meaning for his visit with Amanda, at least not a meaning for her. For him, it had meant the difference between life and death. Should he have told her that? But it was all such a mystery in his own mind, he didn't know how to voice it so that it did not sound like rubbish. Still, maybe he should have said something. Should he have fabricated a meaning for her? No, he could not have brought himself to do that. Anyway, nothing was ever gained by evading the truth. If he *had* told her about his experience with Amanda, would it have done any good? He didn't think so. After all, it had been *his* experience. Helena was so focused on her own pain, she wasn't open to hearing about other people's experiences. Besides, he wasn't sure, himself, what had happened to him that day, only that after years of being dissected joint by joint from himself by himself, in her presence he had felt whole again. Should he have said that to Helena? But it sounded so irrational. He could not voice such irrationality. There were no words to turn something mystical into an explanation that would not sound plain foolish. Words would have trivialized something deeply felt. Was that why he had never uttered the words he might have said, never telling Helena that he loved her?

Helena disappeared from his view, but he could still see her, the shape of her skull, the bones beneath her skin. He was familiar with that hollow-eyed ravaged look. If he rolled up her sleeve, he knew he would find evidence of needle marks.

A different Helena came to mind. Helena coming in from the snow, cheeks pink, green eyes sparkling, snowflakes caught in her hair. He had met her at the door, brushed the snow from her hair, put his arms around her, his body shaking with the pain of pure joy. She was alarmed, thinking that something terrible had happened while she was out. He could not speak to tell her that everything was fine. He had been so full of exquisite pain he could not speak.

That had been good pain, but he knew a lot about bad pain, too, how at first the mind is cauterized by it. That's the easy part. When the blood starts to flow back into the brain, that's when it becomes unbearable. You have to get to the place where pain is bearable before you can think of a way out. You have to try and fill your head with good thoughts so there's no room for bad thoughts. The process takes discipline. It takes strength. It takes time. You have to think of something besides your own misery, even if, at first, you can do it only for minutes, seconds. The time will grow longer.

But it was just as well that he had not said those things, for, in the end, all a friend can do is hold your hand and try and keep you from doing something foolish, hold your hand until you're ready for the miracle. You can experience a miracle through another person, which is what had happened with him, but you have to be open to receive it.

The process doesn't happen overnight. It takes a long time to get to the open position. That was a bit of news he could have imparted. Some never get over a severe shock, was another gem. That's what the books and the counsellors never told you. Most of the people at the Drop-In Centre had been stopped by shock. Some had once had successful lives, friends, and careers, before the thing happened that made them not want to be part of the ordinary world.

Bruno had been married with a family, had a job, a place in society before things went wrong, before he started drifting, started drinking. In a way, Bruno had been successful in dealing with his pain. He had found his place in an underground society as an independent entrepreneur, a dumpster diver, a scavenger, picking bottles and cans out of garbage containers and cashing them in at recycling depots. He had a career. Picking. He would not accept welfare. He wouldn't even collect his pension, though he was nearly seventy. He wanted nothing to do with governments.

How a person deals with pain is a defining factor. Some people fixed themselves at the cauterization stage, some dealt with pain with drink and drugs. Most of the street people did that. But that caused other problems to do with health and relationships. And the pain could come back, like the eruption of an illness lying dormant for a while before re-emerging with a vengeance.

Then there were those who fought like wildcats against pain, who would not let themselves be destroyed, who would use any means or any person available as an object to save their own egos. Veronica was like that.

"Fuck, does this mean we have to stay in?" He could hear her voice as clearly as if she were standing here now, holding back this same rag of curtain. Was it really nearly two and a half years ago?

"What a dump!" That was Veronica's appraisal of his apartment, as well as his life. She had been right. She had been right about a lot of things. Veronica was a very smart girl.

"I might think you're still in love with your wife." Had she said that the same night, regarding him with those eyes that never seemed to look at anything but saw everything? "Except I doubt you've ever felt that emotion. You're pitiful." She probably said that, too, that night. She had said it more than once.

Veronica was another blight on his conscience. He should not have brought her here to his rooms, he should not have feigned feelings for her, although to be fair to himself he didn't think he had done that. She had presumed. But wouldn't any woman under the circumstances? No, he was not proud of his actions with Veronica. Her legs had been what first attracted him. They'd been standing in front of him at the Pizza Hut booth in the food hall. His eyes had travelled up, up from the legs to the hips, the flat back, the fall of golden hair. Maybe there hadn't been anything wrong with that, men are attracted to women, after all. But when he had realized that she was emotionally unstable, badly damaged in fact, he should not have pursued. She needed someone who was strong and firm, who would not give in to her tantrums or her emotional wheeling and dealing. She might be healed by such a person. But it was the old story. Fucked-up people find each other and fuck each other up even more.

He had watched her leave much as he had just now watched Helena, through the same window. Except, then, he'd had to scrape ice from the glass and the figure he had been tracking with his eyes had disappeared into a storm. And, although he saw Veronica occasionally around the university, that was the last of their scenes. For that was the night of the phone call. When he packed a bag and called a cab to get him to the airport, she had not yet returned from the Crown. When he got back from the Coast a few days later, she was gone.

Benjamin let go the curtain and turned from the window. He picked up the whiskey bottle. He found his last cigarette on the table and took it and the bottle with him to the armchair that at one time had been his worry chair but was now his thinking chair. At one time he had worried and agonized nonstop nearly twenty-four hours a day, scarcely taking time out to sleep, and even his sleep had contained his worries. When the day came that his thoughts were less clouded, he decided that he wanted to get control of his worrying. He set himself a specific time each day in which to do nothing but worry. During that time he let himself worry about anything that was bothering him and especially about the thing that had destroyed his life. At all other times during the day or night he did not let himself worry because it was not the appropriate time.

That this technique worked surprised him. Maybe because his upbringing had been comprised of god's law and his studies had necessitated discipline of the mind, he was programmed to follow rules. Although at first he was tempted to worry outside the allotted frame, this disappeared with time. It was a slow process, but over the months that became years, his worry time became shorter and shorter. The day came when he found himself impatient with the process. Instead of being confined to his chair worrying, he wanted to be up and about, getting something done. One day he almost forgot to worry. That was the beginning of the end of his worry time.

Benjamin took a short pull at the bottle, cradled it on his lap, closed his eyes and settled in to what he liked to do best — think. Ordering his thoughts, trying to figure things out, this had always been his passion. It was what had made him a promising scholar.

Helena, he thought, and let his mind freely fall. How excruciatingly wonderful to see her again. Yet, he felt that he had been through an ordeal. The emotional turmoil of seeing her, that had been difficult. More disturbing was her condition. Even in the hospital when she had been bruised and bandaged, she had looked better than now. Then she had been in bad shape physically, now she was suffering from soul sickness. She was bent on self-destruction. He had known that even before he'd seen the grief in her eyes. He had seen it in her defeated posture, her skeletal appearance, her mouth that grimaced in place of a smile.

He had watched people travel the passive route to self-destruction — willing themselves into sickness and death. It was not hard to destroy yourself if you put your mind to it. Some people ate or drank or drugged themselves to death. Some people stopped eating. Helena was doing a combination of these things. He wondered if it was a conscious act. A lot of people were not aware, perhaps did not let themselves be aware, that they were killing themselves. They felt sick. They couldn't eat. The body reacted, provided physical dysfunction until they became seriously ill.

But why do some people decide on self-destruction while it never enters the heads of others whose troubles are just as severe? A moral abhorrence of such action, was one answer. Faith, he supposed, was another. Some people, like Esther, seem to be born with faith and some people find it. He had found it. Before that, he had been on the path to self-destruct. Ten years ago, just like in the old bible stories he had learned at his father's knee, a mighty wrathful God had smote him down. He had gotten even with Benjamin for all those student years of shouting that God was dead and that the bible was a myth, for quoting long passages from Nietzsche about man being superman and able to chart his own destiny and everything being permitted.

God had shown him a thing or two. The main thing God had shown him was His existence. Hell exists. Benjamin knew that now with certainty because he had been there. If hell exists, reasoned Benjamin, then God must exist. So then his attitude was, 'Okay, you sonofabitch, you may be out there and you may be stronger than I am but you're a mean old devil and I don't have to respect you or like you.' Thus started a long ongoing battle wherein Benjamin tried to kill God. But the more he tried to kill God, the more God killed him.

His father had taught him that God, although stern and sometimes cruel, is just. The problem was that justice for him would have been to burn in hell for eternity. That was what he deserved. That was what a man who had killed his mother deserved. There was no way around that fact. Justice was no good to him. He needed forgiveness, he needed love. But he believed in neither. Until three summers ago, when he had visited the Island. Until that summer, for seven long years, he had been filled with an incoherent rage. Since that summer, he was a changed man. Or, at least, a changing man.

Benjamin upended the whiskey bottle, set it on the floor and lit his last cigarette with a cardboard match that he found in the chair cushion. He stretched out his body, put his head back, closed his eyes and drew smoke deep into his lungs. He thought about the letters that began Dear Benjamin and ended, Your Loving Father. He still had them, all of them. He kept them in a tin box high up in a corner of his closet. One of them was dated August 22, 1970. That was the one that started: Your letter has caused a great deal of anxiety and worry to your parents ...we can not believe that you would accept a graduate position at the university there and marry this young lady with no thought of your duties. The letter went on, a father's plea to a son: ... my thoughts ... the laws of, and duty to, the state or the group have precedence over the wishes of the individual. What sort of country, corporation, household, universe, could you run if this were not the case? And apart from the law, and perhaps even more importantly, is the personal carrying out of one's duty to others and to God, although I know your thoughts on the subject of God....

This matter cannot be resolved in any other way than by you returning to your country and facing the consequences. Many young men have applied for conscientious objector status. You are accurate in your understanding that one of the questions asked is do you believe in a Supreme Being? ...Most unfortunate that your beliefs in this regard have altered since your youth ... may be a choice between submitting to the draft or going to jail ... and are you certain of your motivations? Of course, I share your ideas about this war, or any war, and none of us can know with certainty our country's motivations in waging it. It may well be, as you say in your letter, a sop to the munitions factories in Texas that have a strong lobbying position. It may be that our country is shoring up its own economy on the bent backs of unfortunate peoples in third world nations (your words). But in spite of all its imperfections, no other country on our planet promotes and allows as much freedom as does ours. Your mother and I have no desire to see you go to war. But will you forgive yourself for not facing the problem squarely? We understand that this opening in the graduate program seems like a heaven-sent opportunity for you. You mention that this is a great chance to work under the supervision of a man who is a respected historian. But please remember the temptations of Satan and how he can be an extremely appealing force.

Think of the future. You may never again be allowed to visit your home! Your mother and I will never be able to visit you with clear consciences and feelings of good will. We, you and your parents, will never be able to look into each other's eyes without feelings of shame. Be careful son, be very very careful in your decision ... the right decision always involves obedience to the law. That is the lesson we learn from the story of Abraham. Also, the importance of the law. The law must take precedence over the wishes of the individual ... without the law it is all darkness. Your idea about our coming to live with you in Canada cannot be taken seriously. Even if we would uproot ourselves and leave our home, a home we have worked for so many years to establish, we could not ourselves defect with a clear conscience....

Please, please, telephone us to say that you are coming or even to discuss these matters. We will accept the reversal of charges. Your mother sends her love and hopes to see you soon.

After a while he stopped reading the letters. After a quick scan in case they contained anything of importance, which they never did, he tossed them into a box. After a further while he tossed them in unopened. His parents did not attend his wedding. By then, his father had ceased to write. Instead, his mother sent long, newsy epistles, which he dutifully read although he found them boring, full of the neighbours and community life around the synagogue. He could scarcely remember the people she was talking about. He had lost his connection to home. He was very busy at that time of his life, with his studies, with his new wife.

The fatal letter, as he thought of it, he received during Christmas exams. He was teaching an introductory course that had three hundred students; he was trying to finish his own dissertation. He had stuck it into a pile of papers on his desk that he meant to deal with when he had time.

The very day that he returned from his mother's funeral — by that time the amnesty for draft dodgers was in place — his hand came upon the letter. He was cleaning off his desk and there it was, the hand of God to strike him down. He slit open the envelope, unfolded the paper inside and, after a couple of paragraphs about the weather and Myrna Bercov who had had cancer but they operated and thank God caught it in time, and Myrna's son who was out at the West Coast now and doing very well in private practice with two darling little girls whose pictures Myrna had shown around at the last ladies auxiliary meeting, read: That polyp I was telling you about in my last letter, it looks like it's cancer all right. I have to go for treatment, then they may want to operate. Well, that's life for you isn't it? The rest of the letter went on about the bazaar and the benefits of the hot tub at the new Centre for his father's stiffening joints. It ended: My dearest wish is that I would see you before I die. I don't know why I would get cancer. It doesn't run in our family. But the doctor says the greatest cause of these things, and many more, is stress. I guess stress is the big thing nowadays. I hope you're not mad at me for not attending your wedding. You know how your father is. It would have been difficult for me to go. But sometimes I think I should have gone and faced his disapproval. Sometimes I think about that at night when I can't sleep.

Benjamin could not remember the next year of his life. It was all one big smoky spaced-out haze of alcohol and drugs, painkillers he called them. Somehow, he had gone on and gotten the doctorate, although he knew he had disappointed his supervisor by not doing as well as expected. The university had given him a position, but the quality of his work had fallen off, he was merely going through the motions. Still, he managed for a few years to hold things together, at least he thought he was holding things together.

He could not pinpoint exactly when he started to despise his students—their materialistic goals, their superficial aspirations, their petty grievances, their blatant stupidity, their mean and petty lives. He could not mask his contempt. He stopped being a good teacher. The most startling comments came out of his mouth — rude, contemptuous remarks when some timid little bastard dared ask a question. The gossip about him making lewd suggestive remarks to some of the young women was true. What else did the little cunts, as he thought of them then, want? Why else would they wear jeans so tight the seam was like a g-string separating each buttock, T-shirts that were meant to emphasize the size of their breasts. Obviously, they wanted to be looked at. However, they did not want to be touched. He found that out when one young woman took her complaints to the head of the department.

The department was very good to him. They gave him several warnings, several opportunities to shape up. Since he was bent on self-destruction, that only meant he had to go further to destroy himself. He went to lectures unprepared and under the influence of various substances. His sarcasm developed into verbal abuse. He was very good at this. He had a clever tongue. It was a gift that, up until then, he had tried to use for good. He abused his gift, turned it into a weapon. To take your God-given talents and use them for evil was, in his father's opinion, the worst thing a person could do. He did exactly that. He perpetrated his evil onto innocent victims, one victim in particular, Helena.

By the time she left for the Coast, he had destroyed her cheerful optimism, turning it first into sad resignation, then into cynical pessimism. Worst of all, she became fearful. His brave fearless Helena became apprehensive when he came in the door. She never knew what to expect, never knew what ugly mood he might be in, what he might have been smoking or drinking or snorting. After a while, they could no longer look at each other. Finally, she applied for graduate school at the Coast.

Into his mind came an image of Helena walking toward him. He was waiting in the doorway of the campus watering hole and she was coming toward him with her full free stride, coming from one of her classes, her hair long then, floating around her face in a soft autumn wind.

He shook himself into reality. She was no longer that person, either. Her life, too, had been irreversibly changed, first by him, then by Amanda's death.

Amanda's death, nearly two and a half years ago, a bitterly cold night on the prairies. He was kneeling beside a heat vent holding Bruno's dead body in his arms when Victor's voice called his name. It was Esther on the phone. She had received a call from Reuben.

Benjamin heard again Bruno's words, very faint, a hoarse whisper. "I'm sorry. I'm sorry." He had no idea what the old guy had in mind. But it didn't matter. According to doctrine, in an emergency a lay person can hear confession, can perform the last rites. Such a person does not need to know the details. Anyone can forgive you your sins. You only need one other person to forgive you.

He had found such a person in Amanda. He had poured out his heart to her, everything, the letters, his mother's death, his behaviour toward Helena. He had told her the worst things he had done in his life. She had forgiven him, and through her words he was able to receive his mother's forgiveness. "Your mother forgives you. She would cheerfully have died for you. You have to accept her gift. It's what you can do for her."

What had directed him to Amanda so that she could give him the last rites? He did not know. He had not seen Amanda for years before his visit. He could not remember consciously steering the car in her direction. It had seemed to travel toward the Island by its own volition. He knew that was nonsense. At the very least, it was unsettling. He could not responsibly believe in a force that had directed him toward Amanda any more than he could believe in something called spiritual awakening. How could he, a serious intelligent person believe that he had received some sort of mystical guidance from another person? What had happened, he rationalized, was that he had found solace in talking to Amanda. In her presence, he had felt at peace for the first time in years. A healing balm had congealed around the open wounds of his nerves and his mind. Amanda, with her slow, calm, accepting nature might have that effect on someone, he surmised, but to elevate the experience to the level of mystical empiricism seemed a bit much. What he could not deny, however, was that after his last sight of her waving goodbye in his rear-view mirror, he had felt that he could go on, that he could find a way to go on. He regretted that he had not been able to do the same for Helena.

Benjamin's eyes sprung open. He had a sudden realization. Helena was looking for something, not so she could live but so she could die. He saw again her eyes when she was asking the question about Amanda. Her eyes on his face had been like a fire, flaring up for a moment then quickly dying when he had not been able to say the words she wanted to hear. He saw her bent head, her manner of resignation.

She had come to see him for words from Amanda, words of absolution she could take with her to the grave. She wasn't choosing slow starvation or alcohol poisoning or any of the hundred other slow ways a person can shorten their life. She meant to choose one of the fast routes. He stood up quickly. Where was she now? He must try and find her. Esther. Esther's number must be in the book. Where was his phone book? Did he even have one? He cursed his own lack of order. Where was the damned phone book?

VII: HELENA

I MAY AS WELL BE DEAD, Helena thought. I *am* dead. I'm a breathing dead thing. In order to be alive, you have to have something to look forward to.

She stared at her hand against the steering wheel. She must be back in the car. In the palm of her hand was a mound of round blue tablets.

Soon she would sleep. Sleep. Sleep. Sleep was like a lover calling. How she longed for sleep. Oblivion.

How she longed to stop thinking. The curse of life was thinking. You were never free of it, even when you were asleep. Unless you were sleeping the deepest sleep of all, the one that clicked off your brain. She must get her brain clicked off. She could not stand the voices, the pictures.

It hadn't worked. That thought kept going around and around in her head. It hadn't worked. Ben had not worked. The thing she had counted on had not worked. The belief that she might find a way to die in peace, the belief that had given her hope since she had looked into that mirror in Prince Rupert, the belief that she had carried with her, so carefully, as if it were fragile porcelain, from that place to here, had broken. She had been so sure of Amanda.

She shouldn't have come. She had gained nothing and she had lost everything that she had left to lose. Her belief in Amanda.

Her belief that Amanda had left her a message. Her belief that she had occupied a space in Amanda's mind. That she might occupy that space in heaven, for surely if there was a heaven Amanda would be there.

She was locked out of paradise, deprived of Amanda forever. She was locked into an eternity of dragging herself up and down streets like this. Hell must be like this, eternal grey streets littered with broken glass and empty cardboard food containers, smeared with hacked up gobs of spittle, inhabited by the weak, the sick, the dispossessed, human fallout of a failed experiment.

The time had come. Even though she no longer had the hope that she might die in peace, die she would. She would go into that black hole of torture and stay there for eternity. Eternity is a very long time. Eternity is forever. That's how long she was damned to hell. To suffer the torments of hell for eternity was what she deserved. That was the proper verdict for a woman who had killed her sister. The worst thing you can do. Cain and Abel. The first murder, the worst one. Cain was marked and cast out into the wilderness. That's where she'd been the past few years. That's what she deserved. The hell of the past few years.

What difference whether hell was in this world or the next?

She was regarding the blue tablets when it came to her — she would not be able to swallow so many pills without liquid. For a moment, she became confused. She thought she might become frantic. Stay calm, she instructed herself. Be sensible. There must be water some place nearby. She raised her head. In the direction of Ben's apartment building was nothing. She looked across her shoulder and saw a corner store. It seemed a long way away.

Could she make it there and back? She had to make it. Otherwise, she couldn't have what she so desperately desired.

She raised her right hand cupped with the pills to the left hand that held a small brown plastic bottle. Carefully, she poured the pills back into the bottle. Carefully, she replaced the bottle into the special zippered pocket of her purse. She opened the car door. She stepped back into the dismal day.

Hunched into her coat collar, she watched the toes of her shoes against the cracked sidewalk. How inevitable it all seemed, her footsteps obeying the command of the future.

The network of black branches overhead, a thick and intertwining net, lowered down on her, closed down like the lid of a coffin. She couldn't breathe. She was suffocating. Her mind was shattering into fragments. She could not catch any of the fragments. She felt for her purse.

Deliverance. She carried it with her, under her arm. Her black bag and her pills. She squeezed her arm tighter to the side of her chest. Yes, it was there, solid, a solid something she could hang on to.

Let me get to the store, just let me get to the store. The thought was so vivid she might have spoken it but she was not speaking to any god, not even to fate or chance. She was simply sending her words out into the cold air, air devoid of understanding or mercy, human or otherwise.

She was so tired. She had never been this tired. But she had to get to the store. She had to make it to the end of the block, she had to cross the street. There was nothing else she could do, except lie down on the sidewalk and never move again. She contemplated that action. But someone would eventually come and take her away. To where? A hospital? The loony bin? Back to Esther's? And what then? To lie in bed all day, or on the living room sofa, or in the TV room watching movement on a screen? Going shopping with Esther, going for lunch, visiting art galleries and museums? Poor Esther, trying to keep her sister going, trying to keep her too busy to think about despair. But it wasn't working and Esther was exhausting herself trying to think up new solutions, new activities.

She must rid Esther and the world of the burden of her personality.

And this body. This repulsive body. This smelly, repulsive body. This repulsive skin, hair. The thought of her digestive tract caused her to feel something akin to horror. Swallowing food, having it pass to her stomach, becoming waste. Elimination. Blood. What leaky smelly disgusting objects human beings were, she, in particular, was. She couldn't do it another day.

At the corner, she looked both ways then stepped off the sidewalk to cross the street.

She became aware that she had been standing a long time in front of the cooler. I'm in the store, she thought. The drinks were all too sweet. Still, she must make a decision. If she lingered, people would notice, they might call the authorities. They might take her handbag away from her. Choose. Choose, she ordered herself. She opened the heavy door, reached in her arm and grabbed a can of soda. At the counter, she waited for her change. This is silly, she thought. What does change matter to me now? Still, she waited, and when she received it, put it in the proper change purse in her bag.

When she arrived back at the car, she felt calm, in control. The drink business had confused her momentarily, but now she knew each step she had to take. She felt good about being able to solve a problem, and she felt confident that she would be able to apply herself to the project in a detached manner.

She slid between steering wheel and seat, closed the door. Her hand knew where to go, inside her bag, straight to the zippered pocket.

But now an old man shuffled past. A woman with a shopping bag was heading her way. People were stopped for traffic at the corner. A man and a woman were chatting on the sidewalk. She could hear their laughter outside her metal container. She felt eyes on her. She felt Ben's eyes on her. I may as well be in Grand Central Station, she thought. What she was about to do was an intimate act. She needed privacy. She had to find a lonely place.

Almost noon now, but the clouds had lowered and the day's

greyness had intensified. The car was moving, probing the misty air, searching, slowing at certain locations that offered promise. One of these was a street beside a deserted schoolyard. The tires rubbed against the curb and stopped.

Helena sat a minute. Through a wire mesh fence was an expanse of brown grass and bare ground. In the field were soccer goal posts and, nearer the building, playground equipment. An eeriness leant itself to the scene, as if the children had suddenly vanished taking all their noise and life with them. This was the right place, lonely and abandoned. Had it been ordained since her birth, or had life randomly dumped her here?

Staring through the window, she let herself puzzle for the last time as to how it had happened? What had directed her to the place where, because of her own wilfulness, she had catapulted the car over the edge? Had she been born with a certain personality that destroyed other people? Had Amanda been her victim? She had always insisted on having her way, she admitted that. Throughout their childhood and later, Amanda gave in because Helena would not. Amanda wanted to go to Art College but she took Nursing because Helena before her had refused to take it, choosing Philosophy instead, a decision that had greatly upset their parents. If she, Helena, had not insisted on always having her own way, maybe Amanda's life would have been entirely different. Maybe she would not have gone to the Coast where she ended up a passenger in a rented car on a stormy night.

Oh, why couldn't she have been less critical, less arrogant, less bossy, less tyrannical, less domineering, less cruel? Why couldn't she have married some nice fellow and trotted off to the suburbs and become a preschool volunteer? Why did her life have to be so damned complicated?

She poured the pills into her hand. She looked at them. This is what her life had been working toward. The last years of drink, drugs, and men, she had been on a self-destructive course that had to end somewhere, some time. Many prostitutes ended up this way. She had been a prostitute; she had prostituted herself. She had lived off the avails of men, but it was more than that. She had not only sold her flesh, but her intelligence, her talent, her human dignity, her soul.

She was glad she hadn't told Esther or Ben the sordid details of the last few years. All they knew was that she had travelled for a while. In their minds, at least, she would retain a certain amount of dignity. And now, in a few minutes, there was no danger that she would, in a weak moment, reveal the facts.

Loss, loss, loss. Loss of grace, loss of Amanda, loss of the good space of her sister's mind, loss of the good vibrations she had received from that space, keeping her from real harm, giving her some direction.

Some people's lives worked toward a good end. Those were the saints, the people who contributed to the human race, scholars, researchers, teachers, doctors. Prizes and accolades went to such people. They were blessed with children and grandchildren, a good life, good work.

Her life had been working toward a bad end. It wasn't just Amanda's death. Amanda's death had been some sort of culmination of the wrong turns of her life. Amanda had been goodness personified, a light of reassurance and consolation. She, Helena, had never been a good person. Hadn't Ben just said that? Ben spoke the truth. She was a despicable person.

Her life had arrived at this handful of pills. And what had it all been worth? Nothing. Life was a straight ruler you walked, step after weary step, to the edge of the cliff, before you stepped off into oblivion. Any happiness you might find along the way was always taken away. You were not allowed to keep any of it. Paradise was dangled before you like a carrot, but it was another illusion to keep the human race going. We make up myths to get us through but none of it is true.

She picked up the can of soda from the seat beside her. Staring straight ahead, she pulled the tab. She talked her way through it — keep your mind on the project, don't let yourself think of anything else. Don't let yourself think of Esther or Ben. Don't let yourself think of anything except what you are doing. Success demands full attention.

She swallowed as many pills as she could manage with each gulp from the can. She realized immediately that she had chosen the wrong soda. This one was pink and very sweet. But it would have to do. She swallowed and drank until the pills were gone. It was actually quite easy. She should have done this long ago. The last few men she certainly could have done without. She was starting to feel quite good. She had solved a problem. Now that it was too late, she knew the answer. She had discovered the solution. Why doesn't everyone do this, she thought.

She put the bottle back in her purse. She finished the last swallow from the can and set it in the drink slot beneath the dashboard. She didn't want to mess up Esther's car. Then it struck her. Esther's car. Poor Esther. They would find her in Esther's car. She should have gotten out of the car, found a park bench. Damn. But it was too late now. She was starting to feel drowsy. How long would it be? A couple of tablets took some minutes, maybe fifteen, to take effect. She lay her head back against the head rest to wait.

The night of the accident entered her mind. She could not remember clearly the events or the sequence of events. It seemed that she had drunk quite a bit in the bar; it also seemed that she had been perfectly sober. And had she really been arguing with Amanda? Had she really accused Amanda of being their parents' favourite? But that was such a childish remark. It had been raining, that was certain; that had been in the police report. She had been picked up wandering on the edge of the highway, in a zombie state of hypothermia and shock. That was also in the police report. The policeman had made her read the report for accuracy before signing it. But had the police report really happened, or was that only part of her nightmare? Had anything really happened?

Helena felt terribly horribly ill. Something was wrong with her stomach. She could feel it bubbling like a cauldron. She could hear it, rumbling and popping and spluttering. She broke out in a cold sweat. She got the door open just in time.

She vomited as though she would never stop. And after the mess of whiskey, pills, and sweet pinkish pop, the bile kept coming and coming. Her stomach heaved in spasm after spasm. Her stomach was in control of her body. It heaved until there was nothing left to reject and then it dry heaved for another five minutes. She surfaced into grey light. Sober and empty, she found herself staring down at the unbelievable spewing of evil that had come out of her body, all of it in a pool between car and kerb. Tears streamed from her eyes, spittle from her mouth. A long string of saliva mixed with vomit swung down from her lips.

She became aware of a presence. She raised her eyes. Standing on the sidewalk watching her was a boy of about eight. He had a thin face and big eyes and a snotty nose. His eyes appraised her condition in a detached yet curious manner, as though he was quite accustomed to seeing such displays. He took a step toward her, his hand out. He seemed to be offering her something. What was it? A tissue, a tissue that he had pulled from his pocket. She looked at the balled-up wad. She looked at the child's face, at his thin bare legs. What was his mother thinking of, dressing him like that on such a cold day? Then she realized that possibly he had dressed himself, and maybe younger brothers and sisters. He looked like one of the misbegotten of the earth, malnourished and overlooked, the people Ben had chosen to live with. He took another step toward her. His approach, his expressionless face, said, here is my offering, accept it or not, it's up to you.

She reached out her trembling hand and took the tissue. He turned and ran back into the schoolyard. With the tissue, she caught the string of saliva that was dangling from her mouth. It was then she heard the children's voices, laughing, shouting, trilling like birds in the cold spring air. The playground and soccer field were inhabited with young bodies kicking balls, sliding down slides, swinging on swings. She should have chosen a different place.

She shifted her body back into the car. She looked at the tissue in her hand. She put it in a plastic bag that was hanging from the dash and found a box of tissues in the glove compartment. She cleaned around her mouth. She wiped up the tears and slobber on her face.

She put her head down on the steering wheel. Great heaving uncontrolled sobs came from her belly. "Please please please," she wailed, "forgive me, my darling, how I love you, how I didn't tell you that night, how you're part of me. My sister."

She collapsed onto the front seat of the car and sobbed until she had no more tears. Still she lay, exhausted in mind and spirit. She lay until she saw Amanda's face. But it was sad, so sad. And she was the one causing the sadness. You can't do this thing, the face seemed to say. If you succeed in doing this thing you will be killing me all over again. You have to stay on this earth and live for me. You have to try and be happy for my sake.

Helena answered, I don't want to be happy. I want to suffer.

She had a sudden insight into what Ben had been talking about, the difference between good and bad suffering. She was immersed in bad self-centred suffering. She wallowed in it. She felt power in it. She guarded it jealously, holding it close to her heart. The pain of her suffering was all she had left of Amanda. She could not give it up. It was all quite perverse, but she couldn't do anything about it.

Amanda's face was still with her. Words came out of Amanda's mouth. "There are people who love you in spite of yourself. There is such a thing as unconditional love."

"I'd kill such a person. Just as I killed you. The more the other person gives, the more miserable I am to that person. I keep twisting the knife until the other person is dead." Helena realized that she was speaking out loud.

And Amanda answered out loud. "Maybe you can change. People do change."

"They may change for a while but sooner or later they revert to themselves."

"Ben changed. Ben, too, was in love with his suffering. He managed to give it up."

It was true. Ben had evolved, but he was a person who looked for goodness, who believed there was some sort of moral framework to the universe. He just got derailed for a while. She was a person who had never believed in anything except her own ego.

The remnants of her vomit, splattered down the front of her coat, was dank and stiffening in the cold. She had a crick in her neck. She sat up, slowly.

She turned the key in the ignition. I'll stay for you, she thought, but don't ask me to be happy.

She would have to repeat the whole ill-conceived venture in reverse, go back the way she had come, through the grey day, through weeks and months of grey days. For, although she had made the decision to stay, she had no illusion that things would suddenly be just fine. She would get along as best she could, she would do that for Amanda, but that's all she could do.

She had no idea where she should go. Home, wasn't that where people went in time of trouble? But the home she longed for was in Amanda's mind and Amanda's mind was no longer in this world. If she was going to stay in this world, and stay she must, it seemed that she had just made a pact with Amanda, she needed a home to get her through to the time when she could be with her sister.

Ben's voice came through the muddle in her brain. "For some people home is a person."

She would go home to Esther. Esther. The name had always been synonymous with home — Esther as the little mother, Esther as the best pal, Esther as her port in the storm. But

Esther's idea of a problem was not being able to find the right fabric for her new drapes. Nothing bad has ever happened to her, thought Helena. Time is a good thing for her. She looks forward to grandchildren, to George's retirement, to travel, to good times. She wouldn't be able to understand time as a bad thing. She tries to understand my predicament, but how can she?

And it was then she realized that Amanda *had* left her a message. But not through Ben. Directly. That last fateful night as the car had hurtled through the storm on its way to destruction, Amanda had said, "He still loves you." Ben loved her and that was the truth. Otherwise, Amanda would not have said it.

She had been looking for the wrong message, something profound, some magic formula that would make everything better. Like a child, she thought, who wants someone to kiss a scraped elbow and then like magic pain and discomfort will disappear.

She saw Ben standing in his doorway, hands out, palms raised, arms open. She stepped on the gas. She turned the steering wheel away from the curb.

3. A Series of Events in Late Spring

VIII: ESTHER

IT WAS A DAY LIKE any other. Later, and forever after, that was what struck Esther, that on a day like any other your life can change forever, that on a day like any other your life can end. With no warning, you can be hit by a random sniper's bullet, you can be struck by a car while waiting at a bus stop, you can be carried away by flood waters. You can be driving along a country road in Arkansas and be lifted by a tornado. Just like that.

It had started as a good day. She lingered in bed, perhaps malingered — she knew that at times she was self-indulgent. Snuggled into her rosy satiny quilts and cushions, she dozed and slept long after the sun was up. Earlier, she had heard the robins that returned every year to build a nest and raise a family in the elm that bounced its branches against the window. And the squirrels, year-long inhabitants of their huge nest in the blue spruce at the end of the yard, how they chattered as they scampered down and up the trunk and branches gathering twigs and pine cones and anything else they could find. The spruce was more than twenty years old. George had dug it as a sapling out of a ditch near Jasper. One Sunday, all those years ago, they had packed a picnic lunch and headed for the mountains. Delores was a year old, barely toddling. They often went on Sunday excursions in those days. It was something to do when you had a small child, distraction for the child, who would soon fall asleep in the swaying vehicle, entertainment for the parents. It was something to do on a summer Sunday. Happily, merrily, tunefully, she would fry up some chicken, boil potatoes and eggs, peel carrots for salad. She would have made a cake the day before. They would put the big wicker picnic basket into the trunk of their TR5, and away the three of them would go. That car had seen them through many an adventure. It was the one George had owned when she had first met him, the dashing flamboyant young professor. He was so handsome, so mature compared to her other boyfriends, of which there had been a constant stream since her early teens. He was a man of the world. She had never been out of the province, let alone as far as Montreal, George's home, which was foreign and French. She fell immediately, hopelessly, exhilaratingly in love with him.

Oh, that TR5! Esther gave herself over to a few moments of fond reflection. Before they were married, before Delores was born — flying through summer nights, to and from parties and dances, the top down, windblown hair, another couple, sometimes Helena and Ben, or Amanda and Reuben, crammed into the back seat, one time even sitting up on top of the seat which, when Esther thought of it now, had been very irresponsible. But they had been so young! Surely, God would forgive them!

When Delores was in kindergarten, George traded in the TR5 for a white Buick. It was a difficult decision for him, but Delores was no longer comfortable in the cramped back seat and they couldn't afford two cars. They had bought this house soon after they were married. George had been put on the tenure track and she had become pregnant sooner than expected. Not for George the bricks and boards of Helena and Ben. He said that he wanted to live like a professional man, not like an undergraduate. He had been brought up in a grand old house in Montreal and anything that did not attain to this standard he viewed as a backward humiliating step. And although the house was more than they could afford at the time, with the way prices escalated soon after, it turned out to be an excellent and prudent buy. Anyway, perhaps because of an indulged childhood, George never worried about money. As it was, his father gave them the down payment. The house was near the university, allowing George to walk to work, near a lovely large park and swimming pool and schools for Delores, near the river and biking and jogging trails, and it was surrounded by other nice houses that were populated by people like themselves. It was larger than they needed, but they had thought they would have more than one child. When Esther considered her life — a piece of whole cloth, rich, colourful, textured — that was the one flaw. She consoled herself that when, after complications with Delores' delivery, the doctor called them in to his office and explained that more children would not likely be forthcoming, George had not seemed disappointed.

Lying in her king-size bed in her sunny attractive bedroom, Esther watched the leaves of the elm float against the window and felt the rightness of her life. The robins flying back and forth, in and out of the cozy depths of the spruce to the graceful branches of the elm, where they sat a minute seemingly to also enjoy the glorious morning, confirmed her feeling of satisfaction. Yes, she was as right in her world as those robins were in their's — busy, busy, between garden and tree, happily engaged in living as all God's creatures were meant to live, nesting, nurturing and rearing young, teaching them to fly, journeying on when the cycle was completed.

As usual, George had crawled out of his side of the bed earlier, trying not to wake her but, again as usual, he did. Not that she minded. For then, she could think, I don't have to get up yet, and then nestle contentedly down inside the warm covers. Dreamily dozing, she would hear him in the kitchen making his coffee. And although he tried to be quiet, she would hear him opening and closing the back door. Then she would fall into a sound sleep for another two hours.

Esther had always been a night person. When Delores was very young, after tucking her in for the night, she and George would spend what was left of the evening together, usually reading or watching television. At about ten, they would look at each other, mutually rise, go into the bathroom together, brush their teeth, and ready themselves for the night. By the time Delores was a teenager, taking forever to get herself into bed, Esther, who could not bed down until her chick was in the nest, had to stay up correspondingly late. As she grew to enjoy this solitary alone time when the house was quiet, the time advanced further. Into the wee hours, she read books, caught up on the news in her pile of old newspapers, did the crossword, put her photos into albums, manicured her nails, fingers, and toes, sometimes watched the late movie. Conversely, George went the other way. For a while, he went to bed shortly after Delores, then, as her schedule advanced, he went at the same time, then earlier. Such are habits born, unshakeable habits, even dangerous habits.

In the beginning, Esther would get up and have breakfast with George before he went to the university. She would prepare a good nutritious start to the day for him and Delores. Then in high school, Delores stopped eating breakfast because she was always on one diet or another and George said he could get his own, which in those days was a bowl of granola. So there was no sense to her getting up. She was only an obstacle for the other two to stumble around as they found juice, made coffee, opened and closed the fridge door. As she told herself, her sleeping in was an accommodation to others. Now, since George had taken up jogging in the morning, which was very good for him, which the doctor had ordered, which she encouraged, often she did not see him until he came home from work. When he came in from his jog, he would go straight into the shower, shave, dress and be off to the university. He would grab something to eat at one of the many food kiosks in the students' union building. He said that he actually liked Egg McMuffins.

Such was the state of affairs, the morning habits and routine of the Martins, on that fateful morning when Esther heard the lilting melodious song of the robin and thought, all is well with the world, and snuggled beneath the covers to doze and drift and doze again. When she finally woke up, she lay for a while basking in the stream of sunlight coming through the open window. She could smell spring — mud, moisture, young leaves, the new-mown hay of freshly cut grass. Soon George would be finished spring session. Did he plan to teach a summer session? He used to do research in the summer. When had he last given over a summer to research? She couldn't remember, although she did think that he had said something to her about it not too long ago. She should try and listen to what he said. But he so often talked about boring subjects, politics of the office, cutbacks in funding. Well, she hoped he would have some time off. So much needed to be done to keep up a house. This room, for instance, the woodwork desperately needed repainting. She still liked the colours, the carpet and cushions and quilts and blankets and wall hangings all various shades of pink and rose, the walls a creamy white. She would have to order more paint. She had the number written down on a piece of paper in a file folder. Outside, the eaves needed paint. Perhaps she could help George, perhaps they could do it together. Usually, she left the outside upkeep to George but they really should spend more time together, relaxing as well as working on the house. They were getting to an age when they should relax more. Why not? George would be fifty this year. She could scarcely believe it.

By mid-morning Esther was coifed and dressed in a clean and crisp flowered cotton house dress. Unlike many of her contemporaries, she still wore dresses or skirts and tops around the house. She was in the kitchen, busily, happily, whipping up a cake for Saturday's dinner party. The mixer was whirring full tilt ahead, the white batter, smelling of vanilla, swirling like cream around the beaters, when the doorbell rang. She switched off the mixer and wiped her hands on the apron that swathed her thickening middle. She went through the house to the front door, it had been the chimes rather than the bell. Likely it was a salesperson or the Jehovah's Witnesses, someone she would have to get rid of, politely, of course, especially if it was the Witnesses for surely they were good people, only misguided.

On the step was a tall, attractive, young woman with long blonde hair, a thin face, rather strange brown eyes and a wide mouth. Esther turned her own mouth up only slightly at the corners, not wanting to give a salesperson too much encouragement, but not wanting to be rude, either, for, as she often said of those less fortunate than herself, there but for the grace of God go I.

"Are you Esther?" The young woman narrowed her eyes. They seemed to be watching her and yet not watching her. Esther briefly noticed that she was dressed in black leather, pants and coat. She wore a black leather tam on her head. She had lovely skin, very white.

"Yessss." Should she admit it? Was this person going to charm her way into the house by false statements and then case the joint? Nowadays, according to the paper, you couldn't trust young women any more than you could young men. She recalled things she had heard on the news as well as stories of friends. Don't be silly, she told herself. It might be someone who knows Delores.

"We have to talk," the young woman said.

Esther knew a moment of terror. Who was this woman? Was she from the police? A hospital? Come with terrible news? Please, please, don't let it be Delores, she thought. "What is it?" she said.

"George."

"George?" Esther did not comprehend. The name had come

so unexpectedly out of that wide mouth, from between those full red lips.

"You do know a George?" The young woman's lips twisted slightly.

Was it an unpaid traffic ticket? A parking infraction? Did police officers look like this? Dress like this? Perhaps, nowadays, they did. Maybe she should admit nothing. What was this person doing here, anyway, invading her home, her privacy? The onus certainly wasn't on her, Esther, to provide answers. And as for George, she certainly wasn't going to supply a stranger with information that might be damaging to George.

The young woman looked straight at her, took a very deep breath of the fresh sunny morning, held it in a moment, then let it all out with a rush along with the words, "George and I are having an affair." Her voice was cold, efficient, practical.

Esther, as though hypnotized, was caught by those bold yet wary eyes. "You must have the wrong George," she said, then thought, why am I standing at *my* door discussing George with this total stranger. "I don't wish to speak to you." She started to close the door.

The young woman threw open her leather coat. She was so slim, the mound looked like a distortion, like a soccer ball covered with cloth. Esther could see that the leather pants were constructed with a stretch material across the tummy for expansion. "We've been having a relationship for two and a half years."

"You can *say* anything," Esther said. "It doesn't have to be true. I don't have to believe you."

The young woman shrugged. "Ask George." She closed her coat and with her hands folded across the front of her torso, as though protecting her soft underside, as Esther thought later, turned and left. She walked with long, self-confident strides down the walk and away down the tree-lined street.

A student, thought Esther. George must have given her a poor mark on an exam. She wants to cause him trouble.

For some time, she stood at the door. She could not think. She felt like she had been delivered a blow to the midsection. She's lying, thought Esther and kept that thought firm in her mind. For some reason, the young woman was lying. She must be lying. George wouldn't do that. Oh, he might have an incident with another woman. Any man might do that, in a weak moment. But George would not carry on for two and a half years without telling her. George would not deceive her that way for that long. She and George were as one. How can you deceive part of yourself? How can you live with a person, share the same bed, and be living a complete lie? That was not possible. George could not possibly have done this thing, for if he had he was not George, not the George she knew, had known for a quarter of a century.

But why would the young woman lie? Esther had heard that harassment was an issue now at the university and in the work place. She had heard stories of false charges. But to come to the house! To produce that evidence, when surely everyone knew that nowadays such evidence could be clinically tested. But by that time, she could make a lot of trouble for George. She could ruin his reputation. How can you ruin another person with no evidence, wondered Esther? That young woman must have some hard facts to back up her claim. Witnesses, perhaps? To what? To a look, a smile, perhaps George's hand on her shoulder in the classroom. She must have more than that. Pictures? Compromising situations?

What if it was true? What if George had been intimate with that young woman? What if he had looked into her eyes, a mutual understanding passing between them? What if he had sat with her, put his arm around her? What if they had laughed together, smiled at each other, perhaps showered together, soaped each other down, stood together under the shower nozzle rinsing the soap from their bodies.

Esther felt a sharp pain pierce her heart, as surely as if a spear had been thrust through her. She might be having a heart attack.

Stop it! she directed herself. This is foolish. This is more than foolish. This is insane. You don't even know that George knows this woman.

Think! Try to think clearly. The first thing to do is to find out, to ask George. With this direction in mind, she was able to close the door. She locked it, firmly, as though it were not too late to save her treasures.

She went into the kitchen and picked up the wall phone situated near the back door. She dialled George's number. What would she say? The funniest thing just happened.... No. I've just had the strangest experience.... You won't believe.... I shouldn't even be bothering you with this, it's so obviously mad....

George wasn't answering. Esther couldn't breathe. She was breaking out in a sweat. At the same time, she felt cold. Why was she letting herself get so upset? Why was she believing a complete stranger? Why wasn't she waiting until she spoke with George? There would be an explanation. They might even end up laughing about it. No, somehow she did not think that they would laugh about this. Likely it would be more serious than that. She looked at the clock above the sink. Ten past eleven. Was he in class? She couldn't remember when his lectures were this term. She should try to remember those things. But nearly twenty-three years of remembering class times! Still, she should. She knew that she should.

Which day was this? Thursday? She let the phone click over into the department office. Sheila, one of the secretaries, answered. "Oh, hi Mrs. Martin," she said. "He's in his 301."

"301?"

"Yes, until noon. Shall I have him call you?"

"Would you, please?" Esther held the phone a moment before hanging up. She did not want to be alone. She did not want to be alone with her thoughts. With her mind. How would she get through the next hour of her life? The next minute? She could phone Helena. She *would* phone Helena. But what would she say? She must not discuss this with another person before discussing it with George. She could simply chat with her sister. How's the new apartment coming along? How's the job hunting? But if she once opened her mouth to Helena, she knew that she would blurt out everything. She would start wailing hysterically. She must not. She must not betray George. She must not betray the loyalty of her marriage vows. She must not put her burdens on Helena, Helena who had remarkably gotten her life straightened around.

Action, Esther ordered. Do something. Keep busy. Keep putting one foot in front of the other. She marched herself to the counter. She switched on the mixer.

She must not fall apart. People were counting on her. Delores. George. Yes, she must think of George. This must be a mistake and therefore George would need her, need her strength, need her belief in him. She and George may have an ordeal ahead of them. There may be a time of trouble. If that young woman was so bold as to come to the house, she may be bold enough to go to the authorities, the head of the department. She may tell her lies to the newspapers. Every day such dreadful intimate human dramas were displayed for the entertainment of the bored and curious.

Esther suddenly saw the batter that she had been staring at for several minutes. How long had the beaters been going around? She clicked off the button, lifted the motor head, wiped the dripping batter into the bowl with her forefinger, poured the batter into the prepared pans. Her cake would be ruined, peaked in the middle. That's what came of overmixing. Well, she would serve it anyway. Maybe she could pile it with whipped cream and no one would notice.

She must think of other people. She had invited the O'Haras for Saturday. They would arrive in good faith, with their bottle of wine and hostess gift. They had a right to expect a civilized gathering and decent food. She had a responsibility to them. She tried to think of Saturday evening, two days from now. She tried to focus on the details of her little party, tried to envision cloth, napkins, floral arrangement, tried to put those pleasant details in place of her terrible thoughts. But she could not keep her mind focused on Saturday evening. She could not get as far as Saturday evening. Saturday might have been next year, the next century. She could not envision that she would still be here, alive in this world, on Saturday.

She stood with her hands on the stove top and stared. She made herself breathe, out, in, out, in. I can't keep thinking about this, she told herself. I'll go crazy.

I have to find a way to think about this, she told herself. If it *is* true. Even if it is true, there are many possibilities. Maybe he *was* having an affair but isn't now. Maybe he hasn't seen her for some time. Maybe he doesn't know she's pregnant. Certainly, he doesn't love her, or she wouldn't have had to come to the house. Somehow, he got mixed up with her. These things happen. Two and a half years? part of her said. It may not have been that long, another part said. Maybe that's how long they've known each other. That doesn't mean they've been having an affair all that time. Perhaps he even loved her once, or was in love with her, which are two different things. But he was no longer in love with her. He couldn't love that person. He was still *her* husband. They still had intimate relations. Sex, Esther told herself, sternly. Sex. Oh, perhaps not often. Esther tried to remember the last time. The occasions *had* become fewer over the years. But she had thought that normal; they were getting older, becoming comfortable old tabbies. It had not bothered her. Perhaps it had bothered George. So he had turned to that girl. Sex, then. Not love. A sexual affair. They happen all the time. Perhaps he tried to stop it and she kept at him. Perhaps she got herself pregnant on purpose. To hold him. If she knew anything at all about George, she would know that he would feel a sense of duty to the child. But why didn't he share this with me? Esther howled within. Why didn't he share his troubles? If he was unhappy with their marriage why didn't he talk to her about it? George is a man of science, came the answer. He has always found it difficult to speak of his inner life. To speak of feelings.

Why am I thinking this way? Esther shrieked at herself. Why am I believing that girl before my own husband? George would no sooner be dishonest in his personal life than in his research. It's simply inconceivable. It's simply not George.

Still, there had been something about that young woman, something in her face. She had seemed honest, not pleasant, but honest.

Esther scorned this thought. Your first impressions are always and notoriously mistaken, she chided herself. Of course, a con artist appears honest. Otherwise, he, she, wouldn't be a good con artist.

The thing to hang onto here, Esther directed herself, is George's basic honesty. George does not tell lies. George prided himself that he did not tell lies.

With this fact firmly in mind, she felt better.

The phone rang, startling her so that she actually jumped as though hit by an electric volt. She turned her head toward it. It looked like a giant scorpion on the wall. She did not want to touch it. She did not want to talk to George. She wanted to stay in this limbo of ignorance. Even if it was an illusion, she would rather live in an illusion than face a reality in which she could not live. But I have to talk with him, she thought. I have to tell him about that girl. Even though everything may be all right and we can go back to the way things were only an hour ago, I'll have to tell him about that young woman coming to the door. The phone rang for the third time. If it rang again, the machine would answer. She stepped quickly across the kitchen and picked up the receiver but she did not make it in time.

"This is the Martin residence," George's voice said, although it did not sound like the real George. It sounded like an actor in a bad movie.

"Esther?" the real George said. She could imagine him frowning.

"Please leave a message after the beep," George's recorded voice said.

"I'm here," she said.

"You phoned?" George's voice sounded apprehensive, as though expecting bad news. But why wouldn't it? She almost never called him at his office.

The answering machine beeped three shorts and one long. Esther waited until the long beep was finished. "I had a visitor," she said.

There was a long silence at the other end of the line. The machine seemed to be winding off reams of tape. Then, brusquely, "Yes?"

"I don't know her name. I forgot to ask. A tall woman, young, long blonde hair..."

There was another long pause. Has he hung up? wondered Esther wildly. Is he waiting for me to say more?

"I can't do anything about it now," said George. "I'm having lunch with the Appointment Committee and then I have a graduate student coming at two. I'll try to get home as soon as possible, three-thirty or four."

I won't break down, thought Esther. I won't break down on the phone. The secretary may be listening.

"I don't know if I can wait that long," she said.

"I can't get out of this lunch," said George. "It was planned a month ago."

"Can you just tell me ... if what she said is true?"

"I don't know what she said."

"No, of course not." Silence. Esther tried to think.

She could hear him sigh, deeply, impatiently. "What do you want me to do?"

"If I knew," she said, "one way or another. If what she said is true. It would help."

There was another long silence.

"Do you know her?" said Esther.

Another blank silence.

"Can you say yes or no?"

"We'll talk about it when I get home."

"I can't manage that," said Esther. "I have to know how to think."

"It's more complicated than a simple yes or no."

"I need a yes or no."

Something in her voice, some hysterical undertone, must have decided George. "Yes," he said. And then, "I don't think it's serious." And after another tense silence, "I'm late for lunch. It's a very important lunch."

She hung up. She listened to the answering machine rewind tape to the beginning of the message and then click loudly. She had gotten what she wanted. Now she knew which way to think.

She felt a great surge of anger. George was such a fool, such a vain stupid foolish fool! He had destroyed them. He had brought the house down on their heads. And all because of his preening vanity. She hated him. She hated, hated, hated him!

She could not live without him. He was her life. When she thought of living without him, a deep black terrifying hole took the place of thought. And what about him? It was inconceivable that he would not live in this house, in this home that they had built together, that they had lived in for so many years. If he moved out, what would he do? Where would he live? In some dreary one-bedroom apartment like other bachelors? She could not bear to think of George living a lonely bare life. She could not *think* of it. That was not his *life*. His life was as her husband, as Delores' father. She couldn't think whether or not she loved him. It was too late for such considerations.

"I don't think it's serious.' That was the phrase she must hang on to. What exactly did that mean? Not serious. A nonserious affair. Maybe only physical. Physical, but nothing deep, nothing that affects a person emotionally. And likely it was already over. George must have told her that it was over and so she had come to the house hoping to cause trouble between him and his wife. It was over, then. George did not love her. He may have been in love with her at one time, loved her in a superficial physical way, but he had come to his senses. But he was still tied to her. Because of the child.

And then it came to her. The child, of course! George must have wanted more children. She, Esther, had been a failure in that area. He had said it didn't matter. He had not seemed disappointed. But here it was! The proof.

And what of the child? She did not want to think about how a child is conceived — the intimacy, the physical contact. That young woman had been the subject of George's most intimate regard, his looks, his thoughts. She, Esther, had been, and even now was, the stranger. She, Esther, was the outsider, the peripheral hanger-on, the nuisance, the person to be dealt with.

A child certainly added a complication. Although, nowadays, such things happened all the time. When she had lunch or coffee with friends, the talk inevitably got around to the sex lives of other friends, of friends of friends, of their own grown-up children. What of Delores? She had not considered Delores. What would Delores think of a sibling twenty-one years her junior! What would Delores think of her father? She adored her father. They must not tell Delores. Delores would never have to know. She was there, they were here. She was safely out of it. Still, the thought that George had not only betrayed her but also Delores was another dagger in her heart.

How could he have done it? she cried over and over again inside her mind. She said it out loud. "How could he have *done* it?"

He would have ended it but he had not wanted to hurt the young woman's feelings. Esther had a moment of compassion for the unfortunate George. He must have felt distress, trying to get out of a relationship without anyone being hurt. And it must have been painful for him to have to lie to her, his wife, to save her feelings. How he must have suffered shame when he found himself caught in an avalanche of lies. Esther let herself wonder about this suffering. She thought carefully about the past few years. Much of it she could not remember. She thought about the last few months. She could detect nothing, no evidence of his suffering. Perhaps he had seemed a bit distracted at times, but he had always been distracted because of his work. At no time had he acted guilty, penitent, more distant, in a word, different, than he had always acted. He had not been away from home any more than usual. He had always had to attend conferences, various gatherings of the scientific and educational communities. He had always had to attend evening meetings, committees, boards. He had always occasionally had to go over to the university in the evenings, to check on a research project, to meet with someone. When she thought about it, a professor's life offered numerous opportunities for a particularly free lifestyle.

Perhaps I do not know this man I've lived with all these years, she thought. He may be a complete stranger to me.

But if he is a stranger, it must be my fault, she reasoned. I have not made enough of an effort to keep on knowing the young man I married. I'm the one who has failed, her mind carried on. I'm the one who has betrayed him by not being the person he needed, by not thinking enough of him, by not loving him enough. Somewhere during all the years I forgot that he was my hero.

Could it be possible that to that young woman George was a hero?

I'm just as much at fault as George, she thought.

Esther was holding a tea towel and was kneading it spasmodically. Maybe we have time, she thought, time in which I can make it better, undo the wrong I have done. He is still my husband. He is still alive. Death is worse than this. Death is the worst thing. Unless someone has died it is not a real catastrophe. Her aunt used to say that. George needed her love now more than ever. Had she the strength, the wisdom, the understanding to hold her love steady? To not let him down in his need? Yes. She felt powerful. She *would* see him through. Whatever it was, they would fight it together. She felt strong. She would be able to take what came. It was unthinkable that she might lose him. That they would lose each other. He was her *George*. They could not lose each other, not those two who had smiled like that for the camera.

While Esther's thoughts and emotions had been swinging wildly from one extreme to the other, she had kept herself busy with real tasks. Disregarding the fact that Louise of the Lady Anne crisis would come in the morning , she vacuumed the upstairs, polished the bedroom and dining room furniture, put in a load of laundry. She was now in the living room, giving everything in sight a coat of lemon polish. She picked up the wedding photo from the top of the piano. She looked at those bland, unmarked faces. She looked into her own dreamy, asleep eyes. For better and for worse, she repeated her vow.

I ought to have been a better wife, she thought, as she sewed a button on the cuff of George's shirt. She ought to have listened to his stories about what was happening in the department, his concerns about students. She ought to have gone with him to conferences instead of cocooning herself in her comfortable life in this house. She had been lazy. She ought to have been interested in how his book was coming along. She hadn't asked him about his book for months. True, the last few times she had asked, he had been abrupt with her, even hostile. But that was no excuse. Of course, he would be hostile if it wasn't going well, but that was just the time he needed her. She should have persisted, broken through his wall of hostility, been loving and tender.

She raised her head suddenly, as though listening. I should have taken up jogging with him, she thought. I will, starting tomorrow.

She was passing through the kitchen, from dining room to laundry room when it happened. In a single moment, her strength abandoned her. She felt her mind go slack at the same time as her body slumped into a chair. She collapsed into a creature writhing in pain. She existed only as pain. She sobbed, she moaned, she grabbed handfuls of hair at each temple and pulled until her head hurt. She raged, she screamed. Her head pulsed, throbbed. Mucus and drool and tears streamed down her face and mixed together and slobbered onto her apron. She got up and stomped up and down, stomped through the house, raging and screaming, still tearing her hair. When she was exhausted, she stumbled into the bathroom. She bathed her face with cold water, she combed her hair. She looked at her face in the mirror. She saw puffy spotty skin, swollen red eyes. She saw hairs starting to grow from her chin just like her old granny used to have. What an ugly old beast, she thought. No wonder he prefers that beautiful young woman with smooth porcelain complexion.

She looked at her hands. She saw skin, dry and cracked from the long winter, fingernails, rough and splintered. One was broken from doing the vacuuming. That young woman probably had a career, worked in a library, an office, put on makeup every morning, spent her salary on her wardrobe, frequented body shops for manicures and pedicures. All my life I've been a housewife, thought Esther. I should have taken evening courses, kept up with what's happening in the world, made myself into a more informed conversationalist. No wonder he prefers a young woman. She probably listens to his stories. The articles say you should draw a man out of himself. You should keep up with the latest fashions, the latest trends, the latest news. It was my duty as a wife to be interesting and interested. I have failed in my duty.

Between three-thirty and four-thirty, Esther jumped at every sound. When the furnace fan came on, when the hot water tank flared into action, when the fridge motor started, when a squirrel jumped from deck rail to roof, she started, her heart pounding. When she heard a car on the street outside, her ears perked up. If the car moved slowly, seemed to be coming to a stop, she ran to the window. Then she remembered that George walked to the university. Although sometimes, if he had to go across town during the day, if he had an appointment at another place, for any one of a dozen reasons, sometimes he took the car. She could go out to the garage and look to see if the car was there. She would if he didn't come soon.

She became more and more nervous about the meeting. Would he be angry with her? She couldn't stand it when he was angry with her. It didn't happen often but at such times, his Latin background emerged. He became snappish, even contemptuous. He waved his arms, he stomped about.

But why was he so late? She tried to remember, she was sure he had said three-thirty. But maybe she was mistaken, her mind was such a jumble. She needed to speak to someone. Anyone. She needed to hear her own voice, to have at least that much physical release from her tension. But she did not want to use the phone in case he might try to call her.

At five o'clock she grabbed at the phone and dialled Helena's number. I won't tell her, she thought. I'll just ask her about her day. But Helena was not there or, at least, not answering. Where was she? With Ben, of course. They were always together now. They might even get back together permanently. Miracles did happen. People were truly amazing. People did build themselves new lives, they found reasons to live. She had been so worried about Helena when she had first come home looking like a skeleton. Three months ago. So much can happen in three months. Lives can begin, lives can end.

Esther hung up the receiver slowly. It was just as well Helena was not home. I didn't mean to tell her, thought Esther, but I would have. I would have betrayed George. I would have dragged her into it. Because of my own selfish need.

There was something else, too. Esther did not want Helena

to know. She did not want anyone to know. She was too embarrassed. She felt as if she had committed some terrible social faux pas, or as if she had failed an exam or been fired from a job because of her ineptness.

Esther's mind was a whirl of disjointed thoughts, a muddle of wild ideas, but one idea that stood out was that somehow this was her fault, for not being attractive enough, slim enough, witty enough, a good enough cook, housekeeper, and mother. There was definitely something wrong with *her*. Her body. What sort of woman couldn't have children? She had failed in the most basic function of being a woman. She leaned against the wall, pressed her forehead against the corner where two perpendicular walls met, felt the sharp edge against the bone of her head.

I may be a bad person, she conceded. I may be stupid and shallow and self-indulgent, but do I deserve to suffer like this? No one has the right to make another person suffer like this.

Slowly, moving like a sleepwalker, she made her way into the living room. She lowered herself onto the sofa. She posed herself like a piece of crystal on the edge, knees together, clasped hands on her knees. She felt that if she moved anything, any part of her body, it would shatter into a thousand pieces. Her face was stiff, stern. She could feel it so, but she could not relax it. If she did, it, too, would shatter. She must not allow herself to move or to think, or she would break. She would run mad through the house, mad through the streets. She must sit here. She must sit here very straight and still.

IX: GEORGE

THE JIG'S UP, thought George. He leaned his elbows on the table as though he were listening. It occurred to him that they might take back the appointment.

In the pale light of the Faculty Club dining room, George was only dimly aware of the bee-hive of activity around him. He was surprised that the room was still intact — high ceiling, tall windows — that it looked the same as on the many other occasions, hundreds of them, when he had eaten here. His inner vision had shifted so dramatically in the last hour, he found it difficult to believe that the outer world — the murmur of voices, the clink of cutlery and dishes, the disturbance of air as waitresses swished past with coffee pots, water jugs, dessert carts — was as it had always been. It seemed bizarre that people sat around the tables, unconcerned, like lizards on hot rocks, drawing spring warmth from a sun streaming unfettered through tall windows, as if a catastrophe had not happened. He felt himself to be in a surreal space, the light thick with sunrays and dust motes. It was like being suspended in a diving tank preparing to be plunged to the bottom of the sea.

George became aware of silence. Two of the three other men at the table were looking at him expectantly. The Dean, on his left, was setting his white coffee cup into a white saucer on the white cloth. What had they been talking about? Should he hazard a guess, make a noncommittal remark? But even a noncommittal remark might be way off base. No, better to admit his wool-gathering and plead his humanness. "I'm afraid," he said, "my mind was wandering."

It was the right comment. They all laughed good-naturedly. "That's allowed," said the Dean. "Once the reality sets in, you won't have time to think, let alone daydream."

Once the reality sets in, thought George, will I ever be invited here again by this group? Such a thought caused him great distress. George liked these men. He liked this room, liked the view of the downtown core across the river, the river itself. He liked the privileges of having membership in such a room. He had moved above the rank and file, the lower class blue-collar status of so many immigrants. He had achieved what his parents, his father in particular, had wanted him to achieve. For, while his father had made a good deal of money in the restaurant business, he had wanted his children to have class. George wondered what his father would think of Veronica. He pictured his father having an affair with a shadowy someone or other. Quickly, he put the image out of his mind. He did not seriously consider that his father would have done that. His father had a strict, albeit superstitious and irrational and, therefore, mistaken Roman Catholic moral code.

The dessert cart stopped before him. He shook his head at the poppy seed cake, his favourite. Normally, he was a man who enjoyed his food, but today he could have been eating sawdust. A shame, too, since a very good lunch was to be had at the Faculty Club. But George's digestive tract had been disturbed before entering this room, before sitting down at the dazzling white cloth with its bouquet of fresh flowers, the glint of sunlight on cutlery, the sparkle of wine glasses as the waitress filled them with something soothingly cool poured from a bottle wrapped with a crisp white napkin. It had been disturbed by Esther's phone call, or more properly, by his to her.

Think it through, he told himself. Think it through. That's your education and training, thirty years of it, rational thinking through. If only this was a project, he thought on. What do you do when you run into problems with a project? You try another method of attack. But not without first making careful notes. "There are no failures." How often had he said that to his students? You learn as much, maybe more, from an experiment that does not turn out as from one that does.

But why did this have to happen today of all days? When he should be enjoying himself, when he was receiving plaudits and honours, when he should be keeping his mind on the conversation, when he should be having his wits about him. Likely it was not a coincidence. Knowing Veronica, knowing her intelligent scheming nature, likely she had timed her visit to Esther to coincide with his lunch with the Committee.

Yet things had been better between him and Veronica this last while. It was as though they had settled down like any married couple to await a planned event. While there was an undercurrent of agenda to be addressed, she seemed willing to table it for future discussion. The question as to when he was going to bring things to a head with Esther had become mechanical, her manner like that of a wife inquiring of her husband when he might clean out the garage. As for George, he was happy to drift along in what was, for the moment at least, a calm sea. He knew that he would have to deal with the situation, but he had been so busy with end-of-term concerns, with restructuring curriculum for the fall semester, with politicking for the new position. He was teaching a spring course. He had two graduate students ready to defend their dissertations in the fall. He told himself that he would do something in August, when he had more time. George had to admit that, when they were not quarrelling, with Veronica he was still the man he was born to be. He felt able to rise to great heights of heroism. Not that he did, but he could have. As for Veronica, she seemed less agitated. Inward turning of the female during gestation, he decided. But whatever the reason, he was thankful for the peace and quiet.

Now he knew that all this time she must have been ruminating on a course of action. With her usual cunning she must have been planning today's event. She must have been planning to smash his world so that he would agree to her world. Even if he did not, his life would be irrevocably changed. Well, she was correct in thinking that. His life was changed already. His life was destroyed. The old George Martin no longer existed. He would never again be Esther's George, not in the old way. He would never again be George Martin, husband, father, staunch member of the university and the community, upholder of its values. His identity was shattered.

Veronica had timed it so that his moment of success had been taken from him. For, during the announcement, glasses raised high, during the toast, the polite restrained applause, fingers tapping lightly the heel of a hand, George had been distracted as might be a man who has just visited his physician and heard the pronouncement of his own doom. Through the sole meunière he had somehow managed to make polite conversation — someone had returned from a convention in Anaheim; hockey was into the playoffs. Black coffee had been ordered around and now George sat in a mental haze with his elbows up on the table, resting his chin on his thumbs, smiling and nodding at his colleagues sitting around the table with him.

What would they think? he asked himself. These men, his peers, how would they judge him? True, nowadays, such a thing would not be the scandal it once would have been. It had been rumoured, quite a while ago, that Henry, sitting directly across from him, was having an affair. The consensus seemed to be that Henry was a fool, that he was going through a mid-life crisis, that he would regain his senses, and that ever-faithful Mildred would take him back. The episode seemed to be viewed as a psychological lapse as well as an error in judgment but not as a sin or a betrayal of some moral code. These days, what shocked people in his circle was lack of intelligence and, also, what might be termed tacky behaviour. That he had gotten himself into this particular mess with a student and that now there was a child involved would be seen as tackiness of the highest order. It would also be denounced as blatant stupidity. Likely the committee, the faculty, the university, would not want to make a stupid man head of a new research lab. The appointment had been touch and go as it was. He had been worried about his book, that it was not forthcoming would be a mark against him. But, he supposed, they should all understand that sort of thing; most of them had had books held up at one time or another. He could not expect them to understand Veronica.

George very much wanted the position. There was money involved, of course, a raise in salary, a bonus, and there was the added prestige. It was a wise political move in terms of recognition and further advancement. But mainly it was the work. He would be back into research. It was the change he needed. Was he not to have it now, now that it was so close? The formal announcement had yet to be made. Was he not to have it because of ... because of what? What had he done wrong that every man didn't do at one time or another in his life? After all, he was not evil. He had made a regrettable error in good sense. Now he had to clean up the mess, face the music, face Esther, ultimately face Veronica. At this very moment, Veronica's telephone number was waiting for him in his office mail box. Her call must have come about the same time as Esther's.

George groaned inwardly at his predicament. How could he be expected to deal with both women in one day? What could Veronica want? Reassurance for her action? That wouldn't be like Veronica. Her method was damn the torpedoes. And she never apologized, not even if she blew up the wrong ship. Nor would she concern herself with whether or not there were survivors. Veronica would be all right. It was Esther he was concerned about. She was not tough like Veronica. She had lived a protected life. He must think of Esther. How would he face Esther? He could not conceive of life without Esther, life without her stability, without the routine of her. His career and home life were so intertwined, it was all part of the same package. Esther was connected with the university. Their lives had revolved around this institution. They had met here, courted here. How many staff functions, wine and cheese parties, weddings and, yes, funerals, had they attended over the years? He had given so much of his life to the university. His teaching and research, of course, but how many committees had he sat on and chaired, how many conventions had he attended, how many weekend seminars had he helped coordinate, how many fund-raising functions had he been involved in, how many studies and proposals to the government? Now, when he had been offered an opportunity to head a new multi-million dollar research lab, a position that would give him everything he had ever wanted, he would not be able to have it. For even though people took a different view of such things nowadays, if the committee had known the details of his private life, he would not have received this offer. He felt sure of that. His colleagues would tolerate his problem in a superficial way, but at some deeper level, he would lose their esteem. And in the political arena of government and industry funding, the university could not afford to take chances. He was, quite simply, ruined.

George looked toward the large windows. Even the day was turning on him. The sun had been replaced by grey clouds scudding in on a wind coming across the river from the north. Rain pellets intermittently struck the glass.

I always thought I could quit any time I wanted to, thought George. When had he passed some invisible point of no return? Is that when he should have told Esther? But, by then it was too late. Then it would have hurt her so. There was a difference between a husband having a casual affair and his being obsessed with another woman. He had not wanted to be unkind to either of them. And there you were. You try not to hurt people and this is what you get. A complete muddle, turning on you. Everyone upset with you!

Veronica was the one who had caused the disaster. He should be upset with her! He was the one who must bear the brunt of her rash action. He was the one who must now face Esther, face inquisition, blame and recrimination, weeping and wailing and gnashing of teeth. He was the one who must face female hysterics. No, hysterics were not Esther's style. More likely, she'd get all weepy and play the martyr, which, in some ways, was harder to deal with, slow and steady punishment rather than a good blast and get it over with. He wondered if she'd kick him out, in a nice way, of course. At a time when he should be looking forward to his twilight years in the comfort of his home, a home he had worked hard to establish, at a time when most men were looking forward to a cozy fire and slippers and books, he would be lying on a rented mattress in a dark room subsisting on TV dinners. When he got through support payments to both women, he would not be able to afford anything better than one of those dingy student rooms the like of which Veronica was in now.

Maybe that was what he deserved. How could he have been such a heel? How could he have deceived Esther? Esther who was the mother of his child, who unfailingly put his needs first, who always cooked the food that he liked in preference to what she liked, who was basically such a good and kind person.

Hold it, George said to himself. Esther's not a saint. She has her flaws, too. In fact, my sin, if you want to call it that, is her fault. Partly, at least. If she had not always acted bloody superior, if she had not always been so damned condescending of his little masculine foibles, as she called them, in short, if she had made him feel like the lord of the jungle rather than an old tomcat past his prime, Veronica would not have happened. If Esther had accepted his foolish smelly masculinity, his vulgar sexual nature, he would not have become a joyless creature, he would not have had his crisis of death and degeneration, he would not have been attracted to the joy of Veronica. If Esther had allowed him to be himself in his own home, he would not have been attracted to Veronica's room.

Could he help it if he was a man with slightly quirky sexual tastes? Not even quirky, really, well within the realm of normality. But Esther was very conventional in that regard. Even when they were first married, while she agreed to some experimentation, he could tell her heart was not really in it and after awhile he stopped making suggestions. Not that their sex life was unsatisfactory. It was regular at least, regular and routine. But when Esther felt joy in the sex act, and he could not be sure that she felt such release as he experienced, she would carry on about how the physical is a manifestation of the spiritual. If Esther had been more open to having a little fun with the whole business, he would never have looked at Veronica in the first place. And if she had not gone into what amounted to purda at the death of her sister, he might not have continued seeing Veronica after that first night. Not that it was not his fault, of course the whole mess was mainly his fault, but Esther had something to answer for, too.

Esther was so self-satisfied about her own comportment, her own actions. She never looked at him, really looked, but if he faced her with that accusation, she would say, but dear, I do look at you. I'm looking at you right now. And she would be, her dark eyes aglow with affection and admiration. But she didn't *see* him. If she truly saw him, she could not have failed to notice his restored energy, his changed appearance, the changes in his daily habits. For a woman who watched every little detail of household arrangements, food partaken, food not partaken, who tallied leftovers and laundry as though she were a tax auditor, he had been constantly surprised that he had gotten away with so much. Often he ate lightly at home because he knew that he would be dining or snacking with Veronica. He took up jogging as an excuse to see her more often.

Such changes he could refer to an annual check-up and doctor's orders. But his glowing countenance, his smoother brow, the way he seemed to dance rather than shuffle through his days, she never mentioned. Perhaps she thought these were due to his new diet and exercise routine. More likely, he decided, it was because she had not looked at him for several years. He knew that Esther loved him, but she loved him as she might a child rather than as a man or even as an intelligent adult human being. The house, raising Delores, their social circle, their budget, these were her interests, about which she made the decisions. She constantly, albeit gently, made jokes about absent-minded professors who wouldn't know how to get along in the real world of daily living, of business and finance and ordinary people. She told such stories widely with a teasing condescension that amounted to pride in her voice. She didn't want him to be different. She loved him. But if Esther had expected more of him, demanded more of him, demanded that he take some responsibility for mundane tasks, he might have felt more a part of her life and the life of the home. And she could have taken a greater interest in his life, the important aspect of his life, his work, which she regarded as little more than a science kit project for the school fair. If Esther had appreciated his intelligence, had supported his intellectual endeavours, Veronica would never have happened.

The truth was that, in spite of her university degree, a degree in education which, let's face it, he told himself, was a job-oriented training program rather than an intellectual exploration of ideas, Esther was basically a simple soul. It always amazed him that he had married a non-intellectual. In fact, he had thought her to be more intellectual than she turned out to be. He was a little surprised when she made a career of being a wife and mother. Of course they should have had more children. Esther was the sort to be mother hen to a brood. But that, at least, was not his fault.

Why had he married Esther? Had he been drawn to the side

of his nature that was missing? No, George did not think that it was anything as elevated or complicated as that. They'd had a lot of fun together, the gang of them — Helena and Ben, Amanda and Reuben, he and Esther. They had been tremendously compatible as a group. And Esther's body! How he had lusted after that trim little body with its round wiggly bottom. Why does the lust have to end, thought George sadly. Lust gives the intellect a break.

Which was a necessary condition of balance in life. He had a moment of regret thinking about Veronica. With her he was able to suspend the dominance of his intellect, give it a rest, so to speak. *Yes.* How that word had seemed to hang in the air above their heads like the blade of a guillotine, a shining blade of thin flexible steel. *Do you love me? Tell me yes or no. Yes.* His gut reaction. For once in his life he had responded without equivocation, without intellectual qualification. And with that word, something inside him had loosened, something confining had fallen away from around him, as though a cage in which he had been enclosed had shattered, and all he had to do to be free was step out of the rubble and walk away. *Yes.* How astonishing that a simple act of honesty was able to do that for him. But at what price?

When George returned to his office after lunch, there was a second memo in his mail box, the same number as on the first memo, without a name. He decided that he may as well get it over with. He dialled Veronica's number. She caught it on the first ring.

"I did it."

"I know you did it." He made his voice as cold and clipped as possible.

"I told you I would."

"And you have. Congratulations."

"It had to be done."

"I don't have time to chat."

"I need to see you."

"I'm afraid I'm rather tied up at the moment. I'll call you when I'm free."

"I need to see you today."

"That's impossible. You've made it impossible."

There was a long silence. George knew that her brain was darting here and there, trying to come up with the best way around him, the best way to deal with him so that she could get what she wanted. "Do you think this was easy for me?" she said. "Can't you understand that things couldn't go on, that something had to be done?"

"I would have handled it," he said, "in my own way. I needed time to arrange it so everyone could have what they wanted. I could have handled it with some tact."

"Oh, Georgie, when will you understand? This is not a perfect world."

"I have to go," he said, stiffly, "I don't have time for this."

"I need to see you," she said. "Today."

He said nothing.

"If you'd think of someone else for once in your life," she said, "you might realize that I'm upset." As she spoke, her voice changed from hard insistence to soft vulnerability. He thought of her body. He thought of the way she was when she had just stepped out of the shower.

He thought of Esther. Esther was waiting for him at home. His home. Their home. She was upset, too. Understandably so. He must go home.

He thought of Veronica waiting for him in her dusky room. He thought of her places that were like warm moist silk. He thought of her smell.

"I can only stay for a few minutes," he said. "And I can't get away until three-thirty."

It was nearly seven. Veronica had kept him too long, longer than George had intended. But she had told the truth when she had said that she was upset and it took some time to settle her down. He walked quickly, one arm swinging freely, the other carrying his briefcase, for even on a day of crisis, it would not have occurred to him to leave his office without his briefcase full of papers.

Now he must face the next hurdle. Esther. He must go through the next fire, Esther waiting for explanations of his actions, for motives of those actions. Would she give him the third degree, ask for times, dates, details? What would she do? Hurl things? Shout? Make a scene?

Try to think sensibly, he told himself. What *will* Esther do? What can she do? What is the worst she can do? Leave him? Divorce him? No, Esther was not likely to do either. In fact, looking at the situation clearly, George realized that he could not possibly have lost Esther after all these years. It was not thinkable that he would not go on with his life with her in the home they had established together. That *was* his life. Any other life was out of the question.

At his corner, he lifted his head. There was his house, at the turn in the road. It looked like a nice, comfortable, old-fashioned house where nice people lived and nothing really bad could ever happen. He could not believe that he would not go in to find Esther contentedly preparing the evening meal, the radio on, or perhaps the small television that they had bought to keep her company when Delores left home. It was on a shelf outside Esther's range of vision when she was puttering about, but she said she liked to hear the voices as she worked. He could not believe that he would not open the door and go in, that they would not say hello and kiss, that she would not say how was your day and he would not say how was yours, and they would not sit down to an uneventful supper.

He turned down his street. As he got closer to the house, as he could see more of it through the old poplars lining the street, it seemed uncommonly still. There was no light in any of the windows, not even the kitchen side window that he could see because the sidewalk curved. On such a dark, overcast day the light should be on. Had Esther gone out? His heart lifted a moment. He might not have to face the firing squad after all. But as he got closer still, he felt afraid. The street, the scene, it did not look right. The house did not look right. When he paused a moment on the front sidewalk, it seemed to him that the splinters in the wood siding pulsated in an odd manner, that the windows were watching him with a cold blank stare. Get a grip, man, he told himself and stepped through the familiar hedge. But as he rounded the house the feeling of the unfamiliar where the familiar should be persisted. The brick walkway beneath his feet, the back yard, even his own physical being, seemed strange. He felt himself to be a foreign figure in an alien landscape.

The kitchen was dark and quiet. He stood a moment and listened. The fridge motor was the only sound, the green clock numbers on the microwave the only light. He set down his briefcase, he took off his coat and draped it across the back of a wooden chair. Esther must be home. The door had been unlocked. He went through the dining room to the living room. The drapes were closed. He saw a shadow on the edge of the sofa, a rounded shape in the gloom. He realized that it was Esther.

He said nothing, only moved around her to his wing chair and sat down. They sat thus for several minutes. Was she waiting for him to speak? Who was supposed to speak first in a situation such as this? George knew from long experience in dealing with colleagues, superiors, students, that it was best to wait and see what the other person had in mind before revealing his own interests.

After several minutes, George started to wonder if Esther was all right. She didn't seem herself but, of course, that could be expected under the circumstances. Still, the way she sat there, so still, her face frozen into an awkward expression, her limbs rigid, he began to be concerned. Had she had some sort of seizure, was she paralyzed into a contorted state? But just as he wondered if he should do something, she came to life. "I expected you earlier," she said in the voice of one who has not spoken for a long time.

"You know how busy we are these days," he said. "I got here as soon as I could."

There was another long silence, during which George kept his mind in neutral.

"I suppose you'd better tell me about it," she said.

"What do you want to know?"

"What do you think I should know?"

"I don't think it's terribly serious."

"It *is* your child?"

"I think so, yes."

"What do you propose to do about that?"

"I don't know."

"When are you going to know."

"I'll have to give it some thought."

There was a pause. They looked at each other. "Do you think we can go on from here?" she asked.

"Do you want to go on?"

"Yes."

George got up out of his chair, crossed the room and put his arms around his wife's shoulders, drawing her head to him, pressing her face into his shirt front. He sank down beside her on the sofa. She buried her face in his shoulder. He closed his hands on her arms. He hung on for his life.

"There, there," she said. "Everything is going to be all right. I expect you're hungry."

"I need a drink more than food," he said. "What a day I've had."

X: GEORGE AND ESTHER

"HOW DO YOU FEEL?" Esther brought two cups in saucers, two plates, and cutlery for two to the table. She returned to the counter for cream and sugar, for cold butter, homemade cranberry preserves, frothy juice.

While still in bed, George had heard her downstairs in the kitchen preparing his breakfast. At least, he assumed that was what she was doing. She was making a good deal of noise that made him think that breakfast would be more than the dry cereal of late years. It would be like the old days, French toast or muffins or pancakes. Did that mean that the torment of the past few years was over, that he had come through a dark place and found Esther at the end, that through the love of Esther he was to be forgiven and taken back into the fold?

Through the love of Esther, he was to escape Veronica. Through the forgiveness of Esther he was to be done with the whole complicated muddle. After his long trial of being separated from himself, of living in two compartments of his brain, he was to be born again, whole, clean, new. He was to re-enter the ordinary cheerful world. He would miss the part of himself that had been connected to Veronica, but this was the best, the only, solution. Surely, a mature man, a learned man, can put aside the physical part of his nature and aspire toward something higher. Without that aspiration there would be no advancement of the human species.

"Not too bad," George said, for he sensed that it would not be prudent for him to feel too good.

He was standing in the doorway between hall and kitchen. He watched Esther's broad satiny back at the sink, against the window. Outside, a tall flowering plum was in leaf, casting its particular green glow into the room. How he wished that he could simply resume his life, have his cup of coffee, go to the office, deal with the mountain of paperwork awaiting him on his desk. But he knew that it would be more complicated than that, that something would be expected of him here.

Was that why he had dressed more carefully than usual? When he put on a brown tweed jacket over a white shirt, had he felt the need to fortify himself, to feel professional and businesslike? I look ready to face an examining committee, he had thought as he looked in the mirror to knot his tie. He noted the puffy skin beneath his eyes, the eyes themselves, paler than they used to be. He had brushed his hair, he had pared his nails, he had flossed his teeth, he had splashed on aftershave. He could malinger no longer. As he descended the stairs and made his way along the hall to the kitchen, he felt a flutter in his chest and noted that it was fear. What was he afraid of? Esther was taking it well. But he was not so stupid as to think that this was anything but an interim period. During the hours and days around a catastrophe people are in a heightened emotional state that bears them up for a short while, but this condition is outside reality.

Last evening, he and Esther had both been in a euphoric mood, as if they had come through the bombing of a city and were amazed to find themselves still alive. After confessions all around, after tears, apologies, joyous exclamations, after George's "you don't know how I've wanted to tell you, to get this off my chest," and Esther's "the truth shall set you free," they had acted like courting lovers in a delirium of discovery, although the evening had not ended in consummation. After a good dinner and copious amounts of wine, exhausted by so much ecstasy, they had fallen asleep almost instantly in each others' arms in their kingsize bed and had slept soundly, spooned like babes in the woods, as though returned to their lost innocence.

This morning George realized that it was not going to be that easy. He realized that now would come the difficult part, getting down to daily living, testing the relationship to see if it would, after all, hold.

"I have a bit of a heavy head," he added, still in the doorway. "But I slept like a log."

"I mean how do you feel about what happened yesterday?" Esther turned to get something out of the fridge and beamed on him a sudden smile, her brown eyes kindling. She came toward him. They hugged, they kissed, a rather awkward kiss, more a brief pressing together of lips.

"I think it's a good thing it did happen. I've been out of control."

"But how do you *feel*." Esther held him away from her. Her voice rose with intensity. He must have looked bewildered. "Do you feel angry, sad?" she coached.

George had known the minute he woke up this morning that Esther would want to talk things out. Women always did. They seemed to find comfort, even redemption, in the process. He could resist, but he did not think that would be wise. Likely, she would ask a lot of embarrassing questions and likely he would have to lie to save her feelings but better to have the discussion and get it over with.

In the shower, with the hot water sluicing down his body, cleansing him pink and new, he concluded how truly amazing Esther was. It was incredible that he had ever thought that she would be destroyed by the knowledge of her husband having an affair. Why, only yesterday, he had actually been afraid to tell her, afraid that it would kill her. Only yesterday he had thought that she would be angry, or coldly silent, or a blithering heap on the carpet. But none of those was Esther. Esther was made of sterner stuff than that. He had tortured himself for nothing. He should have known that Esther would be forgiving. He should have known that she would be merciful. He should have placed the whole mess in her capable hands a long time ago. Esther was his friend. He had always told Esther his troubles, she had always understood. He was so lucky to have her. He must not lose her.

"Relieved," he said. "Mostly, I feel relieved. You have no idea what a strain I've been under."

"Oh, I know. Here, sit down. I'll bring the coffee. It must have tortured you every day, that you were doing something wrong."

"Wrong?"

"Lying. Betraying people. The people you love." Esther charged toward him, coffee pot in hand. She poured two steaming cups. She returned the pot to the stove. She turned back to the table and sat in the chair beside him.

"Yes. You'll never know how I've wanted to get out of this muddle, how I've wanted to get my life back in order."

"I'm surprised you stood it as long as you did." She put her hand over his, which was lying on the table top beside his cup of coffee. She squeezed his hand.

"I think I suspended thought."

"Oh, it must have bothered you so! You with your sense of what's proper."

"I didn't let myself think of such things."

Esther jumped up abruptly. He was startled. But it was just that she had remembered her muffins in the oven. She took them out and brought them to the table with a board that she placed beneath the hot pan. With a metal spatula, she lifted a muffin from its cup and placed it on a plate for him.

He let her wait on him. She seemed bent on pacifying him, almost to the point of obsequiousness. He found it distasteful.

But she seemed to want to do it and he did not have the heart to stop her.

George looked at the steaming muffin on his plate. "You were up early," he said.

"I couldn't sleep. My brain was working so furiously, it wouldn't let me sleep."

George wished that he did not have to know about the workings of Esther's brain. But he also knew that that was a vain wish. "Working?" he said. He broke his muffin in half. He dug his knife deeply into the slab of yellow butter.

"Trying to solve the problem."

George watched the butter melt into the crumbly texture of the muffin.

"For the longest time it just went around and around in my head. There didn't seem to be a solution. I must admit that at first, yesterday, I simply wanted you to be done with your escapade and come home. But then I began to see that that wouldn't solve the problem. I began to see that this young woman belongs to me as much as she does to you, that she's *my* responsibility as well as yours. If I had been able to fill the house with children. No, don't protest. I know I've been a failure in that regard. But if we're truly a couple, we're in this together. In a sense, we both had this affair. And, another thing, we could never be happy together knowing that we had caused someone else's misery." As Esther spoke, she ran the spatula around the rim of each muffin and with a flip of the blade popped each onto its side.

George watched his wife's mouth open and close, trying to comprehend the words coming out of it. "Oh, I wouldn't worry about that," he interrupted through a mouthful of butter-soaked blueberry muffin. "Likely, it won't take her long to get over it."

"There is her to be concerned about of course." Esther took a deep breath. She kept her eyes on the muffins, holding the spatula over them like a sword. "But there's also ... her condition."

George chewed slowly. He swallowed. "There *is* that, yes."

"Something will have to be done about the child."

The child. George did not like to think about the child. Children did not belong in the world of lovers and mistresses. They belonged in a world of husbands and wives, of homes in the suburbs, of Saturday morning gym classes, of picnics in the park. More specifically, a child did not belong in the dark side, the quirky side, of his nature. A child belonged in the sanctioned regular life of society. "Yes," he said. "I suppose it will."

"I suppose it doesn't yet seem like an actuality to you." Esther smiled an amused superior female smile that seemed to say, "You men." "That's biological, I suppose," she continued. "A woman has a child inside her, growing inside, so of course she's aware of it. To a man, a child must always seem somewhat abstract until it actually appears." She put another muffin onto his plate.

George looked at the muffin. He wasn't sure that he wanted another one. "Yes, I suppose that's it."

"Whatever will that young ... I can't keep calling her 'that young woman' or 'she'. What is her name?"

"Veronica."

Esther flinched as though the name was further cause for wounding. She rallied. "Veronica then. What will she do with a child?"

"I don't know." He could not envision Veronica with a child, a baby, a squalling baby in the night. When he let himself think about it, he did have concerns in this regard. But, on the other hand, he was sure that Veronica had gotten herself pregnant on purpose. She was the type. She certainly was not the type to get pregnant unless she meant to. She had manoeuvred herself into position. Was that his fault? She was a big girl of nearly thirty who had always lived in the real world. She must know that sometimes such manoeuvres did not work. She would be furious, of course. She always was when she didn't get her way. "Perhaps she'll adopt it out," he said. "That would be the sensible thing to do."

Esther seemed to be holding her breath. "Somehow I don't like to think of your child being put out for adoption to strangers."

George, too, felt regret at this thought. He would always feel regret for the child. He liked children, when it came down to it. He would not have minded if he and Esther had had more children. He pushed down the feeling. That was the loss he would have to take. He could not expect to get out of this scot-free. "Well, I suppose we don't have to cross that bridge until we come to it," he said.

"I don't suppose…" Esther darted a quick glance up. Her eyes were glowing. "Well, I was wondering about us adopting it."

"Us?" George was genuinely shocked. He reached out his hand for more butter.

"You and me. After all, it is half yours."

"I don't think she would agree to that."

"You never know. And maybe even if she, Veronica, doesn't like the idea now, maybe she'll change her mind. I mean, by the time it's born. I mean, it does seem like the perfect solution. We can give a child a wonderful home. No one would question you and I adopting a child in our middle age. Lots of people in our situation, in our circumstances, adopt children. Oh, they'll think it a bit wild. Some people will. A wild notion. You won't guess what crazy thing Esther and George have done, they'll say. But it would offer a solution. I'd love to have a child around the house."

George looked at his wife. Her energy of purpose struck him like a force from across the table. She positively beamed. Strength seemed to emanate from her pores. She had become Joan of Arc, armoured and mounted. Even without the child, she had a job to do. He had given her the task of saving their marriage. After years of a routine ordinary existence, finally, finally, she had been called to battle.

"I really don't think you should get your hopes up for the child," he cautioned.

"But if she doesn't want it, well, then, I don't see why we shouldn't have it."

"We don't know that she doesn't want it. Maybe she'll marry," George attempted to steer Esther in another direction.

"That *would* be the best solution. After all, I do believe a child should be with its own mother. It's not my child. It's her child. But I want you to know, I would be quite willing, if that's the way things went."

He did not know what to say. He tried to look at her directly but, without him willing it or wishing it, his eyes slid off to the side.

Esther became brisk. "When do you think you'll see … Veronica?"

"I hadn't thought about it."

"I suppose you may as well get it over with as soon as possible."

"Yes."

"What exactly are you going to tell her?"

"Simply that I won't be coming around any more."

"How do you think she'll take it?"

"It doesn't matter, does it? It has to be done."

"I hate to think of her there, in her room, or some place, going about her daily round, unaware that the blade is about to fall. I hate to think of her being hurt."

"Somebody has to be hurt."

"She seems like such a courageous person. Defying the world. For you! The way she took chances, the way she left herself vulnerable to being hurt. Even in coming to the house. Facing me! The wife!"

"Perhaps it's best not to think about such things."

"How can you help thinking about such things? She's had such an unhappy life."

"You know?"

"You told me. Last night. She's the girl who came to your office that day, when we got the phone call. She was broken up about some fellow."

"She's pretty tough. She's a survivor." It's true that she's put up with a lot from me, thought George, but she did it because she wanted to. In the end, people do what they want to do. In the first place, she came here to probe me for information about Ben, then she liked the idea of having an adventure, now she wants normalcy, the respectable life of a married woman. Maybe she deserves something more from life, but my responsibility is with Esther.

"...Financial arrangements," Esther was saying.

"Financial arrangements?"

"I don't know what's fair. But I think we should be as generous as we can be. She'll have to move to better accommodation. Those student rooms are no place to raise a child. And a child needs a great many things."

"She is capable of getting a job." George polished off his muffin and crumpled his paper napkin onto his plate. He thought of Delores. Certainly, finances were connected to children. "She seems to be enthusiastic about her career."

"Even so, we must keep up our end of things. It will make you feel more a part of it. It will make you feel more like a father."

George had not considered that he might want to feel like a father.

"We'll just have to manage two households," Esther cheerfully announced. "We'll all have to work it out so that everyone is happy."

"What if she marries and the fellow wants us out of the picture?"

"I suppose that might happen."

"I'm not saying it will or won't. My point is, we can't take the whole thing over." George meant "you," but he decided to be tactful. "It's her child. Her life."

"Well, every child needs and has the right to know both its

parents. To have a sense of identity." Esther straightened in her chair. She seemed to brace herself. "Oh, I admit when she came to the door, when I first found out, I was thrown for an absolute loop. Last evening, too, I just wanted it all to be over, the pain and confusion. But at some point during the night my thinking started to change. Or maybe my subconscious started thinking. But I dozed and woke and dozed and woke, and finally woke up fully knowing that I must decide what is the best thing to do, the right thing to do, and then keep that thought firm in my mind and not let other thoughts in. The thing that came to me is that you are an adult human being and I shouldn't be telling you what to do. I don't want to be your jailer. Perhaps you shouldn't stop seeing her. I mean, whatever she decides about the child. Until the child is born, she'll need your support, I mean emotionally, to keep her spirits up. You can't just leave her ... them. Aside from the child, you've been friends. What right do I have to destroy that friendship? Friends are not easy to find. No, you must continue to see her."

"You wouldn't mind?"

"As long as you don't love her, as long as the affair is over ... I'm not sure I could deal with that, it not being over I mean, although I understand some people do. Some people, some women, don't mind. Nowadays, people have all sorts of strange relationships. But I think I would. Mind. Yes, I'm sure I would. But as long as you're just friends, well, then, I don't see why we can't work it out so that we all get along. Oh, I'm putting this all badly, but you know what I mean."

George looked at his wife's bright face, pink and screwed up from the effort of trying to accurately relate her thoughts and intentions. "You astonish me," he said quite sincerely.

"She loved you. I can't be against someone who loved you. And it seems to me she deserves some consideration. All these months, she's the one who's suffered. She's the one who knew about another woman — me."

"What if she objects?"

"I don't see why she should. We're all intelligent adults."

"What if she wants to be done with the whole business? Cut her losses and get out? Give the child up and start over? Perhaps we shouldn't interfere with that."

"I can't see how she could possibly want to do that." Esther looked at him, an expression of pained bafflement on her face. He could see the futility of trying to get her to understand a situation not of her own devising. He got up from the table and took his dishes to the sink.

George walked briskly along on the rather cool late spring morning swinging his briefcase. He couldn't believe it. He was to have it all. Everything. Both women, his career, his comfortable home and lifestyle. Esther had decreed it. She had insisted on it. He was to continue to visit Veronica, but now with Esther's knowledge. Everything was to be out in the open, open and above board. It would be good to be done with the lying, at least most of it. It would be good to make things up to Veronica, at least to a certain extent, since he had made her so miserable. Bless Esther for thinking it all up. It did seem a little hard on her but, after all, she had volunteered. Volunteered to take on the task of helping him. He knew he was a bit of a heel. He was not exonerating himself. It was a terrible business. But it wasn't his fault any more than it was Veronica's. And Esther's, for letting him get away with things, for spoiling him. What is a man to do? Any man will let himself be spoiled if a woman insists on it. What was *he* supposed to do? But imagine! After all these months of worrying about Esther, what she would say, what she would do, she was willing to share. A qualified sharing, to be sure. Still, he was to have Veronica with Esther's sanction. Veronica, of course, would be livid. To have Esther in control of their relationship, to have Esther deciding when they should see each other, allowing their happiness, their sex life, for George had no doubt that the sex part of it would ultimately be resumed since he couldn't even imagine a sexless relationship with Veronica. Veronica would find this insufferable. And yet she would have to put up with it. Otherwise, she would be out of the picture entirely. Well, she had certainly boxed herself into this one. She had underestimated the force of goodness, specifically, Esther's goodness. But, then, how could she have done otherwise? She had had very little experience of goodness in her life.

At the end of the street, he turned. He could see Esther standing on the front step. He waved his briefcase. He saw her raised arm in the distance. "What will you do today?" he had asked as he kissed her good-bye.

"I don't know," she had answered.

"Perhaps you should get out," he had said, for it unsettled him to think of her alone in the house all day thinking up ever more complicated scenarios for him, for the three of them, to act out on a stage of her own creation.

For some reason that he could not understand, he felt sad. Why should he feel sad when he was to have it all? But there was something about the way Esther stood on the step of their home, something about the passing of time and happiness, and Esther waving in the distance as though she were sailing away from him, the space between them ever lengthening. There was something about loss, for they *had* lost each other. The old George, the old Esther, those two who could never lose each other, had done just that. Their young selves were lost to each other. For a moment, George felt something quite profound. He shrugged off his sadness and turned and continued on his way.

When he arrived on campus, the place he thought of as the boundary between his two worlds, he felt himself to be in a new landscape where he was not sure of the rules, where he did not know how to act, how even to think. The barrier that had kept things separate and in order was no longer there. His two mutually exclusive lives had been brought together. What had formerly been unacceptable to him, to *him*, to who he really was, had become acceptable. His inner reality had been compelled to embrace a formerly unacceptable outer reality. The wall had been pulled down. He felt a great deal of discomfort, his mind confused to the point where he felt physically uncoordinated. He wondered if this condition was one from which he would ever recover.

XI. BENJAMIN AND ESTHER

THAT SAME AFTERNOON BENJAMIN RECEIVED a telephone call. "Is Helena there?" Esther's voice came through the receiver.

He had not seen Esther since Amanda's funeral and, before that, only a few times in as many years, but he knew her voice immediately, sweet and light with a musical lilt, but now strained and anxious, high and thin. He was on the alert. "No," he said and waited.

"Ben?"

"Yes."

"This is Esther."

"Esther, how are you?"

"I need to talk to Helena."

"She's not here. Have you tried her apartment?"

"Yes. She's not there. I thought she might be with you."

"No. I'll be seeing her later today."

"You wouldn't happen to know where she is?"

"No." He was beginning to suspect that this was not a casual call. However, his antenna for trouble was directed toward Helena rather than Esther. Helena seemed to be stronger with every passing day, but there was still the possibility of a relapse. "Is anything wrong?" He held his breath. "Is anything wrong with Helena?"

"No, no. I shouldn't be worrying you like this. I just wanted to talk with her about Reuben and the children, you know that he's planning on marrying again. Helena was concerned about the children. We were talking about it just the other day. She...," the voice broke off, then reasserted itself. "I need to talk with her. She doesn't have a job yet?"

"No. She may be at the university. You know she's decided to finish that PhD?"

"Yes, that was wonderful news."

"Do you want me to give her a message?"

"I need to see her. I need to see her right away." The voice changed in tone to one of frantic intensity.

He heard a hollow flap, like the wind taking a sail, and then a series of gasps.

"Esther. Esther, what is it?" He made his voice stern. "Esther, tell me, what is all this about?" The command brought a howl from the other end of the phone. "I'll come over," he said. "Are you at home? I'll be right over."

This got a response, a loud "No!" then, lower, "No, I can't stay here another minute." She got it out between sobs, "I'm going mad. I have to get out of this house."

After some disjointed negotiation they settled on meeting in a park that was close to Esther. "Are you sure you can drive?" Benjamin asked.

"Yes, I'll be all right," her voice had fallen to a thin whimper.

"You're sure? I can pick you up." This past month, feeling that he and Helena needed a car, Benjamin had taken on the responsibility of ownership. He called it caving in to middle-class capitalism. Helena's response was that buying a ten-year-old Toyota was a slight bow, not a cave-in.

"No, it's all right. I'll be careful. Don't worry."

The park was beside the river, down the hill from the university, below George's jogging path. When Benjamin arrived from his place on the other side of the valley, Esther was already there, wandering about in a daze at the edge of the parking lot. When he got out of his car, she didn't seem to notice, although he slammed the door soundly behind him. He approached her and touched her elbow. Slowly, she turned her head, slowly looked up at him. Her eyes were red, her complexion splotchy. Still, he detected the old Esther, cute and perky, with dark brown curls and what he had always considered a doll-like face, a face of the fifties, although that was a little before her time, but she retained an innocence that seemed to get lost in the sixties. In stature, too, she seemed an earlier product, petite, dainty, even though she'd put on weight.

She stood in confusion, like a child waiting for direction. "Here, let's walk a bit," he said, guiding her shoulder with his hand. "We'll find a bench."

Whether it was the walking or his presence, she seemed to recover somewhat and so he kept her walking. They talked about the old days. "We were so close for a while." Her eyes narrowed into the distance and he recalled with fondness her myopic squint. "We were so close and then we all drifted apart." Her voice was a lament. "Life is cruel the way it does that to people. We were three sisters. When we were children, when we were growing up, we were complete. A circle. Three men joined our circle. We thought we would live happily ever after," she said. "What happened?"

They gravitated toward a bench. They sat. Apart from a city crew cleaning out a nearby swimming pool, they were alone. The day was blustery. Esther was wearing a heavy coat, something woolly and dark. Still, she shivered. Her hand was resting limply on her thigh. On impulse, Benjamin took her hand in both of his to warm it. Her hand was plump and soft. His was thin and bony. "Esther," he said, "how very nice to see you."

Immediately, she began to wail, not cry, not sob, but wail, a long keening wail. He put an arm around her shoulders and drew her to him. The tears streamed down her face and fell unheeded into her lap. Her face was a rigid grimacing mask. She did not attempt to hide it. A jogger glanced their way, then quickly turned his head and jogged on. After some minutes, the wail subsided into low guttural gasps and heaves. Benjamin turned her head to his shoulder where she shuddered and convulsed a few moments longer. After a while she was still. Then in a thin voice punctuated by stops and starts, she told him the whole story.

In the silence that followed, Benjamin felt suddenly tired. It's a good thing we met in a park, he thought. Esther was right to want to get out of the house. This was a story that needed fresh air and space and the light of day. In the night and the dark, such stories became frightening.

Although he had heard countless renditions of suffering, this one struck him profoundly. He still thought of the six who had formed such close ties in a smoky den so many years ago as his family, their lives and his inexorably intertwined. He had been an outsider and they had drawn him into the warmth of their circle, three sisters who had been so eagerly and innocently seeking experience, embracing life, throwing themselves into the causes of the downtrodden, the dispossessed of the planet. The Cave, he could see so clearly yet, walking through the door and there they had been, three laughing faces, Esther's fresh and pretty, Helena, tempting and provocative, Amanda the naive blue-eyed blonde. It was her first year and her sisters were introducing her to the sophisticated life of a university student. In spite of what had happened between him and Helena, the other two couples had set a standard of behaviour and values against which he measured his own. Amanda's death had destroyed something important for him, not only because he loved her but because she, and she and Reuben as a couple, were part of his mental life. He admired them for taking a difficult road. They had done it for each other without regret. As for Esther and George, during his bad years, it had been a consolation to think that they were still here, an intact entity on the planet. Now, it appeared that that belief was an illusion.

"I shouldn't have burdened you with all this," Esther's voice threatened further tears. "But I had to say the words. I had to speak them out loud to someone. I was fine this morning. I couldn't believe how well I was taking it. I was full of plans and optimism for going on. Of course, I was deceiving myself, holding myself together with some sort of manic glue that was bound to come unstuck. Which it did shortly after I waved George off. While he was there, in the house, I could keep catastrophe outside myself. But then I was alone with my thoughts and the catastrophe got inside me. I was plunged into the blackest hole. My mind was plunged into it. I couldn't get out. It's hard to explain. I felt frantic. I couldn't stand it one more minute without telling someone, someone who could say some words to me, some sensible words. I needed another mind to share my thoughts with. That's when I picked up the phone. You happened to be at the other end. Well, at least you saved Helena from having to hear it all." By now Esther was sitting with her face forward, staring at the ground. "Please don't tell her any of this. I'll tell her another time. Soon. But I should be the one to tell her. I don't want her to get it second-hand."

Benjamin stared at the men cleaning out the swimming pool. Later, he could not have described what they were doing. His mind was busy. He did not want to be the one entrusted with this knowledge. He did not want to be the one chosen to be here, in Esther's path. He did not want to keep things from Helena. He did not want to have to find words, consoling words, helpful words for Esther, not here where he was personally involved. He feared his words would sound insincere because his feelings around the situation were so strong.

He waited for her to speak again, to give him some direction for his words. "I would have been a much more interesting person all these years if I'd had a career," she said, her voice empty of tears but weary.

"I don't think you can assume that," he said, cautiously.

"It's true. I've spent my life cooking and cleaning and running a household. No wonder George took up with a younger woman, a more interesting woman. I'm so boring."

"I doubt it very much."

"Dull, boring and unattractive."

"That's simply false."

"Smelling of garlic and onions."

"I certainly find you attractive."

"You do?"

"You were always attractive. You had so much energy. You used to remind me of Debbie Reynolds in *Singing in the Rain*."

"I did?"

"Yes. You had Delores by then. You were finishing up your degree. You had that big house to manage. And George was an upcoming young professor, which demanded a lot from you. And you were so young. Yet you managed it all. I admired you very much."

"I should have carried on with teaching. By letting that go I became too much the dull little housewife. Not like Veronica."

Benjamin felt instant alarm. "Veronica?" There could not be many Veronicas around. It was an unusual name.

"That's the name of the girl. Oh, when I first heard the name it hurt so. But I must get used to it. I must say it."

Benjamin sat stunned, staring straight ahead. Only his mouth moved. "What's her last name?"

Esther turned to him, her forehead creased. "I don't know. I just realized, I don't know."

Benjamin's mind felt like it had collapsed in on itself. He could think of nothing to say. But, Esther's voice continued. "She's terribly attractive, tall, blonde, very slim...."

Oh, sweet Jesus, thought Benjamin. "I spoke to that relative of yours today," he could hear Veronica's sad voice. "He's kind of cute.'" Had she done this deliberately, in a fit of pique at being rejected by him? He must not think that. Good Christ! What had he been called to do? He couldn't continue with her if he didn't have feelings for her. Was it his fault if he had not had such feelings? He should never have slept with her in the first place. Okay, he admitted that. But once that fault was committed, was he supposed to put himself in bondage to a woman he did not love?

"What are you going to do?" He was amazed that his voice was calm and in a low register.

"Help him, of course," she said. "He's got himself into trouble. If it were business or work trouble I'd stand by his side. We've been together so long. We're responsible for each other."

"Forgive and forget, then."

"I don't know if a person can will themselves to forget. As for forgive, well, it's not up to me to forgive him, is it? I mean, it's not my job. I don't have that authority. He's done a terrible thing against himself. He has suffered a personal disaster. I must help him forgive himself. It *is* terrible. It does hurt. I wish he hadn't deceived me. It's the deceit that tears at me. The exclusion from his life, the fact that he didn't *share*, that's what hurts. The invisibility." She started to weep again, this time softly into a tissue that she pulled from her pocket.

"How about ... the young lady? What does George propose to do about her?"

Esther wiped her eyes and blew her nose. "He can't abandon her. In her circumstances. Even though he doesn't love her. She helped him through a bad time. Amanda's death was harder on him than I knew. It started him thinking about his own death and that he hadn't lived up to his own expectations, that he hadn't accomplished anything important in his work. You see the fault is mine as much as his. He should have talked to me about Amanda and how he felt about his life. I should have left the way open for him to talk to me. But it's over between them, *that part*, anyway. Still, he must continue to take care of her. And then when the child comes, well, he must take responsibility for that. Don't you think?"

"But ...are you sure you won't mind?"

"Lots of women have to deal with ex-wives. Or maybe a better way of putting it, she'll be like one of his students. He'll be kind to her, but as far as the other is concerned...."

So George was to keep living his double life and with Esther's blessing! How in hell had he managed that?

"I'm sure we can all live happily together," said Esther. "There's no *reason* why we can't. We're all mature, intelligent, educated people. We can make it work. As long as we're not small-minded, as long as we don't lower ourselves to indulging in petty emotions."

He didn't manage it, thought Benjamin. Esther did. "Are you sure you won't start resenting Veronica?" he asked. "After a while? Perhaps even just the time that George will spend with her?"

"I never resented the time he spent with Delores. Why should I resent this young woman? Veronica." He could feel her beside him, stiffening, bracing herself to say the name, as if she were about to take a blow.

"On a practical level, won't it be expensive to keep two households going?"

"Yes, we'll have to work out the practicalities. But ... Veronica... I must start thinking of her as being a real person with a name, does have a career in mind."

I suppose Esther will end up babysitting, thought Benjamin.

"What do you think?" she asked.

"About what?" he evaded.

"About it all. I need an outside opinion. You see, I'm in such a state of emotional turmoil, I don't know if I'm thinking straight. I trust your ability to think straight, to tell me truthfully what you think."

"I think..." What do I think? Benjamin asked himself. I think that I want to say some easy words and get out of this quickly and cleanly, he answered himself.

He might slide out from under taking a stance. In fact, did he have the right to take a stance? Would not a stance influence Esther's decision? Did he have the right to influence her decision? But he had the uncomfortable feeling that he *did* have a responsibility here. No matter how he would rationalize it in the future, and he knew that he would, the fact was that if he had acted differently with Veronica this woman would not now be sitting here beside him weeping. Could I help it if I didn't love Veronica? he tried to excuse himself. No, but you could have handled it better, he told himself. At the very least, he could have listened to her, shown her some understanding. He hadn't wanted her hanging onto him so he had got rid of her the way you get rid of a pest. He had been so busy with self-indulgent wallowing in guilt and misery, he hadn't had time for her. If he had so much as discussed her feelings with her, perhaps he could have helped her through a tough patch, helped her to feel better about things, so that she did not feel unloved, abandoned, and thus ricochet off him and into George's life. Now he owed *this* woman an intelligent ear, a serious endeavour to find a solution to her problem. But how to do this? It sounded like she had made a decision. Even though he could not endorse her decision, should he support her in it? Should he tell her not to be hasty, to give herself some time to think this through. Was this a time for truth? Did he owe her the truth? What are the rules here? Is there a time for truth and a time for lies? He was caught in lies already. Would another matter? Would a lie be more helpful in this situation? But if Esther considered his opinion, or worse, if she based her decision on what he was about to say, and if he were to lie, her future would be influenced by, if not founded on, lies.

"I think that you all will constantly be living with lies," he said. "You might start out with good intentions, you all might, but the situation is one which will demand lies. You will be putting George, and Veronica too, in a position where they can't help but lie. You will suspect that George is lying and you'll start to despise him. You may continue to love him but you will not respect him. You won't trust him. Even when he isn't lying, you'll wonder if he is. Your love will become a despairing thing. Instead of saving George you'll destroy him and you'll destroy yourself because you'll be dragged down into the lies and ultimately into some sort of evil that will come out of telling lies."

"Evil? Isn't that a bit strong?"

"Evil happens when people's minds get twisted, and that comes about through telling lies."

"You don't have faith in the human ability to be truthful, honourable? To *try*?"

"Yes. Yes, I do. But the first step here, in being truthful and honourable is for George to feel that he has had a personal disaster, that his integrity has been shattered. You feel this, but does George feel it?"

Esther did not speak for a long time. Benjamin was tempted to say words to sway her. He might say, "George always had trouble thinking that he might be wrong." But he sat silent.

"Maybe you're right," Esther finally said. "One thing that does bother me ... he hasn't apologized. Oh not that I want him to flog himself or grovel, but I would feel better about things if he had said a simple, I'm sorry. I'm sorry for hurting people. If he admitted his wrong. To be honest, I have to say it has crossed my mind that he doesn't consider that he's done anything wrong. He has not told lies because anything that isn't a blatant lie isn't a lie. Betrayal and deceit don't count."

"So he will continue in his lies and you will be encouraging him to do so."

"So he must give up that y... Veronica."

"As long as there are two women the lies will continue."

"You're saying." Esther paused. "George must choose."

Benjamin was silent.

But Esther would hold her belief a moment longer. "Do you really think that's necessary? I don't ask him to choose between me and Delores."

"Esther. You see how already you're being pulled down into the lies? You don't really believe that George's relationship with ...Veronica is the same as his relationship with Delores."

"Yes. Yes, I do. Oh, it wasn't. But now it is. Maybe he did

love her, or at least thought he did, but he doesn't any more."

"Has he actually said that?"

"I don't know. I can't remember. Yes, most certainly he did, last evening, I can't remember exactly...."

"All right. This can be easily solved. Ask George. In a straight manner. And demand an unqualified response."

"He'd be angry. He'd think I didn't believe him, didn't trust him."

"He has been lying to you for more than two years. Why should you believe him? Why should you trust him? Why should he suddenly become truthful?"

"I believe him." Esther's voice was emphatic, even stubborn.

"You see what you're doing to George? By believing his lies, his possible lies, you're encouraging him to tell more. You're indulging him."

"Perhaps I *have* spoiled him. But why can't we spoil people a little. People need a little spoiling in this world."

"Not when it allows them to be self-indulgent. Not when it doesn't demand of them to live up to what is best in them. Not when it doesn't demand their truth." Benjamin took a deep breath for what he had to say next. "Maybe you're trying to spare yourself."

A long silence followed. During it, Benjamin thought, I'm going to find out what she's really made of. Is she the complacent, self-deluding person I've always thought of her as being or is she more than that.

"Perhaps you're right," she said, finally. "Perhaps I don't want to know the truth." Again, she was silent. She appeared to be thinking. "I can see the complications," she eventually said. "By not facing the truth, a person can stand between another person and his truth. And a person's motives might be good. You want to be kind, you want to protect the other person. Still, it isn't always easy to know what the truth is."

"The truth *is* difficult."

"What if I insist that the truth is that George is still in love with that young woman when he isn't? Isn't that just as bad as thinking he's not when he is?"

"But it's not up to you, whether he is or isn't. What's up to you, what you can control, is your choice of whether or not to cut George free to make his own decision."

When Esther spoke after another long silence, her voice had a new, serious, introspective tone that Benjamin had not heard in it before. "You may be right," she said. "Perhaps I have barged ahead with my own plan. Perhaps I haven't asked George what he wants."

Exhausted, they sat together on the park bench for some time lost in their own thoughts, contemplating all that had been said. Benjamin did not think that Esther would make up her mind today. She would need time for further consideration. She would vacillate back and forth maybe many times before making a final decision, and maybe she never would. People did that, went on for years in inconclusive situations, unable to take the action that would change their lives, even if it was for the better, clutching the known rather than face the unknown.

The city crew gathered up their machines and their tools into the back of a large truck, climbed into the cab and slowly drove away. The park was empty and silent. The squawk of a magpie slashed a jagged discordant streak across the grey afternoon.

4. Two Years Later

XII: GEORGE

"CONGRATULATIONS!"

"Thank you. Thank you very much."

"That fellow in California who threw you a curve. What happened to him?"

"His research went off in another direction."

"Good luck that."

"Every time you roll the dice you have a fifty-fifty chance."

"Right place at the right time."

"Being prepared when you get the chance."

"Main thing, you got the damn thing published. As one academic to another, I know what a relief that is."

George watched Henry's mouth and wrinkles. Since the faces of the two men were inches apart, he was able to see the enlarged pores in the other man's collapsing skin, the cheeks and jowls that were starting to sag. Through the thinning hair, patches of scalp were visible. It seemed ludicrous that Henry had had an affair, that a woman had been attracted to him. Then George reminded himself that Henry was only a few years older than he was.

He became aware of a silence and Henry regarding him expectantly. He moved his head in such a way it could be construed as either affirmative or negative.

"I hope they take it. *Science* is a prestigious publication. It would be good for the department."

George nodded again, a definite affirmative. Henry must be talking about his team's submission. "They'll take it," he encouraged. "It's a fine piece of work."

"You know the science journals. Editors a bunch of supercilious assholes."

Henry moved off. I still have all my hair, thought George, watching his colleague advance toward the food. Maybe a little greyer every year but still there. And I'm in pretty good shape even if I have given up jogging.

George took a moment to view his associates milling around the hors d'oeuvre table, holding aloft goblets of champagne, creating a great hum of voices, eruptions of laughter. He wondered if they still gossiped about his affair with Veronica. Probably not. Yesterday's news. Other choice departmental tidbits had surfaced since then. Scandals were numerous and quickly forgotten.

Others moved in. "Congratulations. Congrats. Well done. Way to go. Nice work."

"Thank you. Thanks. Thank you very much."

George still liked these men and women, some of whom he had known and worked with for twenty years. He still liked this room. He still liked the privilege of membership in such a room. The champagne and hors d'oeuvre in the Faculty Club were first rate. He looked through the tall windows near to where he was standing, looked out, way out over the river valley, the wide sluggish North Saskatchewan, the north embankment, the buildings that were part of the downtown core. If he looked sharply down he could see the sidewalk below where he used to jog on his visits to and from Veronica in what seemed another life.

It *was* another life, thought George. Sometimes he had trouble remembering that life.

He lifted another glass of champagne from the server's passing tray.

Why shouldn't he drink champagne? Why shouldn't he celebrate? If we're the privileged class we may as well act the part. Had he really said that in that other life? Had it been he, George Martin, who had said those words? Esther should be here. The thought was out before he could stop it. Quickly, he reined it back in. He would not think about Esther. Today was *his* day. If Esther was here, she would be swanning around the room taking credit for *her* George, *her* book, *her* triumph. In her warm, effusive, motherly, hovering way she would appropriate his occasion.

"George, good work." It was Cindy MacGregor a young professor in his department. He liked her; she made him think of Delores. The young women of today, he marvelled, the way they juggled careers, babies, households. They were a force of nature. "And besides getting the book off you've been busy in other ways. I've been hearing good things about what your lab is doing. You have some promising graduate students."

"The sabbatical helped."

"Yes, I'm looking forward to mine next year. But no shop talk today. How's the little one? A new father at your age, that can't be easy."

George had hoped his domestic life would not become a subject of conversation today, but Cindy with two young children was very much interested in the topic and coping with same.

"Sleep deprivation has taken on new meaning. But you know about that."

"Two of you under the same roof going through the pains of creativity in more ways than one. How did you manage it?"

"It had its moments. Still does. But she defends in the fall. Things should be more relaxed after that."

"Thank god my husband isn't an academic. Two in the same family must be quite the circus at times."

Circus? Perhaps that did describe his life. The roller coaster rather than the merry-go-round.

Cindy moved off and another attractive young woman took

her place. This one had lovely long blonde hair swinging freely and was tall and slim, although at present she had a slightly rounded abdomen under the straight cut of her black sheath. "Well, Georgie, you've pulled it off." There was something irreverent in her voice, something that was, at the same time, mocking and affectionate.

"*We've* pulled it off." He could be generous where he did not feel defensive. Veronica did not want his life. She had her own. And there was truth in his statement. In living with Veronica, he had discovered many things about her that he would not have guessed. One was her strict regime fuelled by a profound work ethic. When Polly was born, she became obsessive about her schedule. Otherwise, she said, she wouldn't get anything accomplished in this life. As it happened, her obsession kept him on track, her schedule kept him on schedule. He spent hours in the lab then further hours at home in his study, working long into the night. He was pleased to learn that he could work again like that, could put in the hours it took to write a book.

In finishing the book he discovered that he had not lost it after all, the ability to focus, to put his thoughts down on the page in a coherent fashion, the ability to *think*. He had been afraid for a while, afraid of what the two women were doing to his mind. The events of that time had threatened to destroy his intelligence and his confidence. As he thought of it now, it was amazing he had stood up to it as well as he had. His life had been a hopeless mess. But he had cleaned up the mess and put his life back in order.

"My dominatrix, cracking the whip," he murmured the words for her ears only.

"And don't you love it."

"Are you ready to go?"

"You can't very well leave yet. It's your party. Stay a while and enjoy your fifteen minutes of fame. I'll pick up Polly at the daycare."

"*Ta ta* then."

"Goodbye." She kissed him full on the lips and he felt the old fire. Something to look forward to — the bottle of champagne on ice at home for later in the evening when Polly was safely tucked between the sheets.

He watched her willowy figure thread its way through the crowd toward the door. How complicated his life had been two years ago. How simple the solution had been in the end.

The next morning, a glorious sunny morning in spring, George woke up in his new kingsize bed, minus the satiny quilts and cushions, and was immediately enveloped in a shroud of gloom. This happened some mornings, he didn't know why. He thought it might be a dream he could not remember, only a feeling remained, a sad melancholy longing for something vague, unnameable, out of reach. He had never given much credence to dreams, never used to remember them. But lately he'd been having a recurring dream of loss. The loss was connected to a deadline, and a great deal of anxiety surrounded the situation. He had to give a lecture, catch a train, an airplane. He had to find what he had lost in order to meet the deadline. He had to find his notes before the lecture began, he had to find his suitcase before the flight took off. He would run from place to place in frantic search. The dream had no resolution. He always woke up before the class started or the plane left.

He wondered if he had drunk too much at yesterday's department party or later in the evening when he and Veronica had celebrated privately. He'd had to drink most of the bottle of champagne since Veronica wasn't drinking much these days. He dismissed the thought. He never suffered from hangovers. He didn't have a heavy head. All he had was the residue of a dream.

George malingered beneath the warm sheets, beside the warm body of Veronica, Polly curled into her curve. Often she brought the child into their bed in the night, a holdover from breastfeeding days when she said it was easier than to sit up with her. In another curl, inside Veronica, was the new one to be born in the fall. Soon he would have two to babysit. It was his morning for the familial duty. Veronica as a teaching assistant had to instruct a class at ten. At two o'clock this afternoon he had a meeting with a grad student and, of course, he would look in at the lab, but he had no teaching duties during the spring semester so his time was flexible.

He looked at the red numbers of his bedside clock. He would give himself ten more minutes max, then he would jump up and face the new-fangled coffee station Veronica had recently invested in. Its little packets of various strengths and flavours and its complicated procedure of dialling the brew was a formidable challenge first thing in the morning.

The bright morning sunshine streamed through the window with nothing to intervene. The elm that had bounced its branches against the window had been cut down. The robins that had lived there had fled. George missed the elm, the floating leaves, their particular shade of new spring green against a cerulean sky. He missed the robins that used to wake him at three in the morning with their rising of the sun song allowing him to snuggle back into the blankets with the pleasureable knowledge that he didn't have to get up for three hours. However, Veronica wanted a vegetable garden, she wanted to puree carrots and peas so that Polly would not be ingesting the additives and chemicals in commercial baby food. The roots of the huge tree discouraged a garden, its shade was a further detriment to plant growth. The tree had to go.

Esther had to go. A giant garage sale was organized — dishes, pots, pans, knickknacks, including the Royal Doulton minus the shattered Lady Anne. Esther was consulted, through Delores. She stated that she wanted nothing. Veronica stated that the whole place had to be repainted, refurbished, redecorated. Although George liked the house and its convenience to his work, he thought it would be easier to sell and buy a modern place in the suburbs.

"Oh yes, you'd like that wouldn't you, hide me away some place where you don't have to introduce me to the neighbours," had been Veronica's response. He surmised that she did not want to give Esther the satisfaction of forcing her out, but an even stronger motivation in her wanting to stay seemed to be that even though she hated Esther, she loved the house. She had never had a house before, not even as a child when she had lived in basement suites and trailers with her deficient parents. And this particular house in an old established neighbourhood of professionals reeked of a certain class to which she wanted to belong, a class exuding respectability, prestige, and social stability.

Such outbursts from Veronica were a source of dismay in George. Why was she still so scrappy when there was no longer a reason for it, when in nearly every issue she seized victory? Had she become so used to fighting to get along in the world that it had become her modus operandi? Or was it that fighting had been a fundamental part of their old relationship, that the sexual tension it aroused had given their union its bite, its excitement. If so, in his opinion, for the new relationship to work, they had to find a replacement.

In the end they fell into a sort of verbal sparring, keeping a light teasing quality in their voices while each knew there was an element of truth behind words and tone. But before they arrived at that solution they'd had to go through early days, when the new relationship had not yet taken hold, when it was being tested, and neither of them was sure how it would turn out. They did not voice their uncertainty, that would have been too dangerous, but they approached each other with a measured wariness, almost a shyness. Because their old relationship had consisted mainly of the physical, they did not know each other. Even Veronica seemed to realize that a wild romantic fling was quite different than settling down into domestic bliss. Without voicing it, they knew they had to reinvent their relationship.

Their first summer in the house, Veronica threw herself into the renovation project with frenzied zeal. She wanted no trace of Esther left behind. She hated Esther all the more for letting her win by default. The enemy had simply left the field, left her without anyone to fight. She did not completely trust George's feelings in the matter. Would George have left Esther if Esther hadn't left first? When she broached the subject to George he told her to stop talking nonsense. "Haven't you got what you want?"

"I didn't get it the right way. I didn't want her to hand you over to me. Don't you see she still controls our lives?"

To which he had replied, rather wearily, "Do you have to speak to me in that shrewish tone? You always boast about lifting yourself out of the gutter and becoming an educated professional person. Why don't you speak and behave as though you are one?"

Paint cans and long-handled rollers appeared. Design books and wallpaper catalogues littered the tables and chairs. The kitchen was first on the list. Out went the solid oak and country cottage kitchen cushions and placemats. In came a stark white modern kitchen prepackaged, requiring only easy assembly according to a chart even a child could follow, so implied the instructions. George wanted to get in a contractor but Veronica thought it would be good for him. "Get your head out of your ass," as she put it in the tone reserved for poking holes in what she called his sublime egoism. The project turned out to be fun. It took him back to his youth when he used to tackle all the usual minor home repairs himself. Veronica helped him. He was surprised to learn that she was very good at grasping the concepts of construction manuals. He also learned that she liked having projects, that she attacked each new one with great enthusiasm. And even though her pregnancy was becoming more obvious by the day, she was still narrow in the shoulders and better than he at reaching into far corners of inside cupboards to fit the screws.

At times, George had the impression that he was playing house with a child, with someone like Delores. What am I doing with this young girl, in this ludicrous situation, he would wonder, hammering nails into drywall, traipsing around to the various hardware and building materials outlets when he should be in his lab working.

But it was in these ordinary things that they became a couple. They were too preoccupied to continue to worry about Esther or how their relationship had come together. The house, preparing for the new arrival, the start of classes in the fall, these concerns filled their days. And as time went on, life for the George Martins settled down. The months before Polly was born were especially productive. Veronica was a female animal with accelerated hormonal activity preparing the nest for her young. George was astonished. Wild and promiscuous in her youth, she became superorganized and supermotivated, as though the energy she had formerly put into being miss party girl was now directed into her child and her house. It seemed that with her own little kingdom where she felt safe, she had never been busier or happier. With her prince to protect her, she could surrender her battle station. Her nature, stunted and deprived from a lifetime of struggle and rejection, when transplanted grew and blossomed. This expansion included her former lover, her husband. She teased him unmercifully but looked at him with tender eyes. She saw his faults, all that was pompous and vain about him, and called him her dear old teddy.

She had little sympathy for his keeping the ghost of Esther alive in himself, so he was careful not to let her see it. Veronica seemed satisfied that with all the changes they had made, they had gotten rid of Esther. George knew that, in spite of Veronica's attempts to eradicate her, Esther was everywhere — in the gardens which she had planted and tended with such devotion, the walls which she had delighted in painting and wallpapering, for even Veronica was not successful in getting rid of the walls that held the house up around her or the perennial shrubs that were so well established their roots were impossible to eradicate. George also knew that getting rid of Esther in the house was easier than getting rid of Esther in himself, which in his view, was only to be expected. He sometimes thought that he should have insisted they sell and buy new, but he always concluded that that would not have solved the problem.

As life went on and Veronica advanced in her studies, she brought that professionalism to the relationship. Was she not supposed to be, after all, a doctor of psychology? She should be able to view things rationally, in perspective. As more time passed she even came to accept her default win. What the hell, as she put it to George, I've got you and I've got myself a life. What do I care about Esther?

The new life worked partly because they both had busy lives and they both loved Polly. But in the last analysis, it worked because both of them knew it had to. For her part, Veronica had fought too hard to get him for it not to work. As for George, from the beginning, standing in the eerie darkness of the old kitchen, the only light coming from under the microwave hood, Esther's note in his hand, he knew that he must make it work. Esther demanded it.

My destiny has been subverted, he thought as the red number on the clock shifted to the hour and he knew that he must get up before it shifted again. A devious god with a wicked sense of humour had reached down a long arm and placed a detour sign on the clear unencumbered smooth highway on which he had been travelling with Esther, and pointed him to a side road of pot holes, twists and turns.

But perhaps these three beside him were his destiny. Is this what he had been travelling toward all his life? Sometimes, when he looked at Polly and cuddled her to his chest, it seemed so. But he didn't believe in destiny. What was that existentialist rot Ben used to spout during their Cave days? At every moment we are free to choose. In fact, we must choose. Not to choose is a choice in itself.

This is the life I've chosen, George said to himself swinging his legs over the side of the bed. But on his way to the bathroom, he had the uncomfortable thought that Esther had chosen for him, and that Veronica, smart, sassy Veronica was accurate in her assessment.

Polly was slumped against the side of the stroller. George bent and lowered the seat back and gently eased her into a horizontal position. He adjusted a light blanket to shade her face from the sun and continued walking along the path that circled the park until he came to the bench near the playground equipment, the same one he used to sit on while watching Delores on the swings and slides. He braked the stroller, spread himself on the bench in the sun, and wondered why Esther was so mean.

How could she have done it? How could she have been so thoughtless of him? His Esther. All the years they had gone through together. Best friends, he had thought they were best friends. Best friends should be tolerant of each other, should understand everything, should forgive anything. The affair had been a bad decision. Okay, he admitted it. Lots of people make bad decisions, especially men when it comes to women. But to just up and abandon him to a thoroughly modern young woman when she knew he was a traditional old male!

And to leave him a note! After twenty-two years of marriage. True, as she had pointed out in the note, if he had been home, she would not have had to leave him a note. True, the reason he had not been at home was that he had been visiting Veronica, but hadn't Esther given him permission to do so? Not only permission, but instructions to do so. They could not abandon Veronica, she must be taken care of, especially in her vulnerable condition.

And now, two years later, she was still being mean and thoughtless. How could she refuse to talk to him on the phone?

She knew him so well. She would know how he suffered. She would know how he needed her, needed to talk to her. How could she be so spiteful as to not allow Delores to give him her phone number? The red rash on Polly's little bum, what the hell was it? A runny nose and sore throat, what do you do about that? Those interminable nights of walking the floor with inevitable colic, if only he could have picked up the phone and called Esther. Those evenings when Veronica dashed out the door to her three-hour evening seminar leaving him to mop up the kitchen and bed down a teething child, a child who, although Veronica expressed milk into a bottle for the bedtime feeding, preferred the real thing to plastic and screamed her head off unless he bounced her in his arms for endless hours. How he had longed to simply pass a screaming baby into Esther's knowledgeable arms. In spite of Veronica's confidence in the matter (he had raised one child, he was an intelligent adult for Christ sake), he couldn't be expected to know anything about babies. He was a middle-aged academic.

Esther must know that he needed her help in dealing with Veronica. There was no rest, no coming home as it were. His homecomings consisted of having a child in one arm and groceries in the other. If he got home first he was expected to get supper going and keep Polly occupied. He could not be tired with Veronica. She would not allow it. "Get with the program," she would say. "Women have been doing it for aeons." He longed to come home in the old way, to have Esther meet him at the door with a martini and a good hot meal. He longed to lay his head in her lap and tell her how tired he was, how he was too old for life with a young wife and toddler. He fantasized Esther stroking his head and offering cooing noises.

He had no one to take care of him, *him*. He had courted a sexy young woman without a thought in her head except pleasing him in bed and woke up to find a highly motivated intelligent career woman, a woman he did not understand, a woman whose values, whose ways of doing things, even her personal habits, were different from his. While he applauded her academic efforts, he simply was not used to it. His mother, Esther, had been wives and mothers and homemakers. He couldn't understand this woman who left her discarded clothing on the bedroom floor, who barged into the bathroom when he was brushing his teeth and elbowed him to his side of the vanity, whose idea of entertaining was nachos with the works.

It was bad enough that Esther had abandoned him, but she had also encouraged Delores to do so. Delores had emailed him some time ago with the message that she would not be visiting this summer. She had not visited last summer, either, but he had hoped that time would change her attitude. How could she so easily discard the memories they shared? Planting a tree together, she with her little shovel, her small hands helping him place the roots in the hole, helping him hold the watering can, her short legs racing outside each morning to see if it had grown overnight. He saw the picture so clearly in his head. But that wasn't him in the picture. It was a young man whom he recognized only as a vague acquaintance.

His phone calls to Delores were becoming more and more strained, so much so that lately he felt that he did not know the person at the other end of the line. After they dispensed with the weather and an overview of what she was doing academically, there seemed little else to say. He knew that the boyfriend she had such hopes of a few years previous was off the plan. That had been revealed in phone calls back and forth shortly before Esther left. He and Esther had discussed it, Esther typically taking the sentimental position, "Poor Delores. It's so sad," forcing him into the practical position, "It sounds like she's better off without the jerk." "But it's always sad when young love doesn't work," Esther countered. "The young go into it with such hope, such expectations."

Perhaps Delores had someone else now. He didn't know. She was reluctant to discuss deeper personal issues with him and he was incapable of broaching such subjects. He realized with something of a shock that their conversations had always skimmed the surface, clever repartee rather than heartfelt talk. He also realized that this was not likely to change, especially now with her hostility toward him because of Esther.

Still, he kept phoning and when he did, he tried to bring up the subject of her mother's life. But she simply would not talk about it. Likely, she had orders not to. He wondered if Esther had found someone else but he dare not ask. And he could not hold the thought for long. It was inconceivable. How could she have found someone else? How could she give her smiles, her attention, *herself*, to someone else. She was part of him, part of those two who had been young together. But he wondered about the young man who had been half of the couple. As in the picture with Delores, he did not know him. He could not find him.

He missed Esther and Delores, but most of all he missed himself. When Esther left, she took the essential part of him with her, leaving him without anything of himself that was solid, that he could get a grip on, leaving him with the question. Who am I? Who am I supposed to be? He didn't realize it at first, the shock waves had to subside. Then as the weeks and months passed he realized that he was a man without a past. Esther owned his past, not only everything they had done together but his thoughts, his work, his recreation activities, even the sitcoms they used to watch weekday evenings. He had belonged to her as he had belonged to God or, since he didn't believe in God, to life itself. He had lost this sense of belonging.

George had an insight into marriage. Dissolving a long marriage was not simply dissolving a contract or a cohabitation. It was dissolving whole lives of people, all that had gone before, their past lives and, yes, their future lives. Not only had Esther taken his past but his future, all the future they might have had together, retirement, travel, grandfather to Delores' children, an old age that they were to enjoy together. There was Veronica, of course. Now he would do these things with her. But it would not be *him* who was doing the things. And he could not quite believe in a future with Veronica. He could not envision their growing old together. He would in time, he was sure of it, especially with the two little ones, but the mindset for it had not yet arrived and so he was in a no man's land, crossing from one territory to another, exiled from the old place but not feeling at home in the new.

His mind wandered to the first time he had seen Esther. She was laughing, her face open, vulnerable, her brown eyes sparkling. She was with the group in the Cave, someone had just said something to make her laugh. Ben was there and introduced him around. He knew Ben because they belonged to the same student protest movement, a movement he had become involved in because of a girl he was hoping to bed. He immediately forgot that girl and all the other girls he had ever known when Esther shone her warm eyes on him and offered her hand. The six of them in the group, the other four had already formed couples, had grown into each other in such a way as to become an entity which for a while seemed immune to harm. What went wrong? he wondered. Where had things gone off track? When had it last been right? The night of the storm before the fatal phone call; after that phone call everything changed. That night a bacteria attached itself to the blood vessels of their relationship. The neutrophils patrolling the system failed to leap and seize and gobble up the bacterium. Amanda's death and the entrance of Veronica, the two events seemed connected, *were* connected, Esther being away, Veronica being put in his path. Coincidence. It happened in his work, too; two events coming together at exactly the right time and place, sometimes the results were fortuitous, sometimes catastrophic. That was the way it happened with the immune system, too. George liked the analogy. Viewed that way, the damage of the last few years could be defined simply as a massive immune system failure.

But it didn't seem fair to have his life so defined by this end. Surely, he was more. He was the total of all he had been, all he had done. But he couldn't remember what that was. He couldn't *feel* what that was. And there was no one to ask. The man who had done those things had disappeared and he could not find him.

A slight movement of the stroller, Polly was stirring. He watched her wake up, watched her open her eyes, watched while the sky and the trees entered her consciousness. Her eyes were full of wonder, like someone coming out of the darkness viewing the world for the first time. She saw him and smiled. He leaned forward and picked her up and held her close. She snuggled her face into his neck and lay there for some time. He experienced a rush of feeling for his child.

It was all very simple. An experiment failed, you tried another method. He would simply have to become acquainted with the new George. Survival depended on it. This child depended on it. In that conclusion, some of the old George was re-established. I'm not a bad person, he thought. I only did what half the male population does. Why am I the one made to suffer?

XIII: ESTHER

THE BRIGHT SPRING SUN ANIMATED the Toronto harbour. Lake Ontario was enamelled with intense blue and silver under a cloudless lapis lazuli sky. Pleasure boats were out in full force. Toronto Island across the water was a green mirage. Although it was nearly seven in the evening, the light was still strong, a low sun filtering through the close-set high rises that lined the shore.

Esther was standing at her balcony door enjoying the view. From the tenth floor, the water and boats and green island was like a picture postcard advertising a resort. When she lowered her head, she could see people moving about, trying to cross the street below before the traffic light changed, scurrying to get home or meet up with friends or pick up groceries at either of the two large outlets nearby. Some were already engaged in evening leisure, strolling along the boardwalk, sitting at patio tables with lattes and espressos or glasses of wine. The boat rental was doing a brisk business. Esther did not mind the intrusion of human beings or even the sound of traffic into the scene. The crowds on the quay kept her company. The activity, the *life*, reminded her that she was part of the human race.

Behind her a small table was set with two placemats, flowers between, candles at either end, wine glasses. A fragrant garlicky ragout was bubbling on the stove, a salad of crisp greens reclined in the fridge. The one-bedroom apartment was in order, but then it was not likely to get out of order with her as the sole occupant. On the narrow balcony, artfully arranged as to colour and height, were flower pots filled with pansies, carnations, kalanchoe, recently purchased. She and Delores had made an excursion to the Garden Centre last week.

Altogether, in spite of the generic one-bedroom layout, the apartment had a homey, comfortable look. Throws and cushions on the sofa and the one armchair, art work on the walls, plants placed strategically, all gave a warm personal feel to the setting. Esther had lived here nearly two years now, she couldn't believe how fast time went. She had refused to be a burden on Delores any longer than necessary. Delores needed to live her own life. Also, Delores insisted on rehashing her father's total moral breakdown and ensuing ruination. Esther, who at that time was still in mourning, did not want to intensify her misery by having someone remind her of it on a daily basis.

Arriving where she was, at this place and time, after walking through the fire, as she thought of it, Esther was so pleasantly surprised at her ability to survive and get on with life that it fairly took her breath away. This ability was due in part to her deciding that all, all, was meant to happen exactly as it had, that everything was part of God's plan. She must accept God's plan. If her belief was worth anything at all, she had to give in to God. Maybe Veronica is part of God's plan for George, she thought. Maybe I was too easy on him. With me, he didn't have to reach.

After a period of seeing the cloth ripped apart, jaggedly as she thought of it, Esther again saw her life as whole, a seamless tapestry, although now with both dark and light threads. Her destiny was to end up in Toronto with Delores and to love the children. The children at the daycare. They needed her. They needed her and George did not. Perhaps it was her destiny to go where needed. She had considered Oxfam or one of the other agencies who took volunteer workers, but she came to the conclusion that she wasn't ready. Perhaps next year or the next. She had time. Many such volunteers were much older than she, people who had retired from their careers and still had energy to offer to the world. She would wait for God to tell her what to do. She was sure He would give her a sign.

She still missed George. She admitted it. She gave herself permission to admit it. She would always miss him. She would always regret him — she had so wanted him to be successful as a human being, but she had learned not to live in that regret.

After her arrival in Toronto, the thought that she had done the wrong thing in leaving, in abandoning George, in pulling her own life down around her, and the ensuing loss of everything, her whole life including George, threatened to destroy her. As she probed the painful place inside herself, the source of those feelings, with a scalpel as it were, and opened it up, the agony was overwhelming. She doubled over with the weight of it and for some months she was like one in shock. She found herself stopped in the middle of a crowded sidewalk, standing rigid, staring, paralyzed with pain. She found herself lying on her sofa or bed staring at the ceiling paralyzed with pain. Delores would call and she could not move to answer the phone. Delores would come charging in to her apartment demanding answers. Have you gotten up today? Have you eaten? Since she couldn't endure the disturbances or the scoldings — this is the stupidest thing I've ever seen, you're going to let that man kill you, you have to smarten up — she put the phone beside her on the bed and willed her arm to reach, to pick up, willed her voice to say, fine, I'm fine, I'm better today.

After that stage passed, for some time she was in a state of perpetual sadness. She felt incomplete without George, he had been her life for so long. She felt like a lost soul wandering the wilderness in search of its missing part. She decided, firmly, that she had *not* done the right thing. She should have taken Ben's advice and asked George to choose. He would have chosen her, she knew that, not only because, of course, he loved her while his feeling for that young woman was merely sexual attraction but, also, because she was the most comfortable option. In fact, after talking with Ben, her intention was to follow his advice. She had it all planned. She prepared a nice dinner, she lit candles, she put on soft background music. They got through the meal. Now was the time to do it. She took a deep breath. She looked at him across the dinner table. He was polishing off dessert, a crème brûlée, her crème brûlée was famous amongst their friends, and thought, he's a child. He eats like a child, with total focus on his pleasure and satisfaction, without giving a thought to the emotional upheaval around him, which he has caused. He has the ego of a child, thinking he can get away with anything and be forgiven. Nothing has ever been hard for him. He had an ideal childhood, his mother adored him, lavished him with food and praise; he was naturally brilliant, his studies came easily. She had come easily. Should she let him take the easy way out? Would she be doing him a favour? She must decide on a course of action then not let herself be dissuaded by herself.

She bought an airline ticket. She knew that she could not tell George until the last minute. There could be no time for discussion or dissuasion. When the hour came she ordered a taxi. As it turned out, George wasn't at home when the taxi arrived. Thus, the note propped against the delphiniums on the table, freshly picked that morning.

The sadness eventually became sporadic rather than perpetual and she was able to convince herself that, after all, she *had* done everything right. She had been generous, good-hearted, toward that young woman. She had made the sacrifice. She had nothing to apologize for. George had to be made to realize the consequences of his actions. By making him face the music, she had done the right thing for him. She had done the right, the best, thing for the child. As soon as she was able, she started divorce proceedings. Since there was no contest, it went through quickly. Her message to George through her lawyer was that the child needed a father, its real father. The child needed a proper home, a regular home, and family. The young woman needed a husband.

Throughout it all, the children at the daycare helped her. They demanded her attention, her response. They would not allow lapses. Their needs, their nurturing took up every minute she was with them. She did not have time to think about George or feel sorry for herself. Every day, barring inclement weather, she watched the dear little darlings as she thought of them, shovelling in the sandbox, sliding on the slides, calling and yelping, and the ones who were dearest of all, those sitting apart, digging listlessly or simply staring at the others. These were the ones she would pick up and cuddle on her knee.

She showed up at the daycare every day whether or not she felt like it — even on her worst days when she wanted to curl herself into a fetal ball and never move again. She could not let them down. And they did not let her down. They made her laugh even when she felt like crying. In the evenings, alone in her apartment, just thinking about them made her smile.

As her self-confidence grew, she gave herself permission to be sad. She accepted the fact that life was often sad. She found more and more that she *could* think of painful things, she *could* endure the pain of thinking. Life was not perfect. She was not perfect. She had failures. Her inability to have more children, for instance. But failures are also part of God's plan. Sometimes they happen to teach a person a lesson. And look at how God had solved that problem. He had given her the children in the daycare. He had found George a young child-bearing wife. George, too, was one of her failures. During the early years of their marriage, she thought him perfect. It did not occur to her to have so much as a critical thought about him. Over time, she realized that he was not a kind, generous person, that when it came to human beings, he did not have a nurturing bone in his body. She put it down to his being a scientist, driven by cold reason. He couldn't even talk about emotions. Hard facts were what he lived by.

She forgave him. It wasn't his fault he was like that. It was his childhood, his mother's indulgence, and his genetic disposition. Forgiveness allowed her to walk in an aura of light. She enfolded George into this aura with her. You're not one when you start out together, she decided. All those wedding cards that talk about the young couple being one. What nonsense. It takes years to become one. Because she and George were one, it didn't matter that he was with someone else. Veronica had nothing to do with her and George's relationship. Their relationship, a changed relationship to be sure, was between the two of them and always would be. As her heart swelled with benevolence for George, she felt closer to him than ever before. Forgiveness put her in direct contact with heaven.

Forgiveness was a great thing. She felt she was born for it, as though forgiveness had been inside her all this time, waiting for the right conditions to grow and multiply, waiting for someone to lavish it on. And here was George! Maybe that was his purpose in her life, to teach her forgiveness. Maybe George was part of God's plan for her evolvement. Thinking thus, seeing the purpose of people and events, her pain became more endurable. And as time further passed, she began to see that George in giving her the opportunity to be a better person had given her a great gift. And one morning she woke up with the thought that along with everything else, he had given her the gift of freedom. She was free. Free! When this realization first came to her, it was like an elixir. She was free to be a person without the influence of another. She could do what she liked. More importantly, she could think what she liked.

During the last two years, she had thought more about her marriage than she had in the twenty-two years of its duration. She thought how, through her marriage and submitting herself to another's personality, another's ego and values, she had lost herself. She thought how in losing George she had found herself, the person she had been in her childhood and youth. It took a while for her to think this through and come out the other side, to accept this correction of her life. In fact, she must learn to love this correction because it gave her the chance to find herself, to know who she was, to become strong in who she was. In order to not go stark raving mad she'd had to dig into herself and find the lost Esther.

Who am I? she asked herself. A nice person, she answered herself. Everyone from the drugstore clerk to the head of George's department said so. But was she a good person? What was demanded of goodness? She decided that goodness was a strange thing. How sometimes we think we're being good when all we're being is self-righteous. In fact, if we think we're good we're not truly good. She had thought she was the great and good and benevolent little wife with her plan for Veronica, accepting the scarlet woman, as it were, the woman who had deceived her, betrayed her with her husband, into her bosom, into her house and family. Now, at this distance of space and time, she could see the gesture for what it was; an egotistical move to puff up her vanity. I was full of myself, my own virtue, thinking how I was such a great, good person, so generous in taking George back and providing everybody with a way out. I was blind, wilfully blind, she could think now. There's no virtue in being blind.

She often returned in thought to the Cave. Every day she thought of Amanda and prayed for her soul in purgatory. Lately, she had given much thought to Amanda's marriage. Reuben and Amanda had thrown themselves into their relationship in the same way they had their causes, with completeness and abandonment, without giving the matter serious thought. Running off to the Coast without considering how they would make a living, having all those children without thinking of consequences. Esther had always been afraid for them. She'd had, still had, the uncomfortable feeling that those who were so careless with life would sooner or later crash.

Now she questioned her own marriage. An emotional distance had certainly been a part of it. At the beginning she had felt it as a lack but George seemed to feel comfortable with the space and after a time she decided that such a distance suited them. She wondered if George was involved with Veronica in the deep way of Amanda and Reuben. She didn't know, she couldn't know, but she thought not. George just didn't have it in him.

Maybe she didn't have it in her, either. This thought came as a revelation. She had always blamed George for the lack of an emotional component in their marriage. But now she had to consider her part in that lack. She tried to remember what had attracted her to George in the first place. He was fun. They had fun together, epitomized by that TR5, whizzing around town summer nights with the top down, Amanda and Reuben or Ben and Helena perched up in the back. They owned the town; they owned the world. Nothing bad could ever happen to such blessed creatures as they, privileged because of their place, their intelligence, the strength of their egos and their youth. She supposed it was a rather shallow attraction compared to what Amanda felt for Reuben. She tried to think of a time when she did feel deeply. Her sisters. The three of them had been like bears hibernating in the Cave, cuddling each other, comforting each other, keeping each other safe and warm. But when she gave the matter a more penetrating analysis, she decided that even then she had not given herself as fully as had Amanda.

She came to the place where when she thought of the Cave and her sisters, instead of regret of loss she felt acceptance for what was right and inevitable. She understood that leaving the safe place is necessary for growth. No one escaped. Escaped what? she questioned. Life, was the answer. What had happened to them was life. To escape life would be not to live, not to have experiences, good and bad. After all, we can't expect to have only good happy experiences, she reasoned. The word "good" is misunderstood. It's all good, because it's all life.

This understanding was one of her major breakthroughs.

The day came when she could no longer see George. She could not see him in his new life: walking to the university, bouncing a child on his knee. She could not see him in their house, his house now, Veronica's house. The place he should have been was blank, a blank spot in her vision like the precursor to a migraine.

She still loved him and she expected he still loved her. This love helped her to find the strength to know that a segment of her life was finished, as was a segment of his. The task now for each of them was to get on with the next segment.

Behind her, the phone rang. She could tell from the display that it was Helena. She *should* pick up the phone. Helena was so good to her, so thoughtful, visiting her last summer, phoning her on a regular basis, following her to Toronto in the first place. Two years ago she had given Helena a terrible shock. She had not told her sister until half an hour before the taxi was to arrive to take her to the airport that she was leaving George. Helena would demand details, would demand that she stick up for her rights. Esther could not face that interrogation and advice. But, then, she'd had to relent and let Helena follow her to Toronto on the first available flight. It was the only way she could get off the phone.

That first month in Toronto, between the commiseration, advice, and loving care of Helena and Delores, they were all in Delores's small apartment, Esther's resolve threatened to shatter. She needed to be alone to mourn properly. Sharing her grief diluted it and confused her. She managed to pack Helena back to Ben with the promise of phoning her every day and letting her come again at a later date and she started to look for her own apartment.

The phone calls had tapered off to once a week but the subject was the same. While Esther was finished with it, Helena was not. "I can't believe that you just walked out of there and let them have the house. It's *your* house. You can still get it back. Let *him* move." Helena wanted to talk about her own feelings of guilt in the matter. "I should have known. I was living in the house for two months, with the two of you, I can't believe I didn't detect something was wrong, that I was so insensitive, the way I went on and on about my troubles and didn't even ask you about yours. You must have been suffering so. And you didn't tell me!"

At first Esther tried to comfort and reassure her. "I wasn't suffering. I didn't have any troubles, I keep telling you, I didn't know about George." But the words did not penetrate Helena's outrage and sense of failure. Now, usually, Esther listened patiently, nodded and said yes, dear, but tonight she did not feel like rehashing it all again. She did not feel like being quizzed about her life or her feelings. She did not want to be bawled out for not upgrading her education degree to get Ontario accreditation. She knew if she did that she could get a job that paid better, but the children needed her and were so dear to her. Helena couldn't seem to understand that she *liked* her job.

And Helena kept chipping away at George and Veronica, listing their shortcomings, citing the faults that kept them from being lovable or even likeable creatures. She did not understand that Esther needed to keep her love strong and alive and not let anyone destroy it. To hate Veronica would diminish herself and certainly not affect Veronica in the least. To verbally abuse George would jeopardize the love within herself, which was her integrity in the world.

Besides, she was looking forward to the evening. She did not want to start it off with Helena's scathing comments about Veronica and criticism of George ringing in her ears. She let the message service answer. She would phone her sister tomorrow when she felt up to it. She returned the phone to its cradle.

And there was the door buzzer.

Esther walked slowly and regally, all of five foot two and dimply plump, through her apartment toward the door. She felt quite trendy in her long skirt, newly purchased loose top, and open-toed sandals. She could almost imagine that she was tall and slim with long flowing blonde hair, the recent Hollywood style. At her recent pedicure, she'd had the girl paint a delicate flower on each of her shiny red big toe nails. As the skirt swished about her thighs, she felt the ordinary world fall away and knew that something extraordinary awaited her.

She reached out her arm and opened the door to a smiling man, not too tall, sturdy but trim, with greying hair and laughing eyes, who held flowers in one hand and a bottle of wine in the other.

XIV: THE LOVERS ELOPE SKYWARD

"I DON'T KEEP THINGS from you. Do you keep things from me?"

"No. Of course not. Well, trivial things, things you wouldn't be interested in."

"How do you know what I'd be interested in?"

"You can't tell another person everything," Benjamin said. "There aren't enough hours in the day. And a person forgets. And so much that happens is insignificant."

"What seems insignificant to you might be significant to me," Helena contended.

They were walking on a paved pathway that wound through the river valley park. To one side was the brown sluggish North Saskatchewan, to the other, a high, shrub-covered embankment falling from the drive above which bordered the valley rim, the same drive where, farther along, closer to the university, George used to jog between his two lives. Up the hill from where they were walking was their new home, the apartment they had taken together.

Along the path, growth was abundant. The green was vibrant, trees and bushes exulted with life. The air was full of lilting fragrance, buoying up the walkers and runners who had turned out en masse to enjoy a glorious Sunday morning.

"I find it hard to believe," Helena said, sidestepping a jogger. "We're an old married couple. An old story."

"With a happy ending." He put his arm around her shoulder and drew her close. Her hair brushed his cheek. An effusion of dark curls framing her face was one of the signs, an outward manifestation, of her return, if not to the happy girl of her youth, at least to a woman who was confident of the future. "I'm ready for a few years of comedy myself."

"Yes, I want to be happy for a while. I'm tired of the darkness. It seemed like we were just climbing out of the pit when Esther was tossed into it."

"But she's managed to climb out, too."

"I hope so."

"You doubt her word?"

"No, but she may not want to worry us. We used to tell each other everything, when we were young, young girls confiding in each other. But I don't know any more. She thought she had a happy marriage. It must have been such a shock for her to find out she didn't. She must have been so upset. But she didn't say a word about it to me. And we were living in the same house!"

"I think it all happened so fast, Ver ... that woman showing up at the door, Esther's decision. And you'd moved out by then. She didn't have the opportunity to discuss it with you."

"Well, she should have made the opportunity. I would have advised packing his bag and throwing it out the door after him. Instead, she packed *her* bags and walked out. It was like going to a nunnery. Renouncing the world."

"But she's done the opposite. Embraced the world."

"It makes my blood boil, when I think what she's let him get away with. Especially the house. Esther loved that house."

"Shhh." He squeezed her hand. "It's her life. You have to let her do what she wants with it."

"But is that what she really wants? Exiling herself away from her friends, away from us?"

"Delores is there."

"Yes, that's one good thing."

They walked in silence a while. In that silence Benjamin thought how he could not possibly tell her about his part in Esther's decision. How could he tell her about their talk on the park bench that bleak spring day two years ago? In the first place, she would be struck with guilt that she had not been there to take Esther's phone call. And if she had been there, would three people's lives now be different than they were? Would Helena have convinced Esther to hang on? Throw the bum out! That had been her stance. Still was. And yet she had liked George. Maybe at some level she still did. Maybe what really infuriated Helena was Esther's total capitulation to the demands of Veronica. And likely she would be furious with him for taking it upon himself to give advice to *her* sister, sticking his nose into *her* family's affairs. The fact that Esther had not followed his advice would be irrelevant in Helena's judgment of the situation.

And how could he tell her that he knew about George three days before she did? He had made a promise to Esther. He had been bound to secrecy. Their conversation, as far as he was concerned, had the sanctity of the confessional. But what if, in a forgetful moment, Esther mentioned the park bench incident to Helena? Or what if Esther assumed that he had told Helena about it even though she had told him not to and so mentioned it herself? And then there was Veronica.

"…What she must have been going through!"

"I don't think she was going through anything." Since Benjamin had been listening to this replay for nearly two years, he was able to tune into Helena's remarks and answer accurately. "She didn't know about George then."

"So she says."

"Don't you believe her?"

"Oh yes. One must believe Esther. But she's good at fooling herself. Likely she knew but didn't know, the way you can know things but you don't let yourself know them."

"I think she was completely innocent of that knowledge

when you were staying in her house."

"George was carrying on for years! She must have suspected something."

"Esther is very trusting."

"Naive might be a better word. Let's face it, she's not swift in some ways. But you'd think she might have *felt* there was something wrong. After all, they shared the same bed! How is that possible?"

"Esther would be easy to deceive. She's entirely without suspicion."

"Maybe you're right. She would have told me. Even if she had just suspected, she would have told me. Or I would have known. I would have sensed something. Sisters can't keep these things from each other. No, she seemed the perfectly happy little housewife doting on her middle-aged husband when the child was gone." Helena thought a moment. "And Esther *wants* everything to be nice. She builds a scenario in her mind, a *nice* scenario. She wants everybody to be happy, everything to be wonderful. Discord, fighting, scenes, they always did upset her. If our parents so much as had a difference of opinion, she would be terribly upset. Now, that woman George has taken up with, she looks like a person who wouldn't be much upset by scenes."

"Esther prefers not to see," Benjamin quickly brought the conversation back to Esther as a topic. As always at mention of Veronica, he felt a stab of conscience. It was conceivable that he might some day tell his wife about Esther's phone call and their talk that cold spring day on a park bench, but how could he ever tell her about Veronica? The fact that he had had an affair with the woman who, in her opinion, had ruined her beloved sister's life would be damning enough, but the fallout of that affair in the intolerant eyes of his wife would be unforgivable. But what if she found out from someone else? What if Helena and Veronica met at a university function? It would be just like Veronica to say something awkward.

"Maybe she's changed. She was telling me on the phone that she's started wearing her glasses. You know how she never would wear them even when she couldn't see traffic signs? Well, it seems she was invited to a party by someone in her building. She saw an attractive man across the room, at least she thought he was attractive, she couldn't see him well enough to be sure and she couldn't be sure of his age. And was he wearing a wedding ring? All of a sudden the stupidity of the situation struck her. She excused herself, found her handbag in the closet, put on her glasses then and there, and hasn't taken them off since."

"She's turned out to be a survivor. Tougher than we thought."

They had come to the end of the path. They stood and looked at the city, the buildings rising tall on the opposite embankment, the slow river. A riverboat with bright flags chugged past carrying a load of passengers, but when Helena spoke it was obvious that her thoughts were not on the scene. "I scarcely saw her those few weeks before she left. After I moved, she'd call and I was too busy to talk. I was spending all my time with you and getting back into my dissertation. She must have needed to talk. The story of my life. Not to be there when people need me. It's a sort of betrayal. I seem fated to betray people."

"There you go again, making a myth out of ordinary life."

"Something I learned from you."

"But I cured myself. Or, at least, I'm curing myself. Let's sit a moment."

They found a bench off the pathway. Benjamin took off his glasses and massaged the narrow bridge of his nose, the deep cleft either side. He held his face up to the sun. He closed his eyes.

Helena's voice invaded his dreamlike state. "I wouldn't elevate my life to the mythic. It's more like a third-rate Harlequin. Except for the time with you."

"What's that? A Thomas Hardy? A Dostoevsky?"

"I hope not. They're so grim. I'd rather be in a comedy."

"Tragedy and comedy are the same, though, aren't they? It just depends on when you tune in to the story. And when you leave your characters. It's all cyclic. Take you and me. Right now we're flying high. But at one time we had fallen with a thud."

"Do you think we'll fall again?"

"If we do, then we'll just have to try and rise again."

"I hope George and that woman are in a tragedy."

"No, you don't. I hear she's pregnant again."

"Where did you hear that?"

"I saw George."

"And you didn't tell me!"

"It was only yesterday. I've been going to tell you."

"My God, two kids at George's age! That must be a comedy. It's amazing, though, isn't it? How everything settles down and nobody cares."

"No one remembers. Half the faces on the history department staff are new. And most people are busy with their own problems. But, here's something else I haven't told you yet. George is up for some research award, quite prestigious. International."

"Sorry, I don't want to hear about anything good happening to him."

"Try to remember the old days. George was a good guy. All his life he's been involved in intellectual pursuits. His life and his mind disciplined to the scientific order. Maybe he had to do something that didn't involve his intellect. Maybe he had to do something outrageous before his life was over."

"Likely I'd be more forgiving if that outrage hadn't involved my sister."

"Esther wanted to work with disadvantaged children. She's finally doing what she wanted to do. Try not to hate George."

"I'd hate anybody who caused my sister such misery."

I can't tell her now, thought Benjamin. Maybe he would never be able to tell her that Esther's misery was his fault — that if he had done as much for Veronica as he did for his unfortunates at the Centre, if he had treated her with compassion, with human kindness, he might have saved everyone a lot of grief. And what of Veronica and George now? Can a relationship that started with revenge possibly turn out well?

Was Veronica capable of love? He didn't know. And how about George? In the Cave days, neither George nor Esther seemed to inquire too deeply into emotions. George was too much the scientist and Esther was too busy being nice. But he didn't know if his assessment was accurate. What can we really know about another person's deep thoughts and feelings, he asked himself, which was why complete honesty between people was impossible. Even if you share information with another person, they can only have a surface understanding of what you're talking about. They cannot internalize your situation. He had told Helena about his visit to Amanda and that she had helped him see things in a different way. But how could he ever explain to her the deep mystical experience of Amanda? Since he was a person who never had mystical experiences, deep or otherwise, he could not even explain it to himself. Even if he tried to tell her, she could never fully understand. She could never *feel* it as he had. They could only share the surface story. The truth is that you can never tell another person everything, decided Benjamin, because they can't know *your* truth.

"What *is* the truth?" A voice inserted itself in his thought.

Startled, he turned his head quickly toward Helena. Had he spoken out loud? Had she read his thoughts?

"Behind George," Helena elaborated. "I can't understand how he would choose Veronica and upheaval instead of Esther and comfort. It just doesn't sound like George."

Benjamin pulled Helena to her feet. "The truth is, it's none of our business. It's up to George and Veronica to redeem the situation for themselves. They're the only ones who can."

They started walking again. All it takes is control, thought Benjamin. He didn't know about Veronica but he was pretty sure George was good at control. As for himself, he supposed he could never entirely control his thoughts. He still sometimes thought about the war. Sometimes, he believed himself a coward who had come north to escape having to face physical discomfort. Sometimes, he believed he had come here because he had felt a need to rebel against his father. At other times, he distinctly remembered that he had, in fact, taken a definite moral stance against the war, against his country's exploitation of weaker countries for its own gain. He could not know with certainty what his motives had been. He could not remember the details. His past life was slipping away in his mind and through time would become ever more dim. He had thrown away physical reminders; he had thrown out the tin box. When he and Helena were packing to move into their new apartment, he had held the box in his hands for a long time. It was all he had left of his mother and father. It contained his father's words, his mother's words. But they were the wrong words. They were not helpful. They were words that would hold him back, that would hamper him in his attempt to get through life. It was better to remember his parents during happy times, occasions of his childhood and boyhood. He had willed himself to toss the box into the large black plastic garbage bag overflowing with all the other residue of a former messy existence.

He had chosen to let go of the past. He had chosen this woman who was walking beside him. Each step he took with her further defined who he was. He was okay with that. He lifted his face to the sun. He opened his ears to birdsong and human voices. There was tomorrow's lesson plan, which, assuming there would be a tomorrow, he must look at this afternoon. But even that was too far in the future. Concentrate on the pathway before you, he told himself. It's all you can know at this moment. This pathway and this woman who is walking beside you.

Helena's step was light. Her spirits elevated by the morning, the scene before her, the man beside her, she did not ask herself if she was happy. Happy was too big a word, too big a thing to be. She was not sad or depressed or anxious, but ... happy? Is happiness even a consideration? she wondered.

She had been happy with her sisters, three in a bed on a cold winter's night. They would climb in with each other, hunker down into each other's warmth, and tell stories. They had grown up and chosen men and taken different paths. That's what happens to most people, so get over it, she told herself.

She had been happy with her sisters because she had not yet experienced anything bad happening to her. She had not been fully aware that bad things could happen. As a young woman, as a student, she had been in control of her life. At least, she thought she had. Then Ben had gone off the rails. Then she had obstinately driven the car that had killed her sister. How could life have been so cruel as to involve her in causing Amanda's death? Life had played a terrible trick on her.

Although she would never again trust life, things were going well at the moment. In the past, she had been too trusting, but she had smartened up. No longer was she the wide-eyed ingénue of her youth, open and vulnerable to the world, who, with stars in her eyes, had married a man and honestly thought that she would live happily forever after. No longer was she the confident career-oriented smart young woman of her post-Ben pre-accident years. But these last two years, through Ben, she had been returned to a version of her early self-confident self, a version who no longer felt that disaster was lurking behind every bush. Still she had learned to keep one ear alert at the waterhole. And in her new wariness, her love for Ben was more realistic. She did not have to trust him one hundred per cent to love him. She could tolerate Ben as a human being and not expect him to be without fault.

She could and did acknowledge Ben's help in her getting her life back together. The day of the pills, as her mind designated the event, she had stumbled her way back to him, crept up his stairs, knocked on his door, fallen into his arms. He had taken her to his bed, lain down with her and held her until she stopped shaking. He had fed her chicken soup and returned her to Esther. Later, he had been the one to suggest that she get a place of her own for a while before making decisions about them as a couple. He had walked her through the steps of returning to her studies. He had assumed that she had overdosed by accident and she did not set him straight. At first, she had been too sick to talk about it. As she recuperated, the words seemed too big, assigning importance to something that was actually quite trivial. And after another while she told herself a version of Ben's story. She had wanted so badly to sleep, she had swallowed too many pills to help her sleep.

Neither had she told him the details of the time they had been apart. That time didn't have anything to do with her life now or who she was now. It didn't have anything to do with Ben. When she had been weak and sick, she had wanted to confess, but thank heavens she hadn't. That sordid part of her life was a secret she did not want to share. She was thoroughly embarrassed and ashamed of it. Her penance was a ritual flogging of herself — how could she have been so stupid? How could she have picked up such sleazy types? How could she have not been concerned about catching some terrible disease? Secretly, she had herself checked thoroughly by a gynaecologist.

Also, she sincerely wanted to spare Ben pain. It was all very well to prattle on about free love but when one actually practiced it, usually there was a great deal of pain to one or more of the people involved. She and Ben had got their lives back on track. Why take a chance of pulling them off the rails again? And as those dissolute years dissolved into the past, they became ever more dim so that she could recall scenes but someone other than she was the actor in the drama. If she confessed, she would be telling Ben a story about a stranger, a stranger who, after all, had only asserted her freedom, the freedom of the individual to act as she chose. To act otherwise would be a betrayal of the sixties revolution, a revolution they had fought so diligently in their youth, a battle that Ben had believed in so strongly he had given up his country for it.

She did not consider these omissions to be lies. The information was not relevant to their life together. She was who she was, not who she had been. These things would not happen again. She no longer drank too much. She no longer collected pills. Her attempt at suicide was part of a distant past. She was like a soldier returned from a war zone who does not want to talk about it, who tries to live in the present. Mostly, she was successful.

Of course, she would always regret Amanda and her own self-centred stupidity. She would always regret that she had been such a mean older sister. But she could not change the past. In the past she had made bad choices, but now she was making good choices. No longer did she feel defined by those bad choices but, rather, by the choices she made now. She believed now that she had a choice, that her future was not foretold by fate. She was not a victim. She would live day by day, making the best choices she could at the time. And she consciously tried to be a better person. She tried to act with more compassion and kindness toward her fellow creatures. She tried to be more aware of what was going on with the people around her. She tried to sympathize with Esther. It was just that Esther was being so stupid, letting George get away with too much. And not only George, but that person, Veronica. To walk away and leave them with everything! It was insane. Esther had not even taken any money out of the marriage. She insisted that she had money of her own, a small investment from their parents' estate. She was sure that if necessary George would help her but so far it had not been necessary. While she, Helena, kept at her about getting the finances down in writing, Esther kept prattling on about how things happened for the best.

Helena had no patience with Esther's putting herself in the hands of a benign God who worked everything out for the best, but she had learned to tolerate Esther's references to such a being. Instead of saying "tommyrot," she smiled sweetly and nodded her head. And she had to admit that in some ways Esther was coming along quite nicely. She was not quite as soggily sentimental as she used to be. While she was still primarily driven by emotion, at times she could think things through using reason. A new pragmatism had taken hold.

Helena was equally pleased with her own progress. The past two years had definitely been a learning curve, she, too, was coming along quite nicely. She had learned to deal with pain — she had learned not to hold on to it, to let it flow in and out. This was an important lesson because everything caused pain — the past, the present, the knowledge that none of them could ever return to their light-hearted youth, the knowledge that she and Ben had destroyed innocence for each other. Ben's smile was not the unguarded smile of the young man she had married. In it she saw a reflection of her own caution, not so much an inability to trust the situation completely, but, rather, the knowledge that things can come at you. Unexpected, dreadful things can happen without warning, but she had learned not to fear the future. She felt strong enough to endure, to accept whatever came. She could live with that as a truth, most of the time.

She tried not to think in terms of mythologies. She tried not to look for deeper meanings. No longer did she wonder why she had chosen that particular spot beside that particular playground where that particular child was standing on the sidewalk with his hand outstretched. It had all been, quite simply, a series of events. Why wouldn't she chose that playground, it had been a deserted place. Why wouldn't she throw up, her stomach a roiling mixture of whiskey and fizzy sweet pink pop.

No longer was the hand that had directed Ben to Amanda mysterious, nor was the happenstance of Amanda's words in the car the night of the storm. "Ben loves you," the words that would eventually bring her up out of the cold black water.

Those words were not Amanda's foretelling of the future, as though she had known that Helena would need Ben, would need her words referring to Ben, to help her sister find her way back. Helena had come to the realization that none of it was a miracle. Why wouldn't Amanda say those words, they were part of the subject under discussion.

She intended walking clear-eyed and clear-headed into the future guided by rational thought. She admitted that she did not know what the future would bring, but at the moment she felt optimistic about her strength and the strength of her will to cope with whatever that might be. She was making good decisions, she was back in control, she felt strong, she felt good. She trusted her new strong self. She had gone through a bad patch but she had emerged the other side. She slipped her hand into Benjamin's where it was curled inside his jacket pocket. They looked up, at the trees, at the river, at other walkers and joggers. Mostly they smiled and even when not smiling, their faces wore pleasant aspects.

ACKNOWLEDGEMENTS

Thanks as always to Willie Fitzpatrick, Dixie Baum, Sue Hirst for suggestions and lots of laughs in the process, to Barbara Scott for her editing sensibilities, to Pat Allan for the title. Family and friends, what would I do without you?

Thanks to the Alberta Foundation for the Arts for providing financial support.

A special thank you to Luciana Ricciutelli, Editor-in-Chief at Inanna Publications, who must have incredible focus and endurance.

CECELIA FREY is the author of fifteen books of fiction and poetry as well as works of non-fiction and award-winning plays. She has worked as an editor, teacher, and freelance writer, and has for many years been involved in the Calgary literary community. Her short stories and poetry have been published in dozens of literary journals and anthologies as well as being broadcast on CBC radio and performed on the Women's Television Network. Numerous reviews, essays and articles have appeared in a wide range of publications including newspapers such as *The Globe and Mail* and journals as varied as *Westworld* and *Canadian Literature*. Her novel, *A Raw Mix of Carelessness and Longing*, was shortlisted for the 2009 Writers Guild of Alberta (WGA) George Bugnet Fiction Award and she is a three-time recipient of the WGA Short Fiction Award. Her most recent publications include novels *The Long White Sickness* (2013) and *Moments of Joy* (2015); and a collection of poetry, *North* (2017).